FROM THESE RAGING SEAS

BOOK 1 OF THE KEELHAUL JACK SERIES

BRITTANY CZARNECKI

ALSO BY BRITTANY CZARNECKI

The Girl Forged by Fate
The Girl Destined to Rise
The Girl with the Iron Heart

Copyright © 2023 Brittany Czarnecki

EBook ISBN: 979-8-9875188-1-6

Paperback ISBN: 979-8-9875188-0-9

Hardcover ISBN: 979-8-9875188-2-3

Cover art and design:

Franziska Stern

www.coverdungeon.com

www.instagram.com/coverdungeonrabbit

Editor:

Crystal Pikko Watanabe

www.pikkoshouse.com

www.instagram.com/pikkotheeditor

Cartographer:

Dewi Hargreaves

www.dewihargreaves.com

www.instagram.com/dewiwrites

Formatter:

Liz Steinworth

www.theartofliz.com

www.instagram.com/theartofliz

This book is a work of fiction. Similarities to people, places, events, or things are entirely coincidental.

For the first reader and fan of this book, April.

CONTENTS

PORT VAIL
VULKAN
MIDSARRA
THE HELM
THE SHIP
GRAVEYARD
ISLE OF THE LOST
THE GREEN SEA
COLD BAY
CRESCENT
COVE

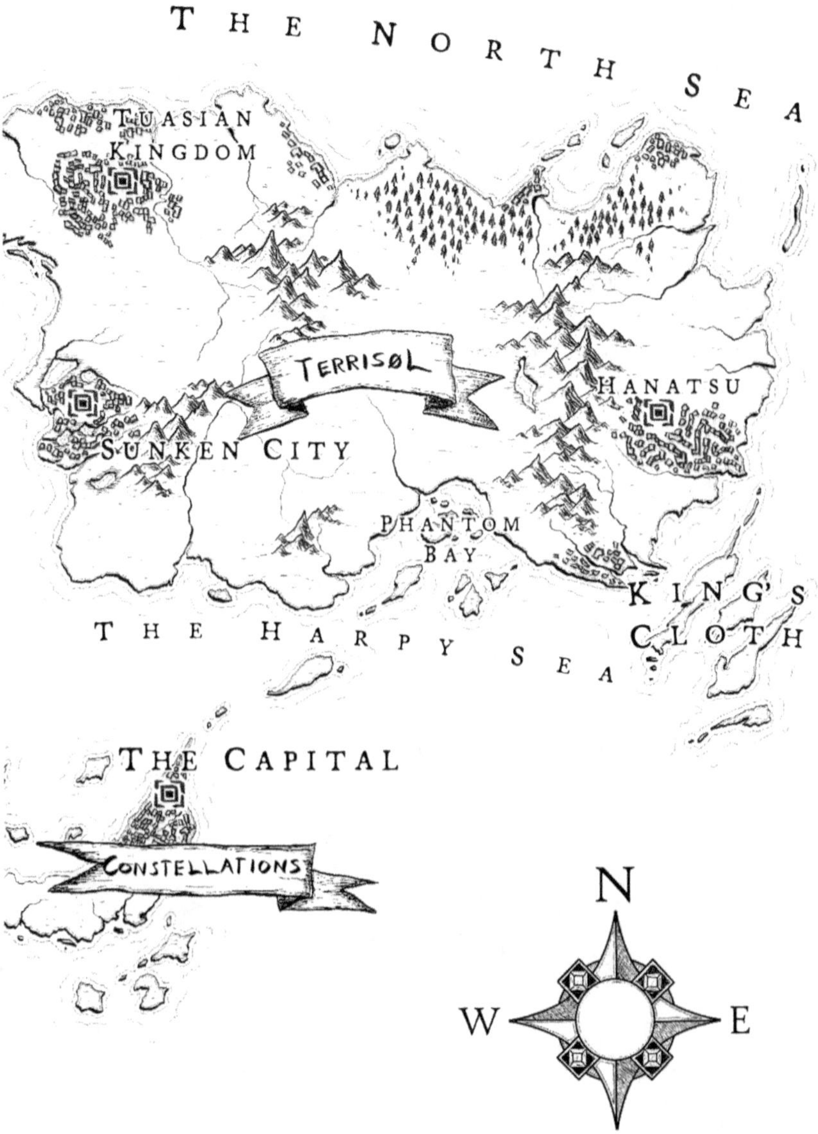

THE NORTH SEA
TUASIAN KINGDOM
TERRISØL
HANATSU
SUNKEN CITY
PHANTOM BAY
KING'S CLOTH
THE HARPY SEA
THE CAPITAL
CONSTELLATIONS
N
W
E
S

PROLOGUE

JACK

The sound of my footsteps scuffing on the cobblestones seems too loud in the darkness of the alley. I glance over my shoulder, but there's no one following me. I'm either too stubborn or too stupid to turn back now.

Knowing that it isn't safe for me to be here does little to stop my feet from taking me to the bar. The splintered wooden doors to the Blue Crab Tavern creak open, spilling laughter into the dark streets of the city. A man with a mug of ale bumps my shoulder as he stumbles past and slurs what I assume is an apology, but he stops when he sees my face. Lowering my hat over my eyes, I enter the tavern, heading straight to the counter at the back.

The laughter and chatter of the patrons slowly dies as I weave my way through the crowd. I know it's risky to stay in the Sunken City, and that my crew will be waiting for me, wondering where I am if I don't get back soon. I'd ordered them all to stay aboard the *Chained Maiden* until my return. I just hope they listen. The governess of this city doesn't exactly like me, and I've been banned from returning ever since I roughed up a few of her guards last year, but here I am anyway. I got what I came for, but now all I want is a moment to think about my next move—and a damn drink.

At the bar, a young woman with blond hair has a look of worry as I approach. I pull out two gold coins from my jacket and slide them over to her. "Ale," I say with a smile. Glancing over my shoulder as she pours my drink, I spot many pairs of eyes watching me, but there's one set that I recognize. A kid sitting in the back of the bar watches me closely. He has dark skin and curly brown hair that tapers down the sides of his head. But those eyes… amber, just like his father's.

A moment after I take a sip of ale, the tavern doors burst open. A sigh deflates my chest as boots stomp over the sticky wooden floor.

"You!" a voice yells at me from behind. "You're under arrest by order of the governess—"

"Do you like your hand?" I interrupt, not bothering to turn around and look at the guards.

"What?" the guard asks.

Now I do turn. The governess' guards are dressed in deep-purple uniforms, with long jackets that end at their ankles. There are three of them, all blocking the door. Many of the patrons have pushed themselves back against the walls, and some slip out of the tavern for fear of what's about to happen.

"Your hand," I repeat calmly, lifting my right hand for the guard to examine. It's carved from oak, and my fingers are permanently extended as if waiting for a hand to shake.

The guards exchange nervous glances. "You're to come with us," the first one says, but his voice holds all the authority of a pouting child. "Don't make this harder than it has to be."

"It's funny," I say, smiling, but it isn't genuine. "How you take something so simple for granted. You never know what you'll miss until it's gone."

"Enough!" the second guard yells, drawing his sword. "This is your last chance."

Around the room, a flurry of hushed voices drifts about,

falling to the stained floor like dead flies. The unease is thick enough that I'm really starting to regret stopping for a drink.

Reaching behind me, I grab my ale and down the whole thing before hurling the mug across the tavern. It makes contact with the guard standing closest to the door. The crunch of bone and cartilage is oddly satisfying, and he cries out as blood explodes from his mangled nose. More people shove back their chairs, hugging the wall as if it might conceal them. The other two guards charge forward, swords drawn. I duck under the first one's blade and grab him by the throat with my good hand, slamming him face down onto the bar as the other stabs his sword toward my gut. Blocking with my wooden hand, I kick the first guard's knee out and square up on the other.

"St-stand down!" he orders in a shaky voice.

A grin splits my face as I reach back in my belt and feel the cold grip of my whalebone dagger.

The guard is visibly shaking, but he doesn't back down. Instead, he raises his sword and swings. I throw myself back, losing my hat on the bar behind me. Moving just in time, I drive my knife forward, slicing the guard's forearm. He cries out in pain as blood begins to trickle to the floor, adding to the stains. The first guard, barely back on his feet after I injured his knee, plows into me from behind. We fall to the floor, fighting for control over my dagger. The guard with the busted nose slips out of the tavern. Smart man.

After I head-butt the guard I'm wrestling with and break his nose, I eye the remaining one.

"I'll ask you again." I slide my copper eyes down to the guard's hand. He snarls and charges, raising his sword as if to take my head off. Sliding from its path, I grab the guard by the back of the neck with my wooden hand, knock the sword from his grasp, and drive his nose into the edge of the bar. Blood explodes from his face as I then lift him and slam him down, pinning him with my wooden hand. I raise my dagger for him to see, and his eyes grow wide with panic.

"No!" he begs. "Please."

My head cocks to one side. "I admire your manners in such a high-stress situation. Most would forget them." Leaning closer, I lower my voice to a growl. "Answer my question, and maybe I'll let you go."

The guard writhes under my grip, fighting to get free, but he won't. He doesn't take long to answer. My face remains neutral and cold, but I'm not enjoying this. I don't want to have to hurt these guys, they're just doing their job after all. But I have a reputation to uphold, even if I hate it.

"Y-yes!" the guard answers. "I like my hand."

I grin and nod my head. "Good," I say, then drive my dagger down. The guard screams, my blade sticking from the bar just between his middle and ring fingers. He turns as white as a sheet as I lean in, a few locks of black hair spilling over my ears. "I'll be leaving now, and if I see you again—"

"You won't, Captain… sir."

"Good, because next time, I'll take it."

The guard nods, so I release him and step back. Tucking my dagger back in my belt, I reach over the bar and snag my hat, placing it back atop my head. The young woman who served me stands there with her mouth agape. I pull out five more gold coins and slide them across the bar.

"Sorry for the interruption, miss," I say, softening my face and smiling. She just stares at me until I turn around and head for the door.

Before leaving, I turn to see the kid at the back still watching me. We've never met, but I know who he is. I just did business with his father an hour ago. I wonder what he's doing in a place like this, but he isn't my concern. As I tip my hat to him, he starts to smile, and then I'm out the door.

The briny air welcomes me back as I stomp down the cobblestone path toward the harbor. My fingers touch the pocket of my jacket where the piece of paper is safely tucked away. I lift my head as the *Chained Maiden* comes into view, with her red sails already unfurled and ready to catch the wind.

Climbing the ramp up to my ship, I pause as I spot a shadow out of the corner of my eye. As I turn, the shadow disappears behind a stack of crates on the empty docks. Smiling to myself, I willingly turn my back and board my ship.

ONE

JACK

The salty brine of the ocean burns my throat as I scream. As my body is dragged through the water. As I drown.

A sense of calm comes over me as my eyes scan the sea, though my lungs scream for air, and my fingers are bloody down to the bone. It's like a hurricane—chaos, and yet at the center, peace. I try to hold on to that, thinking I won't die, not this time anyway. I've been here before and was sure I'd be here again before the ocean finally claimed me. The sea is cold and consistent, always claiming souls that aren't ready to die. But that's how death is, I suppose. You can never be ready for it, no matter how many you've seen die around you. You're never prepared for your own.

Selfishly, I ask the sea to wait and return me to the world above.

I will not die like this.

"Captain!"

Someone stands over my bunk as I startle awake, kicking at my cracked leather boots. With a fresh curse on my lips, I sit up and rub the sleep from my eyes.

"Oh, good, you're awake."

It's Tetra, my shipwright.

"What?" I ask, annoyed that I've been woken, even if it was from a nightmare. Tetra levels her golden eyes on me, crossing her arms defiantly. She's large for a woman, taller than most of my crew, and stronger.

"Well," she says, rolling up the sleeves of her tunic, revealing the black ink that curls across her brown skin. "We're being pursued."

"Right on time," I say to myself as I get up and brush my black hair from my face, though I'm seeing more and more grays mixed in these days. I'm only forty years old, but you can't tell by the looks of me. I try to avoid a mirror, not that my sunbaked skin or crow's feet bother me—I just avoid looking at the man staring back. The man who wonders what the hell I'm doing.

Tetra follows me from my room on the aftercastle, and when the ship lurches, we both stayed balanced. After so many years at sea, my legs are more accustomed to waves than dirt.

"Where's Hraefn?" I ask over my shoulder as I double-check my belt for the whalebone dagger.

"Already in the crow's nest," she answers in her thick accent, as if the word crow has more than one O. Tetra is from the Isle of the Lost. It's a small island in the Southern Sea, full of secrets and danger—a pirate's paradise.

I stay the hell away from that island as much as I can.

As I shove through the door, I shade my eyes from the sun and glance up, watching as Hraefn unslings his rifle and waits. Following his gaze, I spot two large ships gaining on us. Their dark-purple sails tell me they're guards of the governess from the Sunken City, a land we only just left last night. This isn't a surprise.

To my right, my navigator is staring down at a map with his bronze compass in hand. Walking over, I snatch away the map, roll it up, and smack him over the head with it.

"Sundance," I address him with as much calmness as I can muster. "Do you plan to outrun them? Take them on a wild goose chase through all these obstacles?" I spread my arms out and gesture sarcastically to the vast open sea. The governess has some of the fastest ships in the whole continent of TerrisØl

His hazel eyes narrow on me, crinkling his skin and making him appear older than his thirty years. Sundance gets my point and tucks his compass back into his breast pocket and adjusts his glasses. "You'd catch more fish with chum than a spear."

Pushing the map into his chest, I brush past him. "Uh-huh."

All around me, the crew springs into action. Having been in many situations like this before, they know what to do in case of an attack. Though I doubt they'll be firing on us, not with the precious cargo I've got stowed away.

Just then, a cannonball whizzes past the ship and crashes into the sea ahead.

Fuck.

"See anything?" My voice is carried with the wind up the mainmast and to the crow's nest. Hraefn shakes his head, his blue-black hair swishing over the shaved sides of his scalp.

"Not yet!" he calls down. "I think they're warning shots!"

Ace, Hraefn's best friend and a constant pain in my ass, cackles by the mainmast. "They've got some balls, aye, Captain?" His arms are crossed over his chest, posture relaxed and cocky as usual.

I shake my head, trying to ignore him. "Ace, do me a favor and shut up."

"What?" he asks, brushing back his feathery blond hair. "It was an honest question."

Hraefn calls down to his friend, "Your big mouth is gonna get you killed one day."

"One day," Ace agrees with a grin.

Hraefn turns back with a snarl on his lips, just as another cannonball is fired.

The sea explodes on the port side of the ship, rocking the *Chained Maiden*. Her red sails snap in the wind as they hopelessly try to carry us away, but the governess's ships are almost on us. Hraefn swings down from the crow's nest and lands on the deck next to Ace, who gives him a playful shove.

"What do you think they want?" he asks, but I don't answer. My crew doesn't know the details of why we stopped in the Sunken City, and for now, it's better that way. I just need to find out how I'm going to tell them what I'm hunting.

Ace taps my shoulder. "Uh, Captain?"

I follow his gaze back to the ships, which are now on both sides.

"Tetra!" My voice carries out across the deck, and a moment later, she's at my side. "Drop the anchor."

She snorts, then realizes I'm serious and steps closer. "You want to let them board us?" she asks, confused.

"Yes."

"Ha!" Ace slaps a hand on my shoulder. "The captain's lost it. Do you ken who they are?"

I tilt my head down and look at his hand, then back at him. A silent order. Ace removes his hand promptly. "I know who they are," I say, turning back to Tetra, "and I know what they want. Anchor. *Now.*"

"Aye, Captain," Tetra says, shoving Ace aside as she barks out orders to the crew standing by. Men and women rush to obey my order. As we come to a halt, the governess' ships flank us, and moments later, a ramp is slid over. My crew looks at me, uneasy but I just lean up against the mainmast, arms crossed over my chest. The guards spill out onto the deck, swords drawn, but I order my crew to keep their weapons away.

"Jack!" one guard shouts, as he comes aboard. "I have orders to search—"

Ace cuts him off, bringing his cutlass up to the guard's throat so quick I don't even see him draw it. Ace is a master swordsman who has had years of training, though he's only twenty. The guard swallows nervously, and Ace grins.

"That's *Captain* Jack. Now, let's try again."

"*Captain Jack*," the guard snarls.

Ace removes his cutlass and sheathes it, patting the guard on the back. "That's better, lad."

I roll my eyes. Ace always needs to make a show of things.

"Captain, we have orders to search your ship."

Behind the guard, Tsu immerges from behind the mizzenmast. Tsu dresses in dark, tight clothing with a hip-length cape and large hood that shadows her delicate features. Her footsteps land silently as she approaches the guard from behind. Tsu lowers her hood, revealing her short-cropped black hair and a mask that covers her nose and mouth. It's black, with gold stitching that swirls across it. She slides her emerald eyes to the guard's back, then to me, and tilts her head in question: *Do you want me to kill them and toss them overboard?* A kind offer, but I shake my head and look back at the guard.

"What are you searching for?" I ask innocently.

The guard begins scanning the faces of my crew. "Not *what*, but *who*."

Pushing off the mast, I walk around the guard and spot him —the kid from last night. His dark skin shines with sweat and his coppery eyes are creased with worry. I'd spotted him last night following me back to the ship and figured he'd sneak aboard, which was why I ordered Tsu not to be alarmed and to refrain from killing him the second he stepped on the ramp. I assume he's been hiding belowdecks somewhere until he came up with a plan.

We make eye contact, and I nod just once. The kid relaxes against the crates that conceal him under the aftercastle. Above him, on the aftercastle, my first mate watches me carefully. Story always has some piece of advice for me, some wise words as to how I should run my ship. I pretend that it annoys me, but in all honesty, I'm grateful for the old man. He cocks his head in question, and I answer with a slight dip of my chin. *I've got it under control.*

Story's lips curl into an almost smile, an amused one. He isn't worried.

Stepping in front of the guard, I block his view of the kid. "And who is so important that you feel the need to waste my time searching my ship?"

"Caspian Vulten," he answers, lifting his chin.

Caspian, huh? I laugh, scratching at my beard. The crew begins to look around, speaking in hushed tones. "A Vulten? On my ship? I don't think so."

"Either way, Captain, I have my orders." He starts to move past me, but I place a firm hand on his chest.

"Orders from *your* governess mean nothing to me. Get off my ship." His lips curl into a snarl, and around me, the crew is becoming uneasy, and the rest of the guards tense. The guard in front of me bares his teeth and removes my hand.

"The governess—"

"Is back in the Sunken City," I say. "And these are not her waters, which means that here, on *my* ship, I'm king, and you're trespassing." My tone is dangerous and laced with a warning.

The guard looks around, twisting his lips in anger.

I place my hands behind my back and continue. "The Vultens are the most powerful family in the Sunken City besides your precious governess. So tell me, *guard*, why on earth do you think some rich spoiled brat would be hiding on a ship full of pirates heading away from his home?"

The urge to turn and ask the kid this directly is almost overpowering, but I'll get my chance. Right now, I need these guards off my ship. The guard falters for an answer, then shakes his head and says, "His father reported him missing last night.

Apparently, he got into an argument with his brothers and father and left."

I shrug slowly. "So? Some kid ran away from home because his father is an asshole. How does that lead you to be standing here on my ship?"

"Caspian Vulten is… somewhat of a fan of yours, according to his father. He owns a shop in the—"

"I know what Mr. Vulten does," I say, now losing my patience. "Just because the kid likes pirates doesn't mean he's here, and I'd know if I had a stowaway." I step closer, letting my breath wash over the guard's face as I snarl, "Now you have one minute to get off my ship before my sharpshooter puts a bullet through your thick head."

On cue, Hraefn unslings his rifle and eyes the guard with his steely gaze. The guard seems to think about this for a moment, to consider all his options, but there's only one. Letting out a tired sigh, I click my tongue, and Hraefn aims at the guard's head, who finally throws his hands up in surrender.

"Okay!" he yells, backing up, turning to address his men. "Off the ship! Now!"

The rest of the guards start to back away and go across the ramp.

"I'd move a little faster if I were you," I say, turning my back on them. "One minute isn't a long time." At that, they begin to run, and my crew shoves their ramp from our gunwale the second they're back aboard their own ships. I stand there for a few minutes and watch as their ships begin to turn around, heading back to the Sunken City empty-handed.

With the guards a safe distance away, I tell my crew to get back to work and set sail. Story is by my side now. "What was that about, Jack?" His gray hair catches the breeze, and his wrinkled face is pinched up as he stares at me. Story was the first member of my crew, and he's by far the oldest.

"Seems we have a stowaway, Story."

"But—"

"Kid!" I call over my shoulder. "Get your ass out here, now!" The crew around me halts what they're doing to watch. The confusion on their faces confirms that no one knew about the kid, except Tsu, of course. A moment later, I hear footsteps behind me and turn around to face our stowaway.

He's tall and broad, wears a fine pair of pants and a light cotton shirt and has a leather pouch around his waist. Swiftly, I step up to him, snag the pouch, and grab him by the throat, slamming him up against the mainmast.

"Jack!" Story warns, but I ignore him.

The kid chokes and claws at my hand, his eyes wide with panic.

"Why did you follow me last night?" I demand.

Behind me, Ace lets out a cackle. "Would you look at that! We've got ourselves a stowaway. Hey, lad, how'd you get on board without Tsu here takin' your head?"

"Shut up, Ace," Hraefn growls.

My focus is still on the kid, and I release my grip a little to allow him to speak. "Answer me."

"I… I saw you in the tavern," he croaks.

"Aye, I saw you too, kid. That's not what I asked."

He struggles to get free, so I release his throat and grab a handful of his shirt, leaning in closer. "Why did—"

"I couldn't stay there!" he yells, baring his teeth and shoving his hands into my chest. His copper eyes do a quick scan of the faces around him before landing back on me. "Throw me overboard if you want," he says, putting his hands up in submission. "I'll just find another ship."

Stepping back, my brows knit together as I stare at him. The kid lowers his arms and stands up taller against the mainmast, though his hands stay clenched, as if he's preparing for a fight. My mouth quirks up in the corner slightly.

"You're a Vulten, kid. What's so bad that you'd risk your life and board my ship?"

"My name is Caspian," he says defensively, but then his

shoulders round and he looks at his boots. "There's nothing back there for me now."

My arms cross over my chest. "You've got brothers and a father who's the richest man in the city. Doesn't sound so bad to me."

He looks around at the crew, then back to me. "No. I suppose it doesn't."

I narrow my eyes on him, then bark at the crew to get back to work. They move about slowly, keeping a wary eye on our guest. Story and Tetra go to the helm, but Hraefn and Ace stay off to the side, along with Tsu. I step closer to Caspian, and he lifts his chin to me, squaring his shoulders.

"So, what? You wanna be a pirate, is that it?"

"No," he says quickly, then stops. When he speaks again, his voice is lower and his eyes lose all the fight they showed a moment ago. "I mean, I don't know, I just… I just want to be free."

We stare at each other for a long moment, and I nod slowly. When I open his pouch, I find what must be over a hundred gold coins inside. Caspian reaches for the pouch, but I slam my hand into his chest, pushing him against the mainmast as I pocket the money.

"For wasting my time." I turn my back and start to climb the steps to the helm.

"Wait," the kid calls, walking over to the bottom of the stairs. "Does this mean I can stay?"

Turning, I look down at him and grin. "A Vulten, huh? We'll see how long you last."

CHAPTER

TWO

CASPIAN

YESTERDAY

"**W**ake up!"

My eldest brother, Martel, stands over my bed with a grin on his face. "Get up, little Cassy, it's time for work."

Anger burns in my chest, warming me awake. "Don't call me that," I growl, sliding my feet over the edge.

Martel laughs, wrinkling the crow's feet that have begun to form near his eyes.

"Oh, relax. Gods, you're always so serious."

Our mother isn't even cold in her grave yet, and already my family seems to have forgotten that she was ever here. I push my brother aside and grab a shirt from my dresser. The dark fabric matches my skin tone and makes my amber eyes appear sharper.

Martel rolls his eyes. "How much longer are you going to wear that shit?"

"It's called mourning," I grumble. "Maybe you should try it."

The smug look slides from his face. "What did you say to me?"

Well, here we go. "No one gives a shit that Mother is dead," I spit, whirling to face him. He stands a good two inches taller than me, but I look down my nose at him anyway. "You all act as if things are normal. That we should just move on and pretend it didn't happen. Maybe that works for you, but I can't do it."

Martel has the decency to look a little ashamed, but not much. "We all grieve differently, so don't stand there and judge me just because I don't want to dress like an undertaker." He steps closer until we're nose to nose. "And don't act like you loved Mother more than we did just because she babied you."

My anger bubbles over, as it does so often these days, and I shove my hands into his chest. "Fuck you, Martel!"

He snarls and grabs me by the shoulders, hooking his foot around my ankle and shoving me to the ground. My back slams into the hardwood floor, and I struggle beneath my brother's weight. I send my fist into his nose, but my angle is off, and something in my hand pops. A painful cry slips between my lips as I cradle my hand to my chest. Martel lifts me by the collar of my shirt and slams my back against the wall. As he rears back to punch me, my father bursts into the room.

"What the hell is going on?"

Martel shoves me away, touching his nose and dabbing the blood with the corner of his sleeve. My father steps closer, running his dark eyes over me with a look of disgust.

"Dammit, Caspian," he says.

"Me?" I yell, though I shouldn't be shocked he's taking Martel's side. Shouldn't be hurt by the look he gives me, but it still stings.

He pinches his brow together between thumb and finger. "You can't keep doing this."

"Doing what?"

He snarls at the bite in my tone. "This!" He points to all of me. "Walking around here like a dead man, starting fights with your brothers over nothing."

"Martel was the one—"

"Enough!" The rumble of his voice shakes me to my core. "You're a Vulten, start acting like it."

I bite back my retort, swallowing the words like a bitter pill.

My father eyes me, challenging me to speak out again. Satisfied, he turns to Martel. "Go. Your brothers already left. And clean yourself up," he calls after him. When my father turns back to me, he looks ten years older. His dark hair glimmers with strands of silver, and when he frowns it's as if the skin of his brow is permanently wrinkled. "Caspian," he sighs. "Get yourself together. I've got important business today, and I don't want you and your brothers fighting."

Scoffing, I say, "Martel deserved it."

"Fine." He holds up his hands in submission. "Just keep it out of the shop." He adds a half-hearted *please*.

I nod but keep my eyes on the floor.

"Good. Now change your shirt and get going."

After I wrap my hand and change shirts, I head out the door. The sky is clouded over, and the wind promises a storm. I breathe in the brine of the sea and feel that familiar pull. I pause and look back at our house, which sits up against a rocky cliff overlooking the sea beyond. The image of my mother on the second-floor balcony flashes before my eyes, her hair whipping in the wind as she hums to herself. Or the front gardens, where she enjoyed reading or spent hours tending to her plants like they were her children. I see her everywhere I look, and I hate it.

Turning, I follow the path out onto the main road. Horse-drawn wagons bounce by, carrying the rich off for a day of shopping. I curse my brothers for not waiting for me, knowing I have a good two miles to walk. My father's shop sits in the main marketplace at the heart of the city. It's a sprawling four-story brick building with stained-glass windows and yellow flowers that hang from the eave near the front door. My mother chose those flowers, saying the yellow would pop against the dull red of the bricks. I've made sure to water them frequently since she died, trying to keep some part of her alive.

As I push through the doors to my father's shop, I'm met by the laughter of my brothers. They stand over by the counter, hunched over on elbows and leaning in as Martel fabricates a story of what just happened. He catches my eye and winks, and the youngest of my brothers, Damien, who is only three years older than me, barks out a sharp laugh that sounds fake. I turn away, not allowing myself to get drawn into their shit. Not today.

My feet carry me up the wrought-iron spiral staircase to the second floor. This whole floor is filled with antiques gathered over the years from pirates and sailors. It's my favorite part of the shop, and I know every piece my father has.

Not all of this stuff is real, and my father sells lies as often as he sells this junk. But not all of it is junk to me. I've always loved storybooks on pirates, sailing the seas, and fighting sirens or harpies. How sea monsters swallow ships whole, leaving only one man to tell the tale. My mother used to read me those stories as a kid before bed, even though she always thought I'd have nightmares. They were always just dreams.

Pulling over a stool, I climb up and gently slide a small wooden box toward me. The top is coated in dust, but I don't bother to brush it off. I sit down on the floor with the box in my lap and lift the small golden latch. Inside is a human hand, now no more than bones. I pick up the pointer finger and examine the smooth white bone, running my thumb over it. A small gold ring hangs loosely on the bone, with a ruby set in the center. I know who it belongs to, though I've only ever heard legends of him.

Captain Keelhaul Jack is said to be the cruelest and most dangerous pirate out there, killing for the fun of it. There are endless stories of how the famous pirate lost this hand, but I bet they're all fake. I suppose it doesn't matter how he lost it, but I do wonder how my father came to have it. I suspect that my brothers know more about my father's dealings than I do.

"Caspian!" Damien's voice slices through my thoughts. I put the box back and peer over the railing to see him waving at me. "Get down to the storage room," he orders. "Father has one last shipment coming in."

Sighing, I say, "I unloaded the last one. Why can't—"

"Oh, I'm sorry," he says sarcastically. "I thought I told you to do something."

I open my mouth to argue, but he cuts me off.

"I could tell Father how much you like a certain relic of his." He smiles wolfishly, wagging his fingers. He's caught me several times admiring the pirate's hand, along with the ring that still sits on the pointer finger. I can't say why, but it's as if it's calling to me, to that part of myself still buried beneath the surface just begging to be freed, begging for adventure. Damien knows I'd never steal it, but if the relic were to go missing, I'm sure I'd find his finger pointing in my direction.

The storage room is massive. Everywhere wooden crates are stacked as high as the ceiling. Oil lanterns hang on each post, but still the room is dimly lit, which makes it hard to read the writing on the crates. I grab a lantern and hold it up to each one as I pass, looking for the most recent date. As I near the end of the aisle, a pair of hushed voices pull at my ear. I recognize my father's voice immediately as he speaks to another man, whose voice I've never heard before. It's deep and rough, as if he's spent a lifetime yelling. My curiosity gets the better of me.

Following the voices, I stop behind a wooden crate no taller than my hips. Crouching down unnoticed, I try to catch the last half of what my father was saying.

"...gold pieces is the price. Take it or leave it."

The other man has his back to me, and I can only make out his frame, as the lantern in front of him makes him appear to be made of shadows. "We agreed on one hundred. Or are you trying to broker a deal with me?" His voice is calm and cool but there's a threat nestled between the words.

I hold my breath, waiting for my father to decide. He rubs at the stubble along his jaw and narrows his eyes, but I can tell by his stance that he's uncomfortable. My father is never uncomfortable, least of all in his own shop, so who the hell is this man?

"Fine," my father says, seemingly irritated, but his body language says otherwise. I wonder if the man picks up on it as well. "One hundred. But I want a piece of what you find."

I hear the smile in the man's voice when he speaks next. "No, you see, there's no negotiating after a deal has already been made." The man takes a micro-step toward my father, who backs up a step. "You'll give me the piece of the map, I'll pay you, and then I leave. That's the deal. If you can't honor it, well..." The man's left hand reaches down, his tanned fingers curling tightly around a whalebone dagger on his leather belt.

Sweat beads at my temples, but I stay rooted in place. I have no idea who this man is or what my father has gotten himself into, but I know I can't help. Even if I wanted to, I'm not sure what I can do. My father's throat bobs as he swallows. Then, schooling his features as best he can, he nods in agreement.

"Smart man." The stranger takes his hand off the knife and rummages around for some notes and gold coins. My father's nose flares slightly as he reaches into his pocket and pulls out a small rolled-up piece of paper. They both exchange treasures at the same time, my father immediately beginning to count his money. "Do you think I'd hold out on you?"

"Well," my father starts, then thinks better of it. "No, of course not."

The man steps closer, his voice lowering to the point where I almost can't hear it. "Then we're done here."

As he spins on his heel, I duck down behind the crate and listen to the man's footsteps until I'm sure he's gone. Then I hear Father grumbling to himself as he, too, turns and leaves out the back door. What the hell was that? Do my brothers witness this kind of thing often? Our father dealing with who I assume is a dangerous man, and for what? A map? I've never seen it before, and I know everything in this shop, so why did Father keep it hidden? Maybe I can ask him—

"What the hell are you doing?"

Martel and one of my middle brothers, Leon, stand behind me, arms crossed and murder in their eyes. "Damien told you to unload the last crates," Leon says, bending down to get in my face. "Were you eavesdropping on Father?"

I ignore Leon and turn my gaze to Martel. "Do you know what that was about?"

"What?" he asks innocently.

"That guy," I say. "Do you know him? Have you ever seen him before?"

Leon snorts, answering for Martel. "We see all kinds of people come through here. Who the hell cares what his name is?"

I shake my head. "He seemed… off. Father was afraid of him."

Martel's eyes darken as he speaks. "Don't let Father hear you talking like that. Now, come on. Get back to work."

I don't know if it's my anger or the adrenaline from sneaking around that I always get, but I stand up to my full height and say, "No."

Martel laughs in my face, and I lose it. I'm sick of them treating me like shit, always pushing me around and thinking he can control me. Enough is enough. I'm a Vulten just as they are, and Father is right: it's time I start acting like it. Like *them*.

Before Martel can even blink, I rear back and slam my fist into his nose. His head flies back as he stumbles into a stack of crates, sending one crashing to the floor.

Leon is on me immediately, shoving me back until we slam into a post. "What's your problem?" he asks as I struggle against him. Martel shoves Leon away, grabbing my shirt and balling his fist. He rears back, and I tense up as I prepare for the blow.

"What the hell is—" My father's voice makes Martel freeze. "Again?"

"Father," Martel tries to cut in, but my father holds up a hand to silence him, turning his cold gaze on me.

"I can't do this anymore," he says, sounding defeated, yet the fire burns brighter than ever in his eyes. He slides that gaze to the crate we've knocked over, and I swear I see smoke coming from his ears. I look over at the ruined relic, probably something rare or expensive.

Or stolen. It now lays in a hundred pieces that shine in the light of the lantern.

The look on my father's face could melt iron. Coerce a dormant volcano into exploding. "You're worthless," he snaps, voice stinging like acid. And then he explodes. "Do you know what you've cost me?"

I push myself to my feet but stay backed up against a tower of crates. My brothers watch me with slits for eyes as my father lays into me.

"You've always been so much like your mother, never taking any interest in the business. Well, guess what? This is your family, and you will do as I tell you! Family comes first, and if you can't—"

My cackle cuts him off. "*Family comes first?*" I ask. "Oh, that's rich. Especially coming from you."

A dark cloud slides over his eyes. "What did you just say?"

I lift my chin. "You never give me the time of day, but them." I jerk my chin at my two brothers. "You had plenty of love and guidance for them, didn't you?"

If my father is hurt, he hides it well. That only enrages me more. "Do you even know I'm here?" I scream, hands shaking at my sides.

His mouth opens and closes a few times, but he doesn't

answer. I feel tears forming and try to blink them away so my brothers don't see.

My father steps closer, his face mere inches away from mine as he hisses, "Maybe I wish you weren't." His words are like a knife to my gut, and I can't help but falter a little. As soon as the words leave his mouth, I see a flicker of regret in his eyes. Even my two brothers look shocked at the words, but they don't say anything, and it's too late anyway. I shove past him, the loud ringing in my ears muffling my father's voice.

"Caspian!" he calls. "Wait... I..."

The rest of my brothers stare at me as I storm from the shop and into the late afternoon sun. I'm done. Done with allowing them to mock me as if I'm a child. Done with living under my father's thumb and watching my own back against my kin. Done with being taken advantage of. And done with this life that I was born into.

As my feet lead me back home, I pause to look at my mother's gardens, inhaling the scent of the roses before pushing through the doors. I go straight up to my room and start packing a bag and rounding up all the money in the house. I won't be here when my father sputters some half-assed apology. Or when my brothers need a quick laugh and a seemingly easy target. I don't know where I'll go, but that doesn't matter right now. It's like my mother used to say to me: I need to find my own path, an adventure.

This is the start of something new. I can feel it.

THREE

'm beyond relieved when Captain Jack says that I can stay. He might not think I'll last long, but I'll prove him wrong. Maybe this *isn't* the stupidest idea I ever had. I mean, I didn't know what I was doing until I got down to the docks and saw his ship up close.

The black wood was polished and shone in the moonlight, and the wood carving at the bow of the ship was haunting. A woman with her hands chained behind her back and a scream frozen on her lips. The bottom half of her body seemed to be made of waves, but the top half was exposed for all to see. I found myself lost in the terrified look in her eyes and wondered how someone managed to capture such emotion in wood. After I'd peeled my eyes from the ship, I spotted Captain Jack walking up the ramp, and then I knew I had to follow.

I've always been light on my feet, a trade I learned from walking on eggshells my whole life. If my family wasn't rich, I would've made an excellent thief. It's the only thing I have left to offer since the captain has taken all my money and left me with nothing but my clothing.

A young man about my age claps me on the back. "This way, lad." His hair is golden and fluffed from the wind, and his eyes match the pale sky above. He has the same accent as the barmaid from the Blue Crab, though his seems more washed out.

"Name's Ace," he says as I follow him down the deck. He points up to the crow's nest. "That there is our sharpshooter, Hraefn." I don't even look up at Hraefn's cold stare, but I thought I felt his eyes on me. "Tetra's the shipwright," Ace goes on, pointing toward the helm. The strong-looking woman is talking with Captain Jack, though both their eyes follow me.

A dark figure moves out of the corner of my eye. Ace pauses by the stairs and nods to a woman bathed in shadows. "That's Tsu," he says, lowering his voice some. "You don't wanna be messin' with her, lad. Tsu'll cut your head off so quick, you'll still be blinking when it hits the deck."

I swallow hard and avert my eyes, and Ace chuckles, slapping a hand on my back and gesturing for me to follow.

Ace leads me down to the bunks just one level belowdecks, pointing to one at the very end. "You can have that one across from Hraefn."

Great.

I drop my sad bag of clothing and look around. The bunks are nothing like my bed back home. Something pulls at my heart as I imagine my home back in the city, and I wonder if I'll ever see it again. I realize Ace has been talking.

"… and the lasses are right down the hall next to the galley. Our cook, Bas, should be makin' up some supper for us." And with that, he leaves me alone to go in search of food.

I feel extremely out of place, and a small spark of panic catches inside me. I don't know anything about ships or sailing. I can't navigate or use a sword, so what the hell am I doing here? And of all the pirates, I chose Captain Keelhaul Jack to bring me out into the world. He's a dangerous pirate, likely being hunted by more than one region, and here I am throwing myself in harm's way.

Stumbling my way back up to the deck, I make my way over to the gunwale. My legs aren't used to being on the sea, as I've only ever been fishing with some childhood friends before. This is different—the whole ship moans and gives with the waves, making it seem somehow alive. I feel a pair of eyes on me and turn to find Tsu staring from up in the netting along the masts.

"Hello," I try, then immediately feel ridiculous. I can't make out much from her expression since she has a mask covering the lower half of her face, and she stares unblinkingly.

"Oh, leave him alone, Tsu." The sharpshooter, Hraefn, swings down behind me. I barely notice Tsu's shadow as she drifts away.

"She's… intense," I say carefully.

Hraefn chuckles, showing off a mouthful of perfect teeth. His complexion is pale, and his hair so dark that it seems to swallow light. He stands a few inches taller than me, with a lean build and a scar that drags across his left cheek. It disappears under a dimple when he smiles, but his sharp blue eyes are like daggers.

"So," he says and pulls out the coin purse that the captain had taken from me. Hraefn weighs the pouch in his hand for a moment, then tosses it to me. "It's all there. The captain doesn't need your money."

"Thanks," I say, looping the pouch back on my belt.

Ace comes and hangs an arm around Hraefn's shoulder as he gnaws on a chicken leg. "Has he bored you to death yet?" He coughs on his food, laughing at his own wit.

Hraefn rolls his eyes and looks truly exhausted, and I find a smile tugging at my lips. Hraefn shakes his shoulder until his friend unslings his arm. "Ace, don't you have something better to do?"

He taps the bone to his clean-shaven chin and then tosses it overboard. "I'm sorry, I thought I'd spend some time with our new crew member. Is that a problem?"

"Only if he turns into a walloper like you."

"Ha!" Ace smacks him on the back. "Never say I didn't teach you anything, lad."

I clear my throat. "A walloper?"

"Idiot," they both answer, then chuckle.

Hraefn's eyes lower to my bandaged hand. "What happened there?"

I look down, having forgotten about busting my hand on Martel's nose. My fingers run along the dirty bandage. "My brother."

Hraefn studies me for a moment, his eyes flickering with warmth. I shift uncomfortably on my feet. His eyes are beautiful, and I find myself staring. Ace steps between us and then wipes his greasy fingers on Hraefn's jacket, which earns him a punch to the shoulder. "I'll take him to see Nitelocke."

Peeling my eyes from Hraefn, I turn back to Ace. "Nitelocke?"

The concern must show on my face because he smirks and says, "Ah, not to worry, lad. Just a nickname." He runs a hand through his golden hair, then pulls a metal pick from his jacket and starts picking his teeth. "Nitelocke's our doctor."

Hraefn tilts his head toward his friend, his brows raised. "Doctor?"

"Well, he is," Ace protests, then adds, "He's also the captain's master of poisons."

My stomach drops to the deck, and my face must register worry because they both begin to chuckle lightly.

"Don't worry," Hraefn says, leaning back against the mast, his black hair falling over one side of his shaven head. "Nitelocke is a gentle creature."

"That's because poison is a woman's weapon, and he doesn't have the balls to—"

"All right, Ace," he says curtly. "Would you just take him already, or do you plan to talk him to death before we have a chance to put his skills to use?"

My cheeks heat slightly as I lock eyes with Hraefn. He seems intrigued by me and my sudden arrival amongst their crew. He leans in suddenly, and the scent of gunpowder washes over me. "Captain might have use for a boy like you—" He stops himself, then looks me up and down. "How old are you anyway?"

"Eighteen."

Hraefn smacks Ace's chest. "Congratulations. You and Tsu aren't the youngest on board anymore."

My eyes immediately start scanning the shadows in search of the mysterious young woman. Ace proudly proclaims that he's twenty, and Hraefn is just one year older than his friend. I've only gotten a small glimpse of the crew, but I already notice that they are different in every way—all ages, races, and from all walks of life.

Two levels belowdecks, Ace drops me off at the back of the ship in front of what I thought was a storage room. I rap my knuckles against the wooden door, and it immediately swings open. "Ah! You must be the fresh meat."

My instincts tell me to run, to get away from this guy, but then why would they allow me to stay just to poison me? I nod, and the man steps aside, allowing me to enter his room.

Nitelocke isn't what I was expecting. I'm not sure what I expected, but it isn't the man in front of me. He's stout, with a thick head of red hair and a matching beard kept tight to his face. His eyes are gray, almost purple at the edges, but that could be a trick of the light. He wears a leather apron that covers a clean tunic, and his boots look freshly polished. "You hurt already?" he jokes, lifting my bandaged hand.

"It's from my brother," I say but don't elaborate.

Nitelocke clicks his tongue as he examines the wound "Ah. Brothers can be nasty."

Nasty is a nice way to describe them.

"You have brothers?" I ask, following his movements as he wanders over to a wooden shelf housing many glass vials. Nitelocke mutters something to himself and speaks over his shoulder, more interested in the medicine than the patient.

"Nope."

I stare at this strange man as he hunts for something to either help me or poison me with, but then my eyes start roaming the room.

The room looks like a storage area that's been converted for the doctor. Crates line the back wall, and to the left, what look like dried herbs and flowers hang from the ceiling. "Here we are." Nitelocke gestures for me to sit on a stool next to a bench.

"What is that?"

He pops the lid off a glass jar and starts unwrapping my hand. "Just a salve, boy. Now keep still." My hand is swollen, but I don't think anything is broken, and Nitelocke confirms this. He starts rubbing the soothing cream into my skin, and the pain immediately fades, giving way to a cool and tingly sensation. Nitelocke smirks at my confused expression. "It's my own recipe," he proclaims proudly. "Had plenty of practice to get it right."

"How long have you been part of the crew?" I ask.

Nitelocke flicks his finger over my wounded hand, and amazingly, I feel nothing. Satisfied, he turns back to his workstation. "Oh, it's been some years now." He glances over his shoulder with a knowing grin. "But I don't think that's the question you wanted to ask, was it?"

My cheeks heat slightly, and I shake my head before asking what I really wanted to know. "Why does a captain need a master of poisons?"

He smiles and runs his eyes over the shelves. I follow his gaze, where it lands on a small white flower shaped like a bell. Nitelocke goes over and carefully picks up the dried plant and cradles it like a baby bird in his palms. "Do you know what this is, boy?"

I shake my head.

"It's called lily of the valley." He holds it closer for me to see, but I find myself leaning away instead.

"It's poisonous?"

"Very." He puts it back on the shelf. "To animals and people." He turns and straightens some vials on his shelf.

"That doesn't answer my question," I say as he moves on to a stack of dusty books.

His tone is nonchalant. "No, it doesn't."

"But—"

"Careful, boy." He turns around slowly, his gray eyes shimmering in the candlelight. "Jack is a private man and wouldn't take too kindly to some kid poking around, you hear me?"

I open my mouth to speak, but he steps toward me quickly.

"Especially someone he isn't sure about. If I were you, I'd keep your head down, do what you're told, and maybe you'll survive amongst this crew." He holds my gaze for a long moment before breaking it. "Now go on. Supper will be served in the galley." He dismisses me with a wave of his hand, not bothering to turn back to make sure I've left.

I find most of the crew in the galley, hunched over bowls of stew, laughing and talking. Ace waves me over from the back where he sits next to Hraefn and Tsu. I weave my way through the tables and benches, nearly slipping on some spilled ale. "There he is!" Ace spreads his arms as if to embrace me but doesn't rise. "The lad with the silent feet."

Tsu eyes me from where she sits, and I notice she doesn't have any food in front of her. Ace slides over a bowl of stew, then continues his conversation with Hraefn.

"It's not our business anyway," Hraefn says.

I spoon some stew and take a bite and almost spit it out. It's oily and pungent, with a fishy aftertaste.

Ace grins at my reaction. "No, the stew isn't great today, and yes, we're talkin' about you."

I look between them, then set down my spoon. "Oh."

Hraefn drains his ale, then reaches for the flagon. "Ace here thinks there's got to be some other reason you don't wanna go back. Like you killed a man and you're running."

My brow furrows. "I didn't kill—"

"No, no!" Ace interrupts, waving a hand in my face. "Don't

tell us. I love a good mystery." He leans in, forcing me to snap my head back. His eyes narrow as he smiles. "I'll figure you out, Caspian."

I put a few fingers to his chest, pushing him back gently. "There's nothing to figure out. I'm an open book."

"Not a great trait for a pirate," Hraefn points out.

I shrug. "I'm not a pirate."

"You're a stowaway and a thief," Ace says.

"Excuse me?"

He shrugs and takes a sip of ale, leaning back. "It's how you managed to sneak aboard, right? I ken you're light on your feet, so you must be a thief. That's why you're here, isn't it? What was it, kid? What did you steal?" His frantic tone has me shaking my head, but Hraefn speaks before I can answer.

"The captain said he knew he was being followed, you walloper. You're drunk, Ace."

"Ha!" He claps a hand on Hraefn's back, sloshing his ale. "I ken when I've had too much, lad. Don't be tellin' me my business."

Hraefn just shakes his head and sighs deeply. I can't help but smile, and then Hraefn's eyes are back on me. His gaze flicks down to my lips, then back up, and he offers the smallest smile in return.

Breaking his gaze, I turn and look around the large room, taking in the new faces and ones I suppose I'll get used to if I decide to stay. But I notice an absence. "Where's the captain?"

"He eats alone in his quarters," Hraefn explains.

I nod but find it odd that a captain wouldn't want to eat with his crew. But then again, I don't know the first thing about being part of a crew of pirates. "So, where are we going?" I ask Hraefn, but he turns his head down at the question, his face going grim.

I look at Ace for an explanation, and he says, "Vulkan."

It's the only other piece of land large enough to be considered a continent. The rest of the world is made up of islands, large and small, and sandbars. I've read a lot about Vulkan. Most of the north is made up of rocky mountains, all surrounding a massive volcano. Apparently, it's been dormant for hundreds of years, and the people give sacrifices to their gods to keep it that way.

"Where in Vulkan?" I ask.

Hraefn shoves back his chair, snatches up his ale, and storms out of the galley. I look at Ace in question, but he waves it away.

"We're headed for the Helm. The largest city."

"For what?" I ask while looking at where Hraefn disappeared.

"Ah, just pirate stuff," Ace answers with a grin.

"Right."

I haven't touched the rest of my food, which is probably cold by now. I pick up a heel of bread instead and tear off a piece, but then I drop it when I spot a young woman approaching the table.

Her shoulder-length hair is the color of hazelnuts, and her skin is light amber. Her left arm is covered in black tattoos from shoulder to wrist, and when I meet her eyes, I freeze. They're the loveliest shade of brown, and I find myself staring. Ace kicks me under the table as the woman veers away, sitting two tables down from us. "Who's that?" The woman crosses her legs and leans her elbows back on the table.

"Wipe the drool from your mouth, lad," Ace says around a chuckle. "What's the matter? You never seen a woman before?"

My cheeks heat instantly, and I remove my eyes from her.

Ace slides over to me and slings an arm around my shoulders. "That there is Skye."

My heart kicks up at the mention of her name—it's as beautiful as she is.

"She's our translator. Captain picked her up somewhere in the Constellation Islands two years back."

My eyes find her again, but I quickly look down at my cold bowl of stew.

"She's a tough one." Ace scooches away and downs the rest

of his ale before getting to his feet. "Come on now. Best be off to bed. We've got a long few days ahead of us."

Following him out, I glance back over my shoulder once to see Skye watching me with an endearing smirk playing on her full lips.

CHAPTER

FOUR

HRAEFN

The sun glides over the calm sea, creating blankets of
light as we travel toward a place I used to call home.
The Helm is the largest city in Vulkan, and though I
know the captain has business there, *know* we need to go there, I
find it hard to swallow the closer we get.

Spotting Ace down below, I let my mind clear as I swing my
legs over the ledge of the crow's nest. Anytime I know we're
headed to the Helm, I spend most of my time up here. The gulls
that circle our ship tell me that land is close, but I try to ignore
their calls. Instead, I focus on the wind, the smell of the sea—
anything but the screaming voices in my head. The ones that
haunt me at night. One of them is mine.

"Watch it!"

My eyes flit back to Ace, who's sparring on the decks below
with Caspian. He isn't very good, and I'd wager he's never even
held a sword before, but still, Ace keeps at it. I guess if he's
going to try to be part of our crew, he'll need to learn how to
defend himself.

"Hold it like this, you dobber!" Ace wraps his hand under
the guard of his cutlass, then widens his stance.

Caspian mimics his stance, but even I can see from up here

that his eyes are uncertain. I smirk as I polish my rifle and watch Ace knock him on his ass for the hundredth time this morning.

"Gods, lad," Ace breathes. "You could at least make it a challenge for me. It's like fighting a bairn!" He chuckles, and Caspian growls as he gets back to his feet.

Caspian thrusts his cutlass forward, but Ace slides around him and smacks him on the back of his head with the flat side of his blade, tsking at his pathetic attempt. "Hey, Hraefn!" he calls out, knowing I'm watching. "How much you wager the lad loses a limb in his first fight?"

Caspian turns his amber eyes up to me, and I look right at him and shrug, setting aside my rifle and bringing one leg up to rest my elbow on. "Oh, I don't know," I drawl. "He might not be good with a sword, but he's slippery like a fish."

Ace throws his head back and laughs, and Caspian takes the opening.

He arches his blade through the air, only to hit Ace's mid-swing. Caspian drives his weight into the cutlass and pushes Ace back, though he maintains balance. The two dance around each other, Ace with a smile on his lips and Caspian with a snarl on his. Ace isn't even sweating as he dodges another blow and flips his sword through the air, catching the hilt and driving the pommel into Caspian's chest. He coughs from the blow and staggers back but keeps his sword raised. "He's got some fight in him!" Other members of the crew have gathered on the deck to watch the sparring match.

Ace was trained by a master swordsman when he was just a little boy, so I know Caspian is no match for him. If Caspian knew who Ace was, I wonder if he'd treat him differently. Everyone on this crew has a story, but by now, we all know one another's. Well, not everyone knows the captain's. I glance over to the helm, where Story and the captain stand chatting. As if he can sense my gaze, the captain turns his eyes up and catches me staring. He nods once, then turns back to Story, who seems to be speaking in a hushed tone. I don't know what the captain stopped in the Sunken City for, but it seems Story might know.

We've learned not to ask unnecessary questions by now. We all trust the captain with our lives and know that whatever he does, he does for the good of his crew. He's saved a lot of us, in a way, taking us aboard his ship, though I know he had other reasons for selecting us. A crew needs to be made up of various skilled people to be called a full crew. Ace is a master swordsman, Tsu an assassin, and I'm a sharpshooter.

Story was the first member of the captain's crew and is privy to more of Captain Jack's dealings than we are. I'm sure that Caspian knows by now that we aren't saints and that we deal in the illegal sale of alcohol. But this isn't just any alcohol. It's Ostium, banished in every city and town across the globe, save for a few. Sure, we trade in goods at port cities and harbors, but the real business is illegal.

We make frequent visits to the Isle of the Lost and a few small towns around the Constellation Islands. Those are the only places that allow the sale of Ostium, and the only place we don't have to hide the bottles. Usually, we sell Ostium in small vials, hidden inside large bottles of ale with pop tops. But in those places, we sell the alcohol by the barrel. The captain forbade us to ever try the product we sell, saying it's highly addictive. I've seen enough of our customers to know that it's true, but I've also heard that it heightens your senses and intelligence. I can see why people want such a drink, but it's a trap because the more you abuse it, the more you come to rely on it.

Some say that it's been around since ancient times and that people thought that they could talk to their gods if they drank enough. The name means *venom* in a language that is no longer spoken, at least that's what Skye tells me.

I scan the decks, then swing down the mainmast, landing just behind Ace. The fight is over, and I can tell by the look on Caspian's face and his labored breathing that he's been beaten.

"If you want to gain a certain someone's attention, I'd practice some more if I were you."

Caspian follows my eyes to where Skye sits with a couple crew members, Yonis and Remmie. They've been watching Caspian the whole time. I could swear he's blushing. He quickly turns away from Skye and eyes Ace.

"How do you know she wasn't watching Ace?" he asks, side-eyeing me.

"Me?" he asks innocently. "Oh, no, lad. I barked up that tree one night."

Caspian narrows his eyes. "And?"

Ace sheathes his cutlass and rakes his golden hair back. "Nearly got my hand lopped off for it."

Caspian smiles at that then dares another look at Skye. She's a beautiful girl, no one can deny that. She tried to kiss me one night after too many drinks, but I turned her down. She knows I prefer men, and was embarrassed about the whole thing to the point where she didn't speak or even look at me for weeks.

I find my eyes resting on Caspian's new look. One of the crew members has given him a haircut. Now his curly brown hair only rests on top of his head, and the sides have been shaven down like mine. He wears loose black pants and tall boots, a cream-colored short-sleeve tunic, and a thick leather belt that covers most of his abdomen. He keeps the cutlass on his left hip, and his purse of coins tucked into the back. He catches me staring. "What?"

"Nothing." I turn to hide the blush in my cheeks. "We should be arriving in a few hours. Do you know what your job is?"

"Yes," he says, somewhat defensively.

I turn back and stalk toward him. "Don't get too cocky. This is a job, not some fun adventure for you to write about in your diary."

Ace laughs, and Caspian glares at me with those amber eyes before marching off.

"What's your problem?" Ace asks. "We've done this a hundred times."

"But not with him." I watch Caspian go belowdecks, then turn back to Ace. "The captain entrusted us to get him ready. This is a test for Caspian as much as it is for us."

"All right, all right." He holds up his hands, then stretches them overhead. "It'll be fine. Besides, if he gets caught, then it's more coins for us."

At that thought, I punch Ace in the shoulder and walk away, but he calls after me.

"What the hell was that for?"

"Because Ace, you're an ass."

I hear him scoff at my back, then grumble, "That's not even clever."

Later that evening, I stand at the bow of the ship as the Helm comes into view. Ace stands to my left, but it's Caspian to my right who holds my attention. His eyes are wide as we approach the city. There's wonder in his gaze, and I remember a time when I felt the same about my old home. Now, all I feel is a dark cloud hovering over me as the sea pulls us closer.

"What's it like?" Caspian asks, keeping his eyes ahead.

Ace nudges me with his shoulder, making me bump into Caspian. "Ask Hraefn, he used to live here."

Caspian turns to me, and I could've thrown Ace overboard just then.

"You used to live here?"

"A long time ago." My voice is nothing but a whisper. I can feel Caspian's eyes on me, but I turn away to hide the pain that I know lingers on my face. Suddenly I feel bad about earlier. I shouldn't have gotten angry with him, but I can't help it. Coming back to this place brings out the worst in me, and I know I should apologize, but my lips stay shut.

As soon as we dock the *Chained Maiden,* the captain rounds us up. Most of the crew will stay on the ship to guard it, while the rest go into the city. We'll be here for at least a day, and I know the crew is itching to get some good food and girls. The captain stands in front of us, dressed in his usual attire, a crisp white tunic covered by a long blue overcoat that goes to his knees. His cocked hat is lowered, shadowing his eyes.

Ace, Caspian, and I are to go into town and find a man named Bart. He runs the black market in the Helm, and Captain Jack has dealt with him many times, but today he has other business to attend to. No one questions what it is, but we all wonder. I trust the captain and know he'll tell us anything that we need to know, and nothing more.

"You stay along the rooftops," he tells Tsu, who nods once in acknowledgment.

Caspian eyes her, and I know I'll have to explain her silence before he says something stupid.

"Hraefn." I turn back to the captain. "Keep your eye sharp." He looks at my rifle slung over my back. "Bart knows me, but he's never dealt with my crew, so watch out. Just make the deal and get out of there. Sell the rest to the names I gave you earlier."

"Aye, Captain."

As we step onto the wooden dock, the captain doesn't look back at us before taking off. He knows we'll get the job done and trusts us to do it right. Caspian wheels a cart full of ale, some containing small vials of Ostium that we'll sell to Bart. I pull up the hood of my cloak, though the night is clear and warm with a cool breeze coming down from the mountains. I look up at the city as we make our way down the street.

Tall buildings rise around us, all different shades of gray or black stone, with tiled rooftops. I think I catch sight of Tsu following us from above, but I doubt it. She's like a shadow that detaches itself from the human it once followed.

The streets are packed with people, some sitting outside local bars and cafés, enjoying an evening meal. I hear Ace's stomach rumble and shoot him a sideways smirk.

"What?" he asks. "Can't we just stop for—"

"We'll eat when we're done," I snap.

He twists his lips in a frown. "Fine."

Caspian's eyes dart in every direction. They admire the colorful lanterns swinging in the breeze and the flower boxes that hang from every window. He smiles as a few children run by chasing an orange cat that doesn't seem to be having as much fun. This city used to mean everything to me, and I would've defended it until my dying breath.

But that was before.

Sometime later, we find ourselves on the other side of the city, nearly outside of it. The black market looks like any other market, except you'll find things here that you can't anywhere else. We stay close together as we weave our way through the small booths, ignoring the men shouting at us to look at their products. Caspian keeps his eyes down, and I can't blame him. This place is the armpit of the city, and though Earl Thera has tried to be rid of it, I guess even she recognizes the money it brings in. It makes me sick to think that I once swore to protect her and this city at all costs.

At the very end of the row, a large man sits on a crate beneath a tall pine. He has a small table with what I can only assume are stolen gems and jewelry. When he stands up, I hear Caspian take in a sharp breath. The man has to be nearly seven feet tall and is as thick as a tree trunk. His long beard is braided down to his chest, and his brown hair falls in waves down his back. His one green eye scans the three of us, the other is sealed shut by a nasty-looking scar.

"Bart."

His eye slides to me, and he crosses his arms over his broad chest. "And who the hell are you?"

Ace steps up. "We're here on behalf of Captain Keelhaul Jack."

Bart sits back down. "Is that right?" He picks up a curved horn of ale and drinks deeply, letting the amber fluid run down his beard. "All right, then, let's see what you've got."

I nod to Caspian, who cracks open one of the crates and pulls out a large bottle of ale. Bart waves his fingers impatiently, and Caspian hands it over. He snatches the bottle away, then holds up a lantern to the glass. Barely visible inside is the vial of Ostium floating around.

Bart snickers and sets it down. "How much?"

"Three gold coins per—"

"No." He points to the crate. "How much do you have?"

Ace puts a hand on the hilt of his cutlass.

"Sorry," I say. "We have other customers besides you."

Bart rubs his beard and grumbles something under his breath. "You know, I've known Captain Jack for a long time." I can feel Caspian's unease to my right, and my own starts to creep up my spine when Bart grins. It's nasty and dangerous. "He'd sell it all to me if I gave him a fair price."

Ace takes a small step forward and addresses Bart before I can. "Like my friend said, lad. Captain gave us orders, and we're not likely to disappoint him. Now, I ken you think you can cheat us out of our money, but it won't happen. Two bottles, that's what we have for you. Take it or leave it."

My heart starts to race a little as Bart stands up. My fingers itch to feel the smooth wood of my rifle, the familiar weight of it, but not yet. He meets each of our eyes, then clasps a hand on his belly and begins laughing. Ace and I exchange a look. What the hell is wrong with this guy?

When I glance at Caspian, his eyes aren't on Bart, but on the tree line. He's looking for Tsu. As inconspicuously as I can, I reach out, jabbing my fingers into his ribs. He startles and gives me a pointed glare, but he'll get us all killed if this deal doesn't go right. Bart stops laughing and nods his head, though his eyes linger on something behind us. I don't dare turn my back on him. Tsu is out there watching us.

"Very well," Bart relents, rummaging around his table for what I hope is the money.

I clench my fingers into fists, once again resisting the urge to grab my rifle. Glancing at Ace, I nod at his sword, and he sighs dramatically before removing his hand from the hilt.

Bart turns back and starts counting the gold coins. "Six," he says, tucking them into a small leather purse and throwing it at Caspian. We hand over another bottle with the hidden Ostium before turning to leave. But we don't get ten paces away before Caspian nudges me in the side.

"Hey, he cheated us."

Ace's stomach rumbles again. "We watched him count out the coins, lad. Six was the deal."

"Yes, but—"

"Enough. I'm near to starvin'. Let's get something to eat." Ace stretches his arms out, then clasps them behind his head and continues walking ahead of us.

Caspian grinds to a halt, dropping the handle of the wagon and turning to face Bart. Dread pools in my stomach.

"What the hell are you—"

"Hey!" he calls and starts walking back.

My arm flies out, and I seize his wrist, whirling him to face me. "You want to get us all killed?"

Caspian leans in and says, "They're fake." Then he rips his arm from my grasp.

Ace is at my side again, cocking his head from left to right. "What?" Ace snatches the purse away and takes out a gold coin. "You need your eyes checked, lad?"

"No, but apparently you do." He grabs the purse from Ace and walks briskly back toward Bart.

"Fuck." The word comes out in a snarl as I unsling my rifle

and scan the shadows for Tsu, though I know I won't see her. Ace and I follow Caspian, leaving the cart in the street.

"Is there a problem?" Bart asks innocently as he sits back on his stool. Caspian stalks right up to him and throws down the purse.

"Deals off," he says, his tone confident. "Pay us what you owe, or we're taking the Ostium back."

Ace runs up with his hands up in surrender. "Apologies. He's new, doesn't know what he's talkin' about."

"Yes I—"

Ace claps a hand over his mouth, but Caspian drives his elbow into his gut. My attention is pulled over to our right, where a few men begin to emerge from the shadows. Adrenaline warms me as I scan the approaching threats. One, two, three men, and more coming. Bart stands up to his full height, but Caspian doesn't shy away.

"You callin' me a liar?" His voice is deep and dangerous.

Caspian doesn't even blink. "Yes."

Motherfucker!

Bart flashes his teeth and picks up the purse, dumping the coins onto the table. "Look real to me."

Caspian shakes his head patiently as if correcting a student. "Vulkan coins have the helm symbol on one side…" He picks up a coin, revealing the circular rune. "And the first earl on the other. But right here." He points to a nearly invisible slash through the earl's eye, and my mouth drops. It's the common symbol for contraband money, not noticeable to the untrained eye. But of course, thieves know what to look for and can get away with using it in the markets. I regard Caspian in a new light.

Caspian tosses the useless money into the dirt. "My father has the best collection in the world. I've seen everything." He steps closer. My finger hovers over the trigger. "You'll need thicker wool to pull over my eyes."

To my left, Ace smirks—he's impressed. As am I, but this isn't the time for praise.

Bart cackles, the sound grotesque and vicious. "A keen eye for a new pirate." He reaches back and pulls out a hatchet. "Maybe I'll take one to replace mine."

Caspian reaches for his cutlass, but we're already surrounded by men, and I pray to the gods that Tsu is here.

FIVE

The limbs of the pine tree don't even sway as I select a spot and crouch down. High in the tree, I keep a careful eye on my crew, knowing Bart is shady. Caspian seems to be looking for me, then Hraefn pokes him in the ribs, bringing his attention back to our sharpshooter. He's new, and I don't expect him to be an expert on his first run. But still, he should know better than to be actively looking for the assassin meant to keep him safe.

I know he's curious as to why I haven't spoken to him yet, but he doesn't need to know everything about our crew right away. Besides, who's to say he's even going to make it? Maybe Jack will decide he isn't worth our time and leave him in some port town on our next stop. Or maybe the kid will be killed tonight, and we won't have to speculate anymore. I'm not sure why I call him *kid*, since he's only two years younger than me. Maybe it's because my childhood was robbed from me, and I'm envious that he's had eighteen years of freedom before joining us. Although didn't he say that freedom was the one thing he lacked in his life?

How can that be? He's a Vulten, and his father is practically made of money, and yet he ran away from that. I guess I have no right to judge; clearly Caspian left for a reason. But I doubt he considered what it meant to be a pirate before he snuck on board.

When I turn back to my crew below, they're arguing with Bart over the money he's given them. Silently, I pull the twin short swords from the sheaths that rest horizontally across my back. I scan the approaching men, take a breath, then jump.

My boots land without so much as a whisper on the grass below. I hold my swords flat against the underside of my forearms as I dart from shadow to shadow.

There's arguing coming from the group. The voices belong to Bart and Caspian. Great, this isn't going to be an easy night. Just down the path from Bart's booth, I spot two men strapping on swords. One of them wears a vest that holds at least ten throwing knives. Clearly, this exchange isn't going to happen, so I act quickly and silently.

The man with the sword walks closer to the wood line, bending behind the counter to reach for a dagger when he catches my eye. "What the—"

I drive my blade up through his bottom jaw before he can finish the sentence, then catch his weight and carefully lower him to the ground. Peering over the edge of the counter, I eye the next man. He's stretching his arm and glancing down the path, likely looking for a signal from Bart. I glide over to him on the tips of my toes and tap him on the shoulder.

"You ready?" he asks, then his eyes go wide when he spots me. A garbled sound comes from his lips as he looks down and sees my twin blades in his gut. As I slide them out slowly, he gasps for air but only manages to spit up blood. I drag his body out of plain sight, then creep through the other dark booths, listening as the argument grows more heated.

More men begin to emerge from the shadows, though I knew where they were all along. There has to be twenty of them, all armed and frankly very large. An annoyed sigh slips between my lips, pushing heated air on my cheeks. The urge to return to the ship is strong. I'm not a fan of crowds or large cities such as the Helm. I grew up in a large empire, but I can't say that I've ever felt at home there. It wasn't until after I left that I discovered who I am and what true freedom tastes like. Perhaps Caspian and I do have something in common after all.

Crouching down in an abandoned booth, I quickly douse the lantern that swings above my head. My eyes find Bart just as he's pulling a hatchet from behind his back. The rest of his men take that as their signal and begin emerging from their spots, stalking closer to my crew. Hraefn levels the barrel of his rifle at the closest man, but still, he doesn't fire. Beside him, Caspian and Ace already have their cutlasses drawn and backs together as more men seep out of the shadows.

I take off in a silent sprint toward the closest man, swinging my blade through the night and taking his head off. His body drops behind me with a soft thud. At this point, Hraefn spots me, and I give a quick nod before he opens fire.

The loud crack of the rifle echoes through the night, and Bart's men spring into action. Two peel off and head straight for Caspian, but Ace jumps in his path. His sword is a blur as he slices through the men, painting the dark air with crimson ribbons of blood. Hraefn hops up onto a counter and drops to one knee. His barrel follows a man sprinting behind the booths before Hraefn lifts and pulls back the charging handle. He slowly squeezes the trigger, and the bullet tears through the man's temple, collapsing him mid-run.

Two men go down just ahead of me, the bullet having gone straight through the skull of the first one. I leap into the air, pushing my foot off a wooden post and sending my blades down the spine of a large man with an ax. He screams in pain and crashes to his knees, reaching over his shoulders to try and grab me. Pulling one blade free, I slice off his wandering hand, then kick his flailing body to the bloody grass.

The other men have taken notice of me by now. One hurls a knife in my direction. I raise my blade and deflect it, sending the knife off into the darkness. "You little, bitch!" he snarls, pulling another from his belt and throwing it at me.

My body folds backward, the tips of my hair almost touching the grass. The shine of metal sails past my face. I reach into my boot and pull my knife, then roll out of the way and let it fly from my grasp. The knife finds its home in the man's thigh. I rush him, and he panics, throwing up his hands in defense, but I don't strike. Instead, I jump, slamming my foot into the hilt of my knife and driving it deeper into his thigh. I launch myself over his falling body as the man drops to his knees. Behind him, I cross my swords over his throat and slice. Blood sprays from his neck in long spurts, and then he falls face-first, dead.

Caspian grunts as he tries to hold off the weight of a large man with an orange beard. I run to him, sliding under the sword of a man and slicing the backs of his heels as I spring to my feet again. Bart swings his hatchet furiously at Ace, who ducks and dodges with his hands behind his back. His movements are graceful and sure, but his face is split in a grin. He's too cocky. Peeling my eyes from Ace, I head toward Caspian, who finally spots me. With Caspian's gaze averted, the man thrusts his blade forward, slicing Caspian's upper arm.

He hisses through his teeth but doesn't drop the sword. I put my swords back in their sheaths. Reaching in one of my many pockets, I pull out a collapsible staff. With a flick of my wrist, it snaps open to its full length. Caspian stumbles as he backs away from the man, his shirt now sticky with blood.

"Some pirate you are," the man scoffs.

I narrow my eyes on him and lash out, sending the end of the staff into the center of his back. The force of the blow breaks it in half.

Fuck.

The man stumbles forward, then turns to me with murder in his eyes. "Ahh, got a lass with you, huh?" His eyes run over me slowly, taking his time. Rage heats my cheeks behind my mask.

He points the tip of his sword at me and smiles. "Maybe once we kill your friends here, I'll have a go at you."

Caspian gets back to his feet, but I shake my head once, and he stays put.

"Tell me, lass. Are you a screamer, or are you always this silent?"

I wait patiently while he makes his move. Around us, a cacophony of noises dances through the air. The crack of Hraefn's rifle, the grunts of men, the screeching of metal on metal. I push it out, find that silent place inside myself as I eye the man before me. He takes a step closer. His first mistake.

"You think you can intimidate me, lass?"

I only stare at him, which seems to anger him more. Another step. Mistake number two.

"Don't worry," he says. "I'll try not to mark up your pretty face. Although"—he slides his eyes down to my mask— "I'd like to see the mouth that'll be around my—"

Rushing him, I slide between his legs and drive my fist into his groin. He lets out a pained yelp and drops his sword, clutching himself. His last mistake. Kicking out the back of his knees, I pull a wire from my pocket and wrap it around his neck. His hands fly to his throat, but it's too late. The thin metal wire bites into his skin as I force him to his back and crouch over him. I lock eyes with him, his now burning with fear. As soon as they go dead, I rip the wire from his neck, wipe off the blood, and tuck it back into my cloak.

Caspian stares at me with wide eyes, his sword hanging limp at his side. "You… you're…" He clears his throat and tries again. "Thank you."

I tilt my head slightly in response, then turn to see Ace still toying with the giant man. Hraefn has a pile of bodies around the booth where he now stands, trying to get a shot at Bart.

"Would you fucking *move*?" he barks at Ace, but his friend just laughs as he ducks under Bart's hatchet again. Pulling myself up on a counter, I sit back on my hands and watch. Caspian comes to stand in front of me.

"Are you hurt?" he asks.

I take a moment to watch him as his eyes run over me, searching for blood, but he'll find none of mine. Shaking my head, I then lift a hand to gesture at his wound. He looks down as if he's forgotten about it.

I pull out a thin piece of cloth from my pocket and grab his wrist, pulling him closer. His eyes track my hands as I grab a small knife in my boot. Pausing, I cock my head and raise a brow to him. Caspian relaxes and allows me to cut away the bloody sleeve before dressing his wound.

"Thanks." He sounds embarrassed. Turning back to Ace, he asks, "Should we help him?"

Again, I shake my head and sit back, watching as Ace slits Bart's calf. He crashes down to one knee, and Ace steps aside, giving Hraefn a clear shot. The bullet tears through his thigh, and the man howls like a beast. Ace twists his face up and sucks in through his teeth. "That looks nasty, lad. Might wanna get that checked out."

"But Ace." Hraefn hops down from his perch and rests the rifle over his shoulders. "What do we do to people who cheat our captain?"

Ace taps a finger to his chin, then points it skyward. "Now I remember." He bends down, his tone growing cold. "Sorry, lad. But Captain Jack doesn't take too kindly to attacks on his crew. And!" He throws his arm back toward Caspian, rearranging his features into what would pass for genuine worry if you didn't know that Ace is a sarcastic asshole. "Your men bloodied up our new recruit." He tsks at Bart, wagging a finger in his face like he's a dog who messed on the carpet. "What do you think Captain Jack would do to you?"

Bart bares his teeth. "Fuck you, and fuck your captain."

Ace straightens up and pouts. "Well, that's not very nice."

Then he slashes his cutlass across Bart's throat quicker than I can blink.

Caspian looks a little green around the gills, but he doesn't avert his eyes.

"Right, then," Ace wipes off his blade before sheathing it. "Now, can we eat?"

Hraefn smacks him upside the head and moves over to start searching the dead bodies. Crouching over the one closest to me, I pull off his weapons and start digging through his pockets for coins. Caspian watches me closely, and I gesture to another body. He hesitates, then slowly bends down and starts doing the same.

"I want a rack of ribs," Ace says, nearly drooling on himself. "No! Sausage and more ale than my liver can handle."

"Looks like supper is on them." Hraefn tosses a purse full of coins to his friend, and Ace tucks it away. Hraefn catches my eye and inclines his head. "Thanks, Tsu. We can always count on you."

"Yes," Ace continues, turning to Caspian. "I told you she was dangerous."

He stares at me for a moment and nods. "I see that." I can't decipher his tone. Is he afraid of me or disgusted? It doesn't matter, I'm not on this crew to make friends.

"Tsu, will you be joining us for supper? You earned it." My hand freezes over a corpse I'm searching. Snatching my hand back, I toss a bag of coins at Ace, then stroll down the street. I can hear Hraefn smack him again, and Ace's complaint. "What? She did."

"Idiot."

Ignoring their eyes on my back, I head back to the ship. It's a long walk through the outskirts of the city, but as I said, I hate crowds. Ace knows that much at least, and though I've never actually been able to tell him my whole story, I gather that he learned bits from others. Jack is the only one who knows everything about me, and I know all of his secrets as well. I suppose he trusts me with them, and it formed a special connection between us. I don't consider Jack my captain, as the others do. To me, he's more than that. I don't want to say father figure because I doubt I'll ever see a man as my father again, but he's close.

As the *Chained Maiden* finally comes into view, I pause and look back at the city. Laughter pushes through the night from down the busy street. My crew will be out there having fun and drinking until their eyes shut for the night. I don't allow myself such luxuries because I'm afraid that if I give in, I'll remember what it's like to have a family. To have people around me all the time who care, and if I grow attached, it will only make it harder when they die. So, I stay away, shackled to the ship I once saw as an escape, and in many ways, it still is.

My home, Hanatsu, is on the other side of the world, yet I still feel its pull on me. I try to ignore it and focus on what Jack needs me to do, what I wasn't born to do but do now anyway. But if I had a chance to change things, I don't think I would.

As I head down a dark alley, just far enough from people that their laughter and voices are nothing more than whispers at my back, I hear the shot.

Whirling around, my eyes scan the city behind me, though I don't know what I expect to see. If Hraefn fired his rifle, then something has gone wrong, but I also trust my crew. They haven't let me down thus far, and besides, I'm here for another reason than to sell Ostium to black-market rats like Bart.

I turn around and keep heading down the alley, trying to focus on what I need and not what my crew is dealing with. After all, they have Tsu, and if she's there, then they'll be all right. Tsu is the best at what she does, and she's the most valuable member of my crew—at least to me.

Orange glass lanterns swing on curved iron poles, creating a warm glow on the cobblestones as I stroll through the city. Passing a small tavern to my right, I pause briefly just as a fight is starting. Two large men scuffle in the middle of the room, surrounded by patrons who do nothing to stop them, only cheer them on. I'd wager that the fight is over something simple, but the men look too drunk to care. The commotion drifts out into the street through the open door, and just as I turn away, the window shatters.

Turning back, I see one man lying in the street, bleeding from the shards of glass that stick from his arm. People roar and flood out to the street, creating a circle as the other man storms out of the tavern. He picks up the bloodied man by the collar and drives his fist into his nose.

"Hey!"

The voice comes from behind me. The crowd of people part as a Helmsword comes running down the street, rifle at the ready. A Helmsword is a man of the Helm, the city's version of royal guards. They have various jobs—keeping the peace, overlooking trading throughout the markets, and patrolling the streets.

"All right, break it up!" he calls as the people part for him. My eyes run over his uniform—black pants with a long moss-green coat that buttons up to his throat. I can tell by the gold circular rune adorning his chest that he's a higher-ranking Helmsword. Hraefn has a similar pin, though his is stainless steel and still contains the bullet that almost took his life.

I turn my back as the Helmsword deals with the drunk patrons and keep on up the road. I've never been this far into the Helm before. Usually, my business keeps me in the black market. Perhaps I'll make a trip there when I'm done with my other business. The crew will take care of selling the Ostium, but I'm looking to buy something, not sell. You can find anything you want there—drugs, stolen gems, pelts from rare animals, the fins of a siren… Even people, and that's what I'm after.

As I crest the hill, I spot a small wooden building butting up to large spruce trees that stand like giant sentries in the dark. The windows glow orange from the candles within them, and the large door is painted with scrawling letters that read AURORA'S HIDDEN TREASURES. I push open the door, a little bell jingling softly to announce my arrival.

"Just a second!" I hear a voice call from somewhere in the

back of the shop. I take a moment to look around a space that seems much smaller once inside.

Floor-to-ceiling shelves cover every wall, all decorated with mismatched items, some covered in so much dust that I can't make out what I'm looking at. A large elk antler chandelier swings from the pointed ceiling, where red candles drip wax, making it appear as though the antlers are bleeding. Off to my right, a small rounded counter guards a locked cage that contains what I'm sure is the shop's most precious treasures.

Light footsteps turn my attention to a wall of beads and small bones that part as a young woman steps through. She looks to be about thirty, with white hair cut close to her scalp and eyes that appear silver, like moonlight. When she smiles, it's as if her whole being lights up, and I swear her eyes sparkle like the stars.

"Welcome!" She spreads her thin arms out as if to embrace me. "My name's Aurora. And you must be Captain Keel—"

"Just Jack."

She drops her arms, smile faltering for a split second. "Very well." She moves behind the counter, her pale blue skirts swishing silently. Aurora leans her elbows on the surface and looks into my eyes. "So, Just Jack, what brings you to my little shop way up here at the edge of the Helm?"

Her eyes never waver from mine, and an uneasy feeling crawls up my back. I know not to trust this woman. People that have something valuable to sell will always be wary of their customers and do everything to protect themselves and their treasures.

Mimicking her stance, I lean in closer. "You know why I'm here."

Her eyes give nothing away, but somehow they remind me of one of her gods. She's known to be a trickster who uses her looks to lure in men, then uses them to get what she wants before throwing them aside and moving on to the next one. I've read a lot about the Helm and its culture, as with every place I frequent.

I won't be caught off guard by simple lack of knowledge of the place I'm in.

Aurora leans back and smiles. "You aren't going to be any trouble, are you, Jack?"

I grin. "Not if I don't have to be."

She chuckles low, winking as she spins around to face the locked cage. "Excellent. Shall we talk money, then?"

She pulls a long silver key from a chain around her neck and slips it into the lock. The doors swing open, and I'm shocked to see only one item inside the large cage. Aurora gently lifts the wooden box, turns, and places it on the counter. My fingers reach out to touch it, but she slams her hand on the box and pulls it back to her.

"Money," she repeats.

"How much?"

She taps a slender finger to her chin. "Oh, I don't know. Let's say fifty in notes, twenty in gold, *and* you tell me how you lost that." Her silver eyes slide down my left side, gesturing to my wooden hand.

I instinctively pull it behind my back. Her smile turns to a frown.

"No."

"No?" she repeats. "To the price or the story?"

"Both."

Aurora clicks her tongue and picks up the box. "Oh, Jack. And here I thought you'd be a man of your word and give me no trouble."

I narrow my eyes, my anger rising. "I'm giving you no trouble. We're simply negotiating."

"Is that what we're doing?" She taps a finger on the dusty wooden box. "It seems like you're refusing my offer, which I believe was more than fair."

An annoyed sigh escapes through my nostrils. The price in gold is more than fair. I paid Caspian's father one hundred pieces for the first part of the map, but I'm not willing to give her the story she wants. It isn't as if no one knows it; I just like to keep to myself. There are so many rumors about how I lost my hand that I won't give people the satisfaction of telling the real story. Well, I've told one person, but that's only because she's physically incapable of repeating it.

"Come now, Jack," Aurora coos. "Everyone enjoys a good story."

"Fifty notes, twenty gold," I agree, leaning closer over the counter. Her silver eyes latch on to mine, waiting, patient. "And perhaps I can offer you something else."

She sets the box down and leans in, bringing a hand up to my cheek and touching my beard. "Mmm, perhaps you can," she purrs.

Maybe she *is* the trickster god, after all.

Leaning away from her touch, I pull out a small glass vial I keep on me for situations such as this. Aurora's gaze slides to the small vial, then back to me, a wicked grin spreading across her pink lips. "Ostium?"

I nod.

She holds out her upturned hand. "May I?"

Her cold fingers brush mine as I hand it over. Aurora holds it up to the light, tilting it back and forth and watching the liquid slosh in the glass. "Does it really heighten your senses?"

I shrug. "That's what I hear."

She frowns, wrinkling her brow. "You mean to say you've never tried it?"

"No."

"Not even once? You aren't the slightest bit curious?"

"*No,*" I repeat, my tone harsher.

Aurora smiles, sliding the vial across the counter as she whispers, "Liar."

Dammit.

My patience is growing thinner. "Do we have a deal or not?"

Aurora twists her lips, and I begin tapping my boot, feeling the last bit of patience I have slip away into the night. "Fine," she finally says, holding out her hand. "You've got a deal."

I shake her hand, pay her, and only then does Aurora let me open the small box. Excitement courses through me like a child opening a present, not that I'd know what that feels like. But as I lift the lid and behold the small piece of parchment, I can't help but let a small smile curl my lips. I unroll it carefully and glance over the drawing. It's only a small piece, but still, there are only a few more out there, and I know just where to find them.

"Well?" Aurora uncaps the vial and inhales the scent. "Is it all you dreamed of?" she asks as if she were the one who'd drawn the map. I place it back into the box and tuck it into the inside pocket of my jacket.

"Pleasure doing business." I say and turn to leave.

"I'd be careful, Captain Jack." Her voice sounds dangerous, no longer bubbly and warm. When I look back, she's leaning against the empty cage, rolling the glass vial between her fingers. "You aren't the only one looking for that place."

I tilt my head and take a step toward her. "What do you mean?"

A shrug of her shoulder. "Just as I said." She puts the vial down and turns to face me fully. "People will do nearly anything to get what they want. They'll betray their friends, kill anyone in their way and stop at nothing. Tell me, Jack. What will you do to get what you want?"

My nostrils flare as I take another step closer. "Who else is looking for the map?"

She shrugs again with a cocky smirk on her face. "I couldn't say."

"Can't or won't?"

"Both."

An annoyed growl rumbles up my throat as I whirl around, throwing open the door of the shop, but her voice calls to me one last time. "I wish you luck, Captain." I pause, not looking back but not leaving either. "Perhaps the more time you spend in the dark, the more you'll start to see."

Stalking back to the counter, Aurora's smile drips off her face. My boots thump over the weathered wooden floor. Aurora doesn't move as I lean back over the counter, piercing her with my gaze. She blinks and casts a hesitant look to the door, then flits her eyes back to me. "I see just fine." I reach up to tip my hat, and she flinches at the movement. My lips curl into a half smile as I spin on my heels and then I'm out the door.

Drifting through the bustling streets like a ghost, no one pays me any attention as I pass crowded taverns, cafés, and groups of people rolling dice in the streets. Passing one tavern, I spot Hraefn's head of blue-black hair as he tilts back, sending his laughter to the rafters above. I take a second to make sure that Ace and Caspian are still there, and that they all have the right amount of limbs, then continue. Tsu won't be out celebrating with the crew, but I'll have to question Hraefn later about what happened with Bart.

Tsu has always kept to herself, though I think she enjoys my company. I recall the day I found her in a tavern in a small city on Terrisøl. I'd gone in to buy a few barrels of liquor for the crew when a fight breaks out. I expect to see a few drunk men throwing punches, but instead, I see her. She's tiny and quick, dressed in a long black robe and golden slippers that match the scrawling detail of her face mask. Her narrow eyes are calm and calculating as she challenges a group of men who advance on her. I go to pull my whalebone dagger, but the barmaid touches my hand and shakes her head, gesturing back to the young girl.

Tsu stands with her hands behind her back, waiting as the men's anger takes over.

"Hanatsian bitch!" one burly man roars. "You think just 'cause you're a woman that I won't hurt you for that?" Following his pointed finger, I spy a man that lies writhing on the floor, a welt forming on his head. Tsu doesn't speak a word, just keeps staring at the man until he turns purple with rage.

The barmaid speaks in my ear. "Man grabbed her ass. I say he deserved it."

Tsu turn back to her table, and the man charges. As swift as the wind, Tsu slides around the man, grabs hold of his arm, and uses his momentum to swing him around. She kicks at the small of his back, and the man stumbles to me, smacking his chin on the lip of the bar. Blood leaks between his bared teeth. "Don't just stand there! Get her!"

A group of four men charge Tsu all at once. She jabs her pointed fingers up one man's arm, forcing it to go slack, then rears back and punches him square in the temple. He goes down with a loud thud. The remaining three all grab for her, but Tsu launches herself into the air, kicking off one's leg. His knee bends to a sickening angle, and a pain-filled cry tears up his throat. Landing behind the other two, Tsu ducks under one man's swinging arm and drives her fist into his gut. He coughs from the blow, and the other pulls a dagger from his belt. Sweat beads my temple as I watch the blade arch through the air.

Tsu dodges the knife, ducking and twisting away from the blade and letting the man exert himself. His breath comes out in heavy gasps as he tries to slice her but only strikes air. As he tries miserably to stab her, Tsu grabs his arm, drives the heel of her palm into his face, then slides under his arm and twists it back. The knife drops to the ground, and I swear her eyes smile as she yanks it up, popping it out of the socket. The man cries out, and Tsu kicks him to the floor.

The one with the busted knee crawls away, and the other man seems hesitant to attack her again. The first man wipes the blood from his chin and curses at his men for being cowards. He storms over to her as Tsu turns her back, thinking the fight over. He wraps his arms around her small frame and whips her around to the man with the knife. He holds it shakily in his good arm and aims for Tsu's gut. Her leg flies through the air, kicking the knife away, then arches and makes contact with the side of his face. Blood spews from his mouth as he slams to the ground.

Then she throws her legs into the air and arches her back, dropping to her knees and throwing the man over her shoulders.

I smile as Tsu gets to her feet and dusts off her robe before turning back to her table. Patrons part for her, not wishing to be the next victim. The man, stubborn to his core, pulls himself back up. "You fucking bitch!" Tsu doesn't even turn to him. "You should go back to Hanatsu where you belong, serving your men and staying in line."

At that, her back goes stiff. The man stalks closer, spouting insults at her back and digging in his pocket. I see the barrel of a pistol and make to step forward, but Tsu moves before I can. If I hadn't been watching so closely, I would've missed her arm swinging back, cracking the man across the cheek so hard that his feet leave the ground. His eyes close before he even hits the floor, and he begins snoring. Knocked out cold.

I'm so impressed by her skill that I ask her to join my crew on the spot. She says nothing, lifting her mask slightly to take a sip of her ale before nodding her head. And she's been with us ever since.

The black market is mostly vacant by the time I arrive. Many of the small booths are boarded up for the night, and the owners are likely drinking themselves silly with their daily earnings. I walk to the back of the market, scanning the dark tents until I find what I'm looking for. A large cage meant for boars or bears holds a handful of people, all chained together. As I step up to the bars, a man rounds the corner, sharpening a knife. "Can I help you?"

I scan the terrified faces of the slaves, all women between fifteen and thirty. "Where did you get these women?"

"Ah, well, some are from Hanatsu, others from the Constellation—"

"No." I turn to face him. "*Where* did you get them? Who sold them to you?"

The man lowers his knife and looks at me curiously. "Well, Captain Blacktip. He always brings the best slaves."

Oh, I know that all too well.

Reaching in my pocket, I ask, "How much?"

He smiles greedily. "For which ones?"

I look at the girls, then back to the man before me. "All of them."

His eyes light up at the promise of gold. "Well, in that case, I'll make you a deal." He looks over the women, who back away as he approaches the cage. "Let's say, five pieces per girl, and they're all yours."

Bile rises in my throat at the disgustingly low price. "Deal."

The man doesn't hesitate to open the cage. He whips the first woman to get her out, and she falls to her knees. I keep my face blank as he snatches their arms and throws them out of the cage. Their shackled ankles clink as they shuffle outside and stand huddled together. I quickly pay the man, but before I can leave, he grabs one young girl and pulls her in.

"Careful of this one," he coos, running a finger over her plump cheek. "She's a fighter, but I bet you could fuck her into submission."

The woman starts crying silently, and I leave without another word to the man. I lead the women along the outskirts of the city to a small dock. It's poorly lit, and only a few small boats bob with the waves. I turn back, and the women shrink away from me, fear creasing their brows. Slowly, I pull the key from my pocket and bend down, gesturing for one's ankle. She eyes me with suspicion. Like I'm a monster.

"It's all right." My voice is low and gentle.

Warily, she slides her foot to me, and I unlock the shackle, revealing her bloody ankle. I quickly free the remaining women and pull out a small leather purse from my pocket.

They stay huddled together, too frightened to try to escape, even though they're free from their shackles. I count out the money—seventy in gold and some notes.

"Here." I hold it out to the oldest-looking woman. Her brown hair is matted. Her pale face is covered in grime, which accentuates the sharpness of her cheekbones. "Take it," I urge.

The woman takes the purse and looks inside, then snaps her head back to me. "Wh-what are you doing?"

"I have no use for slaves. You're free to go where you please." I gesture to the purse. "Use that to get back home or start over someplace new."

"Why?" the young girl whom the man warned me of asks.

I step closer, and she doesn't back away. "Just because I'm a pirate, doesn't mean I'm a monster."

Her eyes dance back and forth between mine.

"Go, take a boat, and leave."

The women don't hesitate again, and they all pile into a small boat. The young girl catches my eye as they drift over the smooth dark sea.

"Thank you," she calls back, to which I nod, then turn to leave.

Hraefn tilts his head back in laughter as Ace spits up some of his ale. It's contagious, and I find myself chuckling lightly as I sip my drink.

"The look on the poor lad's face!" Ace bellows, referring to Bart. "Tell me, Caspian." He slings an arm around my shoulder, his breath like hot ale on my neck. Hraefn watches us closely, his eyes locked on Ace's arm. "Do you ken how much trouble we'd be in if we went back to Captain with fake money?"

I shrug, mostly to dislodge his arm from me, but he doesn't. "I imagine he'd throw you overboard."

Ace nods in agreement. "That or send Tsu to give us a good beating."

Across the table, Hraefn throws an arm over the back of his chair and eyes me coolly. "You did good tonight," he admits, sounding sincere, though his eyes hold mirth.

I smile, and his eyes lower to my lips just for a second. "Does this mean I'm part of the crew?"

"Let's not get ahead of ourselves, lad." Ace gulps ale, wiping a drip from his chin. "Was beginner's luck is all."

"I don't believe in luck."

Ace shrugs. "And I don't believe in krakens, doesn't mean they're not real."

Hraefn leans forward, a lock of black hair falling between his scrunched brows. "Hang on, you don't believe in krakens? Are you crazy?"

"As I am handsome." Ace slides his cup to clink against Hraefn's, who chuckles and sits back again.

I lean forward, catching his eye. "Have *you* ever seen a kraken?" My cheeks feel hot as his crystal eyes hold me in place.

Then he smiles, wolfish. "Maybe."

"Ooo." Ace scoots his chair closer. "Do tell, lad."

"Maybe another time."

Ace snorts and waves a dismissive hand, rolling his eyes to the ceiling.

"You think I'm lying?" Hraefn asks, sitting forward and resting his elbows on the table.

Ace grins. "I ken you're a tease, so… yeah."

"Ass."

"Walloper."

They eye one another from across the table, challenging smirks on their lips before bursting out into laughter. Ace slaps a hand on my back, making me spill some of my drink. My eyes drift around the tavern as Hraefn and Ace continue to pick on one another. The room is crowded with people, and I can't help but notice a few lingering eyes. Most of these people look like Hraefn—pale complexion and dark hair—so I stand out. I'm not sure if it's me they're looking at or the men I'm with. Perhaps they know who we sail with and have heard legends of the captain.

As I turn back, I find that Hraefn's eyes linger on me as well, though I think it's for a different reason. It's also the only set of eyes that has my heart skipping slightly.

Clearing my throat, I stare at the cup in my hands. "So, what's with Tsu?" Unease settles in my belly as they both halt mid-laugh to look at me.

Hraefn brushes back his hair. "What do you mean *what's with Tsu?*"

"I-I just mean…" What *do* I mean?

Ace cuts in before I can tie my tongue any further. "Tsu is a strange creature, lad. Has been since she joined."

Hraefn snorts. "And what have you been?"

"Incredible," he answers with a grin.

Hraefn kicks him under the table. I smile, but I can't stop myself from asking what I've been wondering since I met the crew.

"Why doesn't she talk?"

Ace lets out a deep sigh, and Hraefn just stares at me, twisting his lips as he considers.

I backpedal. "Sorry, I didn't mean—"

"Sorry for asking a question or sorry for prying?" Hraefn's tone seems hostile, but I don't know why. Have I done something wrong?

"Oh, come now, lad. He's curious, as he has a right to be. Besides, he'd find out sooner or later."

"Fine, but if Tsu finds out, I'll point her blade in your direction."

Ace waves a hand at that. "So dramatic. Besides, it's not like Tsu can tell him herself." That earns Ace a hard smack on his upper arm. "You best watch it, lad, if you wish to keep that hand."

Hraefn snorts at Ace's empty threat and sits back in his chair. Ace turns back to me, and I struggle to sit up straight. I should've kept my mouth shut.

"Now listen, Tsu has a storied past, as do we all, but I'm afraid when it comes to fucked up, she takes the cake—"

Hraefn shoves back in his chair, tipping it over as he storms from the tavern, cursing under his breath. Confusion paints my face, and I start to rise. "Should we…?"

"Do you want to hear or not, lad?"

I do, but I find myself shaking my head. "I shouldn't have asked. Clearly, I upset Hraefn."

"Ah, Hraefn's always upset." When I don't sit back down, Ace sighs and waves me off. "Go on, then. Run along after him." My cheeks flare, with embarrassment or shame, I can't tell. But I grab up our drinks and head in the direction Hraefn went.

The night is crisp and clear as I step out into the streets. People stroll by, some swaying from too many drinks and cackling like fools. I spot a dark shadow to my left and see Hraefn sitting beside the tavern on a stack of crates. I approach cautiously, offering him his drink like a white flag. He takes it without looking at me. "I'm sorry," I say, though I have no idea what I'm apologizing for. He snickers, taking a sip of ale and setting it aside, leaning back on his hands.

He glances at me, knitting his brows together. "Well," he says, annoyed, "are you going to sit or stand there awkwardly?"

I opt to not be any more awkward, so I climb up onto the crate next to him. We sit in silence for a long time, watching people leave the tavern on wobbly legs, their laughter echoing in the night. Finally, he speaks but keeps his eyes forward. "Sorry. This place just brings out the worst in me." He chugs the rest of his ale and hiccups, and I notice his eyes look a little glassy. As I angle toward him, Hraefn shifts away slightly.

"You can talk to me," I offer.

"What? And ruin such a fine evening?" he answers sarcastically, huffing a laugh.

A frown touches my lips. "Is the evening really so bad?"

He turns to look at me, his eyes like ice in the pale moonlight. He lifts a finger to my hair, barely a touch, and then snaps it back to his side. "No," he answers, smiling. "I guess it's not."

I don't know what to say or how to react, so I sit there like an idiot and stay silent, letting my ale get warm between my sweaty palms. Somehow it works, and Hraefn begins talking again.

"You know I was a Helmsword?" I've seen a few men in uniform patrolling the streets after we left the black market.

They wear dark-green jackets and all carry rifles on their backs, identical to the one adorning Hraefn's now. I shake my head. He smiles crookedly, then drops it, turning his eyes back to the street.

"What happened?" I ask after a moment.

"She died," he whispers, half to himself.

"Who?"

His blue eyes well up with tears, but he blinks them away, and I wonder if I imagined it. I set my drink aside and reach out, placing a hand on his shoulder. "I'm sorry. I don't know when to keep my mouth shut."

Hraefn laughs at that, crinkling his cheeks and creating a dimple. "No, you really don't." I go to remove my hand, but he clasps his over mine. "But that saved us tonight. If you hadn't said anything, we'd all be screwed." His eyes twinkle as they hold mine, and heat starts to crawl up my neck. "You did good, Caspian. Truly."

"Thank you."

Hraefn nods then lets go of my hand, leaving a burning sensation on my skin. "I'm sorry for what I said in there." He jerks his chin toward the tavern. "I just meant... all of us have difficult pasts." He snorts humorlessly. "Seems like a rite of passage to gain a place amongst the crew, and well..." He shakes his head. "I just started thinking of my own shit."

"I get it," I say. Not to be nice or fill the silence, but because I *do* get it. My past isn't so far behind me, but I don't think time or distance will make it easier.

I drink the rest of my ale and lay back on the crate, looking up at the stars. Hraefn angles toward me and leans back on his elbow. "And what was so difficult that forced you to flee home?" His tone isn't unkind; he's genuinely curious.

The answer comes easy. "My family." His brows crease together in a question, so I continue. I tell him about my mother's death and how hard that was for me. Then I move on to my brothers and father, how I never felt like I had my own identity or my father's love and respect. I pour it all out, and Hraefn sits quietly, drinking in every word I utter. When I'm done, he lays back beside me and tucks his right hand under his head, letting the other fall between us.

He blows out a long breath. "That does sound fucked up." He turns, our faces mere inches apart. Hraefn smiles big and nudges me with his elbow. "You'll fit right in."

A snort escapes me, and my cheeks flare instantly, but it only makes Hraefn smile even wider. His eyes lower to my lips. I don't look away, even as my neck grows hot, and my heart thunders against my ribs. What the hell is going on? I can't decide, but when he smiles, I feel nervous all of a sudden.

Hraefn's hand brushes up against mine, the touch like a cold shock through my body. I'm frozen in place, too terrified to move, so he does. Hraefn slides closer, his eyes never leaving mine as if asking for permission, but I can't do anything but watch. His eyes drift to my lips again then back up, and then he leans in closer, our breaths mixing as one just before—

"What the hell?"

Hraefn jerks away and stands up so quickly that for a second, I think I imagined him being there beside me. I sit up to see Ace, arms spread out. "You hackit bastards just leave me alone?" A playful smile teases his lips like he knows what he just interrupted. "That's just rude."

I turn my head down, trying to hide my blushing cheeks, but I don't think Ace is in any state to notice anyway. He staggers over to Hraefn and slings an arm across his shoulders.

"Gods, you stink." Hraefn grimaces. Ace only laughs. He doesn't meet my eye as he addresses me, "Come on, we should get back to the ship."

I have no choice but to follow in their wake and try to ignore my still-fluttering heart.

When we get back to the *Chained Maiden*, Captain Jack is sitting on the steps that lead up to the helm. He waves us over, and I glance over at Hraefn. Ace hangs on his shoulder, mumbling something under his breath. Hraefn and I lock eyes for a long moment, and I feel that same nervous energy buzzing in my chest before he turns his eyes away.

"I should get him to bed," he says, gesturing to Ace.

I open my mouth to respond, but he's already turning away, disappearing belowdecks and leaving me alone with the captain.

Captain Jack watches me closely as I approach and stop at the base of the steps. He waves for me to follow. "Come on, storm's coming."

I glance up at the clear sky and furrow my brow in confusion but follow him to his quarters anyway.

The captain's room is on the aftercastle, just past the helm where the giant wooden wheel of the ship is stationed. He swings open the door and steps inside, not bothering to see if I follow. As I step into the room, I'm surprised to see the state of it. I can't say why I was expecting a mess, with maps covering the tables and crates lying abandoned on the floor, but it's the opposite.

The room is large and square, with dark wood from the ceiling to the floors. The whole back wall is a row of windows and a small door that leads out onto a balcony. The captain walks over to a large bookshelf to the right, just in front of a table set with four plush chairs. To my left, I spot the captain's bed through a cracked door, and on his night table, a stack of books spirals up toward the ceiling. A candelabra stands taller than me on either side of his desk, which sits in front of the windows. He lowers himself down, gesturing for me to sit as well.

I force my legs across the room, my steps going silent as I step on an ornate rug. He rubs his beard as he sits back, his copper eyes telling me nothing. "So," he starts, "how did the night go?"

The word *good* forms on my lips, but I know he wants to

know *what* happened. I clear my throat nervously and tell the captain of the fake money. His brows lift in surprise, then lower back to neutral as I tell him about the attack, of how Hraefn had no choice but to open fire, and how Tsu seemed to come out of thin air and killed I don't know how many people. His lips almost curl into a smile when I speak of her.

"Bastard," he mutters when I'm done. "I never liked Bart." His eyes land on the sleeve that Tsu had cut away. "You were hurt?"

"No. I mean, *yes*, but I'm fine. Tsu dressed the wound."

He nods. "And?"

"And… what?"

He stands up and comes around the desk, making my heart thump louder as he sits on the desk in front of me. Captain Jack leans forward, his eyes focused. "*And…* you still want to stay?"

I blink at him, confused. "Of course, I want to stay."

He cocks his head. "Why?"

"Because I have nowhere to go," I say, my voice rising slightly, and a flicker of anger sparks in my chest. Did he think that this mission tonight would help me realize that I don't belong here? That I'd never be a part of the crew? That I'm just some rich kid from the Sunken City who swam out into deep water and can't get back?

With a snarl on my lips, I step closer. He doesn't even blink, not threatened at all. "If tonight was some ploy to get me to tuck tail and run, then sorry to disappoint, but I'm not going anywhere. I'm no stranger to bloodshed." I lower my voice to a growl. "So you either accept me as part of your crew or put me through another bullshit test so I can continue to prove you wrong."

My mouth snaps shut, and I back up a step. Oh god, will he kick me off right here? Leave me in the Helm to find my way back home? What the fuck was I thinking, talking to the captain like that?

After a moment, someone clears their throat from behind. I

spin around to see Hraefn, posted up on the frame of the door. "You wanted to see me, Captain?" He looks right past me, and I turn back to Captain Jack, trying to keep my face passive. He holds my gaze for a long moment, then smirks and stands up.

"No need," he says without taking his eyes from mine. "I got what I needed to know." He dismisses us with a wave of his fingers, and I practically bolt from the room.

Outside, I lean over the gunwale on the lower deck, trying to calm my rapid breathing. Hraefn comes out a moment later and stands a safe space away. "Fuck, Caspian. You're lucky he didn't toss you to the sharks."

My stomach drops to my boots. "He's done that?" I ask, turning to look at him.

He purses his lips and shrugs. "Oh, he's done a lot of things."

I pinch my head between my hands. "I'm such an idiot."

"Agreed."

"Gee, thanks."

Hraefn chuckles and steps closer, leaning over the railing with me. "Relax, the captain just wanted to see if you had the balls to be part of the crew."

"And?"

He leans closer to me, the scent of the sea and gunpowder bathing me. A mischievous smile forms on his lips. "You're still here, aren't you?" Hraefn turns back to the water lapping against the ship. "I'm sure he was going to ask me my opinion of you, but you didn't need me after all. You stuck up for yourself."

I straighten and turn to face him fully. "Would you have stuck up for me?"

His cheeks flush, but maybe it's the crisp air around us. "I would've told him the truth."

"And what's that?"

Hraefn steps up to me, almost forcing me to take a step back. His blue eyes seem to be reading me, digging into the depths of my mind. He tilts his chin down, that stubborn lock of black hair brushing over his brow again. My heart thunders as I eagerly wait for him to speak, to say anything to drown out the buzzing in my head. His lips part into a smile before he speaks.

"I would've told him that you're smart and you know what you're doing. And that every great crew needs an even better thief."

I both smile and frown at that. "I'm not a thief."

He leans even closer, and suddenly I find it hard to breathe, to think about anything other than the closeness of his body to mine. "You are now." Hraefn holds his hand between us, and I hesitate before taking it. "Welcome to the crew, Caspian the thief." Then the sky splits with lightning and rain begins to pour down from the heavens.

A storm is coming.

EIGHT

I wake up before the sun, sling my rifle across my back, and head into the city.

The morning air drags its salty fingers through my hair as a steady wind blows down from the mountains. I crane my neck up, looking at the sinister rocky beasts that stand before me. Just past them, in the heart of the land, sits a massive volcano. The people here never worry about it erupting, though. Some say it hasn't spouted liquid fire in hundreds of years and that the gods keep it from doing so, saving the destruction for the end of worlds.

It's a children's story, one my mother used to tell me every night before bed. The people of Vulkan worship many gods, and there seems to be one for everything. A god of thunder, a god of the seas, a god people pray to for good crops, and even a god of wisdom.

I need that one right now.

Last night with Caspian was a mistake. It's not like I gave in and kissed him, but I came damn close, and I know it won't lead to anything good. Especially since he's a part of our crew now, and I'll have to see and be around him every single day. Getting involved with a crew member isn't forbidden or anything, it's just bad judgment. We all rely on each other to get the job done, and I can't have mixed feelings getting in the way of that. But the more I think about him, the more confused I become.

I've known since I was a small boy that I preferred men over women. It's common within my culture, but still, I kept it a secret for many years. Maybe it's because I joined the men of the Helm when I was fifteen and didn't want my partners to see or treat me any different. I learned pretty quickly that no one I worked with was gay, and I'm ashamed to say that I was embarrassed to tell them, so I didn't. For a long time, my mother was the only one who knew. I remember her embracing me and crying when I finally told her, but still, it took me a while before I felt comfortable coming out.

As I walk the bustling streets of the Helm, passing cafés and restaurants just beginning to open, my thoughts drift to the past. Sailing with Captain Jack, we've returned to this city many times over the years, but it never gets any easier for me. The streets no longer hold excitement in my mind. Bloodshed and ghosts of my past linger on every corner.

I glance over my shoulder, feeling as though eyes are on my back. Shaking the feeling away, my feet continue past the city and through the giant spruce trees. A small dirt path winds its way through the forest, where yellow wildflowers bloom on either side of me. The song of birds follows me down the path, filling my ears but doing nothing to drown out the loud buzzing. I don't know what I'm doing—I haven't been back here since it happened. Maybe it was Caspian prodding at me to talk last night, but that's just an excuse for something I was going to do anyway. I think I need to see it again, then maybe the nightmares will stop, and I can close my eyes without seeing her.

Behind me, a stick cracks. I unsling my rifle and slam back the charging handle, ducking behind a tree to listen. The wind whispers through the grass at my ankles, though I can't make out their message. I poke my head around the trunk and down the path but see nothing. Sighing, I stand up. "Get ahold of yourself, Hraefn." Continuing down the path with my rifle at my back, I can't stop my heart from pumping faster. With each step, my nerves spike, and sweat coats my palms.

Finally, as I crest a small hill that dips into a clearing, I see it.

My home sits in the middle of the clearing, surrounded by wildflowers and encaged by spruce trees. The grass grows tall and wild, as it has more attention from the sun than other parts of the forest. A lump forms in my throat as I walk closer, looking at the shattered windows and crooked doorframe. I can no longer picture what it used to look like, and that breaks a part of me. My mother always loved this little house, nestled away in the forest away from the city. She built it herself when I was no more than an infant.

I grew up here with my mother, never even realizing the fact that I didn't have a father. My mother told me a few things about him when I was young, though I never knew his name. I guess she figured it was better to forget the past and live in the present. I accepted that because my mother was always my best friend and I didn't think having a father would make my life any better.

My mother was amazing. You'd look at her and see a rare beauty. Hair as black as raven feathers that fell past her shoulders and wide-set eyes the color of ancient ice set in a narrow face with delicate features. She was a small woman, petite but strong. Looking at her, one would never guess that she was capable of the things she did. She was everything—a builder, gardener, cook, hunter, and an expert marksman. I learned everything I know about shooting from my mother.

As I step into the house, the floorboards squeak beneath my weight. To my right, the kitchen sits at the front corner of the house, where I always saw my mother's figure in the window as I played outside. I can almost smell her rabbit stew wafting out from the open door, calling me back for dinner. A small sitting area to my left still houses countless books on shelves that line the whole wall. The hearth sits cold and empty, not having felt the warmth of life in years. I crouch down and pick up a broken vase, remembering where it used to sit on the mantel. My mother would pick flowers from around her garden and fill it every day with a new arrangement of colors and scents. Tears form in my eyes at the sudden memory, and I put the vase down, getting to my feet.

How could this place have once held so many happy memories for me? Looking around, more moments flood my mind like a tsunami. A quiet sob escapes my lips, and I crumple to the floor, covering my mouth as tears pour down my cheeks. This was a mistake. I shouldn't have come—

"Hraefn?"

I draw my rifle and aim at the door the second Caspian steps through, hands up in surrender. "Whoa, easy," he says, his amber eyes wide.

I stare at him unblinking for a moment, then angrily wipe my tears away. "What the hell are you doing? I could've shot you!"

His eyes crease with sorrow as he steps further into my past. "I'm sorry… I just…"

Looking at him curiously, I note the way his fingers twitch and how his eyes avoid mine. How his shoulders hunch with uncertainty.

He's nervous.

Getting to my feet, I sling my rifle over my back and brush past him and out the door. I sit down on a small bench under a window and put my head between my hands, trying to calm my breathing. The bench shifts as Caspian sits down beside me. He places a hand on my back. I twist, snatching his hand and bending his wrist back. "Don't," I warn, then release him.

He looks a bit shocked. My mind is spinning out of control with too many thoughts and emotions that will erupt at any moment. The closeness of his body to mine sends fire up my neck, but the ghost of my mother chills me again. I have to get out of here. I stand to leave, then feel his warm hand slip into mine, and I freeze.

"Hraefn, wait." Caspian stands up, his eyes boring a hole in me. "I *am* sorry. I shouldn't have followed you, but, well…" He pauses and looks back at the house. "I didn't know."

I rip my hand from his. "You still don't."

"Then tell me," he pleads.

I shake my head and cast my eyes down to my boots.

"Please." He steps closer, and my heart begins pounding in my ribs to get out.

Glancing back at my house, I wonder if I'll ever see it again. Part of me knows I won't. This place has been gone for a long time, and nothing can bring it back.

I turn to Caspian. "Follow me." We walk around back, where a small greenhouse still stands, virtually untouched by what happened. I step inside, trapped heat of the sun washing over me. Plants and vines grow freely up the curved sides of the structure, reaching toward the sun. I plop down beside a dried-up pond, and Caspian does the same, keeping a good foot between us.

"This was my mother's favorite spot," I say quietly, not wanting to disturb the peace of this place.

Caspian doesn't speak, only watches me intently as I relive the worst day of my life.

As soon as I turn fifteen, I join the men of the Helm, and it's the happiest day of my life. My mother and I celebrate that night with a large boar we cook on a spit and summer wine from a village beyond the mountains.

"I'm so proud of you, my little raven."

I smile at the nickname. So many people pronounced my name as Raven, ignoring the *F*, that my mother started calling me that, saying my blue-black hair fits the name perfectly.

I spend two years with the men of the Helm, keeping the streets safe and serving Earl Thera. She's been the earl of the land since before I was born, and I meet her multiple times during my service. Mostly, I patrol the streets and docks and sometimes watch over deals and trading at the local markets. Earl Thera knows of the black market, of course, but she doesn't think to waste our time there.

"People are going to do what they want," she'd say. "And if you take it away, they'll just find a more creative way to do it behind your back."

Eventually, I move out of my mother's house and stay in the barracks in the city. She understands and doesn't argue for me to stay, saying that I'm a grown man now. I visit her every weekend, however, and help her hunt, practice shooting, and cook meals. It's almost like old times, just the two of us doing what we love together.

One day, all the Helmswords get called into the earl's estate. There's some rioting within the heart of the city, and she worries that it will spread further if they aren't controlled. The earl raised taxes to keep ships docked in her harbor, and the people didn't take kindly to that. We had a poor winter and many crops have failed, so I don't blame the people for causing an uproar for something they couldn't afford. I don't say any of this, though, because it's my job to maintain order, and that's what I do.

My partner, Torfin, and I set off, heading straight into the heart of the city. By the time we get there, many buildings are already destroyed, and people run rampant in the streets. They break windows, set fires, and march toward the earl's estate with whatever weapons they have. I have to pull my rifle on a few people, though I never fire. No one is supposed to carry guns inside the city except the men of the Helm, and so they usually back off when they see ours. But one man comes right up to me and jabs his finger at my steel badge.

"You're no different than us," he spits.

"Get back," I warn, turning my rifle so the butt faces him.

He snickers. "That badge is just something you wear. Don't let it wear you."

The blow to his ribs knocks him to the ground. "I said get back."

A few of his friends help the man back up. He glares at me, eyes wild as they slide to my badge, then back up. "Hraefn, huh? I'll remember you."

We spend hours rounding up people, arresting them for vandalism and carting them off to jail. When night starts to fall, a few Helmswords come to find me.

"Hraefn!" they shout, out of breath.

"What is it?"

"The people," one gasps. "They've moved outside the city, and they're burning every structure from here to—"

The rest of the sentence fades behind me as I shove past him and sprint down the street. Unslinging my rifle, I check to make sure I have enough ammo as I tear down the dirt path to my house. Things are getting out of control, and the only thought I have in my head is my mother.

Every ounce of air I have leaves my lungs the second I crest the hill and see my house on fire, and then I hear a shot and a woman scream. "No…" I break into a sprint, eyes wide as they scan the trees around me, then a bullet whizzes past my ear. Grinding to a halt, I level my rifle, scanning the house. There's a figure in the kitchen window, and my heart lifts.

"Mom!" I cry, but then the figure opens fire.

No amount of training can prepare me for what's happening, and I'm caught off guard. My mind is so focused on my mom that my own survival isn't even on my mind. The bullet skims my cheek, and I muffle a scream, ducking behind a tree as another crack sounds through the air. Bark shatters above my head and rains down on my lap. The people must have gotten ahold of my mom's guns, but where is she? As I lift a hand to my cheek, it comes away bloody, but I don't feel it anymore. My body and mind have gone into full-blown panic mode, and the adrenaline numbs me.

Standing up, I press my back against the trunk and peer

around it. Two figures stand in front of my house, and one lifts a rifle and fires. I snap my head back as the bullet shreds through the bark and strikes a tree just past me.

"Little raven!" a man calls, and my heart stops. They know who I am.

"We just want the guns!" a second voice says.

I can't let that happen. I've seen what these people are capable of *without* guns. What will they do if they get ahold of enough? They can bring down the men of the Helm and attack the earl's estate.

I won't let that happen.

Taking a steady breath, I let my eyes close and say a prayer to the god of war. Then I step out from cover and open fire. The familiar kick pounds my shoulder as I fire. Bullets bite at the ground near my feet as I run from one tree to another. The thundering of my heart mixes with the crack of gunfire echoing throughout the forest. Steadying myself, I crouch to one knee and edge my body around the trunk. I fire at the same moment one of the men does. He goes down screaming and drops his rifle. Pulling back the charging handle, I squeeze the trigger again, but no bullets come.

"Shit, shit, *shit*." My hands fumble in my pocket for another clip when I hear a rifle go off. Then something strikes me in the heart. My back hits the grass, and my rifle flies off to one side as I lie there gasping for air. When I brave a look down, I see where the bullet struck. It's lodged in the steel badge just above my heart. I sit up, grunting in pain as my ribs beg me to stop, but I can't. Forcing myself to move, I crawl to my rifle as more bullets tear up the grass around me. Reaching into my jacket pocket, I pull another clip, load the gun, and spin around just as the man comes running at me.

He kicks the barrel of my rifle, sending it flying into the darkness. Grunting, I drive the heel of my foot into his gut before he can aim and fire. The man doubles over but keeps hold of the gun. I have to stop this.

I fling myself forward, tackling the man and sending us both rolling down the hill toward the fire that consumes my house. I can still hear the cries of the first man as he lays writhing in pain.

Good.

I lose my grip on the man, and he manages to swing the rifle around. A gasp halts my breath as I throw my hands up, just barely pushing the barrel away before it goes off next to my ear. Pain ricochets through my skull. I clasp my hands over my ears as if that will silence the ringing. The man's lips curl into a snarl as he thrusts the rifle up, hitting me on the cheek with the stock. My head whips back from the blow, and lights explode in my vision as I roll off of him. His hand latches down on my shoulder, and then I'm pinned to the grass. The ringing in my ears starts to fade as he shouts to his friend, "Get the woman!"

Mom.

I pour all of my fear and rage into my muscles. Arching my back, I throw the man from me, then swing, punching him in the nose. He curses and lets go of the gun, and I scramble to get it. Behind us, the man I shot somehow gets to his feet and begins to limp back into the house.

Dread floods my veins, and I trip getting to my feet, crashing down on my knees. The man grabs for my ankles, but I send my foot back and make contact with some part of him. My pulse hammers throughout my body as I turn, pull back the charging handle, and fire just as the man lunges for me. The bullet goes through his neck, shooting a fine mist of blood into the air between us, and then I see his face. It's the man from the city, the one who said he'd remember me. Angry tears well in my eyes as I stumble to my feet, chest heaving. I don't even watch as the man dies, I just take off in a sprint toward my house.

"Mom!" I scream as I kick through the door, swinging my rifle in every direction. No one is inside. I run through the back to where my mother keeps a small greenhouse, and just as my hand touches the knob, there's a shot.

I kick the door open and immediately see my mother lying in

a pool of blood, gripping a garden tool. The man who I'd shot earlier is on the floor beside her, clutching the fresh wound to his temple. His eyes are like a wild animal that's been caught in a snare. Dropping to my knees, I gently lift my mother's head into my lap.

"Mom," I choke as tears build in my eyes. She smiles, though it seems to take a lot of effort. I look down at the ever-growing pool of blood and follow it back up to her stomach. She's been shot in the gut, and we both know what that means. "No," I croak. "Mom, stay with me, I'll—"

"Shh, my sweet raven," she coos, her crystal eyes shiny with tears.

I burst into a fit of sobs, my whole body shaking uncontrollably with fear. My soul is racked with guilt.

"Don't let this destroy you," she whispers, lifting a bloody hand to my cheek. "You're a good man, my son, and I want you to be happy."

"But, Mom…" I try to hold back the tears but to no avail. "I can't do this without you. I can't let you go. I can't…"

She hushes my panicked rambling. "It's all right, Hraefn."

"No…"

My mom coughs up some blood, her face going gravely pale. "Don't… don't hide who you are anymore." She smiles warmly, and my heart shatters into a million pieces. "I love you to the end of time, my son."

I stare at her unblinking. My body shakes violently as tears stain my cheeks, mixing with the blood on my face. My mother always knew I felt uncomfortable in my own skin after I came out, even if it wasn't uncommon for our people. She saw me in ways others didn't. How am I supposed to live without her, *breathe* without her? I snap my eyes shut, then blink past the tears, but my mother's eyes are closed and relaxed.

"Mom." I shake her gently. "No, *Mom*! Please!" I sob. "Don't leave me! Please…" But she's gone, off to the hall of the gods in the heavens. I'm not sure how long I sit there with my mother's head in my lap and her blood soaking through my pants. It feels like ages, but then I hear a muffled cry from beside me.

I turn my eyes to the man who'd taken everything from me, and my tears burn tracks down my cheeks. Gently, I lay my mother down, grab my rifle, and stand up. My heartbeat is calm and steady, my eyes as cold as ice.

"No, please," the man begs, crawling back through the greenhouse. "Please, I was just following orders. I just—"

"So am I," I cut him off. The men of the Helm are to maintain order, no matter what. "So am I," I repeat, then level the rifle to his head and fire.

I can't wipe the tears from my cheeks fast enough, though I don't know why I bother. Caspian's face is twisted with pure sadness and hurt from hearing my story. I can't bring myself to look at him. "Hraefn…"

Before he can finish, I stand up and walk past him, back out into the cool air. After I put out the fire, I buried my mother's body in the garden. The fire had only managed to burn the back corner of the house, but that didn't matter if my mother wasn't here to fix it. Caspian comes to my side, not saying anything, just being there with me.

"I just needed to see it…"

Caspian steps in front of me, then slowly lifts his hand, giving me all the time to stop him, but I don't. He rests his palm against my wet cheek and brushes a new tear away with his thumb, eyes glancing over the scar that marks me. He doesn't say sorry or tell me how hard that must have been, he just stands there with me, holding me together by a thread.

I want so badly to lean into him, but a voice in the back of my head tells me to stop. It's my voice. "Hraefn." His hand drops, and the cold air hits my cheek, mocking his absence. "Never mind," he says, shaking his head and casting his eyes down.

I frown, wondering what he was about to say but deciding not to pry. "We should go," I say instead. Caspian looks up at me and nods. Just as I start to go around him, his arms envelop me, and he's pulling me into him. His chest is firm against mine as he wraps his arms around my neck in an embrace.

Fresh tears threaten to fall at the sudden loving contact, but I bite them back. My heart plays an uneven tune as I snake my arms around him, crushing Caspian against my chest. I savor the moment, knowing it likely won't happen again, even though I want more to happen. With fresh color staining my cheeks, I step out of the embrace. Caspian doesn't seem offended. A small crooked smile forms on his lips, and I can't help but return it. It's contagious.

We walk away from my past and back to the present, neither one of us speaking. I don't think we need to. Caspian somehow knew that I didn't want to be alone, even if he had no idea where I was going. I can't express how much it means to me to have someone here to listen. As we walk back, I steal a glance at him. His eyes are focused on the road ahead. Maybe one day I'd tell him how much that hug meant to me.

NINE

JACK

As the sun settles in the center of the sky, I pull my cocked hat lower over my eyes as I spot Hraefn and Caspian. They walk close together, seemingly unaware of the world around them as they chat. I don't have to spy on Hraefn to know where he went this morning. I know the Helm holds too many ghosts for his comfort, but I can't stop coming here just because it makes a member of my crew uncomfortable.

As they get closer to the ramp, Hraefn spots me and takes a step away from Caspian, who looks somewhat hurt by the extra space. "Captain," they both say as they board.

"Hraefn, we'll be leaving at first light tomorrow." I gesture up to the crow's nest. "Be sure to watch our backs."

"Aye, Captain. And who am I looking for?"

I hesitate. I don't need to tell the crew of the warning Aurora gave me, not yet anyway. Looking him in the eye, I answer, "Anyone."

Hraefn nods then goes belowdecks with Caspian.

My business is done in the Helm, but I want to give my crew at least one free day before we set sail again. The *Chained Maiden* is a ghost ship, as the whole crew has left to enjoy the day. All except Tsu.

I know she's somewhere on the ship, but if she doesn't want to be seen, then it's impossible to spot her. I bet my eyes have glanced over her a hundred times already this morning.

A moment later, Hraefn and Caspian emerge back onto the deck, both having grabbed a cloak to fight the chill in the air. "Do you need me, Captain?" Hraefn taps his fingers on the sling of his rifle. I glance at Caspian, who doesn't avert his gaze from mine.

"No." I wave them away. "Enjoy the day." They both nod, taking off down the ramp and disappearing into the crowd of people at the docks.

I know about Hraefn's past, but only because people in this city love to talk. He's never told me personally why he left home, though I can guess. I found out about his service with the men of the Helm and the rebels who tried to take over the city. One Helmsword named Torfin claimed he used to be Hraefn's partner, but after what happened to his mother, Hraefn disappeared, not even coming back to turn in his badge and uniform. I see Hraefn some nights, running his finger over the bullet still lodged in his badge. But still, I don't pry. We all have a past that we'd like to forget.

Walking over to the gunwale as Hraefn and Caspian continue into the city, I recall the first time I saw my sharpshooter. I was with my crew in the Capital, selling Ostium to the Rana, who ruled after his niece's death years back, though I don't like to think of that. My crew is on their free day off, and I decide that I'd like to taste the spoils of our hard work.

I decide on a tavern just inside the city. It's only just past noon when I arrive, so the tavern isn't very full at the time. Only a handful of patrons fill the corners of the place, so I head right for the bar. A dark-skinned woman about my age operates the counter, sizing me up as I approach. After I get my drink, I sit at a table where I can spread out my map and choose our next destination.

Thunk.

At the front of the tavern, a young man leans back on the two legs of his chair, twirling a dart between his fingers. He has a scar across his cheek and hair so black it almost looks blue when the light hits it. I furrow my brow, wondering what he's doing because I didn't see a dartboard when I walked past. The young man looks bored as he sips his drink and, without looking, throws the dart.

Thunk.

I follow the sound, my eyes growing as they drift some thirty feet away to the back of the tavern, where a dartboard is mounted on a wall behind the counter. My attention turns back to the young man just as he throws another one, and it lands exactly where the other dart is. I push back my chair and walk closer, looking at the board in amazement. All the darts are right on the bull's-eye, all fighting for a spot on that small circle. "Amazing," I breathe.

When I approach him, he doesn't even look up at me. "You're really good," I say.

Nothing.

"Can you shoot like that too?"

Still nothing.

I sit down across from him, and finally, he lifts his steely blue eyes to mine. "What do you want?"

"You." I sit back, explaining who I am. Then I offer him a job as my sharpshooter. His fingers twitch as he reaches for the sling across his back that holds his rifle. It looks familiar at the time, though I don't know why.

"A sharpshooter, huh? On a pirate ship?" He snorts, draining the rest of his ale and getting to his feet. "Sure, why not? I have nowhere else to go."

Now, as I walk along my ship and look to the sky, I wonder how we would've fared without Hraefn. He's the best shooter I know. Well, maybe not as good as someone *else* I know, but that's a man from a different life.

I told the crew of our next destination—the Constellation Islands. There, I can sell barrels full of Ostium freely, as the current Rana hasn't banned the alcohol and enjoys a cup himself. I've met him many times over the years, though I can't say I particularly care for the man. His sister, on the other hand…

The Constellations hold something of more importance to me, however—another missing piece of the map. I don't know exactly how many pieces there are, but I know I'll find all of them. My crew will have to be let in on my real reason for these random stops, but that can wait. Not all of them will want to accompany me on such a dangerous journey, but I'm not ready to let go of my crew just yet, even if it will be only a few. Aurora told me someone else is after the map as well, and the more I think about it, the more confident I become that I know. It can only be one person.

Strolling along the aftercastle, I let my mind wander as I think of what I might find. The map will reveal to me the hidden location of a particular ship, and with it, I'll be the most powerful pirate on the seas. I've heard stories of this place growing up, and I know in my heart that it has to be true. Of course, I was always scolded and told that it was just a story and that no place could exist in our world.

It's called Perdita, which means *lost* in some dead language that I'm sure Skye speaks. The legend tells of a captain who built a ship worthy of all the world's gold. He hand selected each member of his crew, careful to pick people who'd be loyal to him. It's said that he made a bargain with a siren, who had fallen in love with the captain. She enchanted his ship, bringing it to life so that nothing could take her down. The ship defends itself in a way, raising the ocean waves to push ships away, sailing out of harm's way even when the winds are dead. The ship became alive, and its captain became king of the seas.

People gave him the name of Captain Armada, for he needed

only a skeleton crew to keep the ship running—she did the rest. After years of sailing, Captain Armada discovered man's hunger for his ship and its abilities, but he wouldn't let just anyone have it. When he grew too old, the captain chose a secret location given to him by his siren lover. There, he beached the ship and left her, burning the only copy of the map to the hidden location —or so he thought.

I keep both pieces of the map in a metal vial on a string, tucked next to my heart. It's not that I don't trust my crew not to snoop in my room—they know better—I just can't force myself to part from it. I'm so close now to finding Perdita, and I won't let anything stop me. With Captain Armada's ship, I'll be the most powerful pirate in the world and won't have to worry about my crew's safety ever again. We'll be truly free. They deserve that much. I used to want this ship for another reason, but now I want it for myself and my crew.

I've been hunting down this map for years now, bribing and trading with anyone who knew anything. Most of them turned out to be liars, but I couldn't risk not following a lead and missing a chance to get my hands on it. I hadn't told my crew what I was doing at the time because I felt like it was a fool's errand. We're still doing our normal business and sailing to our regular places, so why tell them what I'm looking for until I find it?

Well, now I've found something, and I'll need to tell them soon. A heavy feeling settles in my gut at the thought. But no matter what, I'll support anyone's decision to leave my crew and not continue with the journey ahead.

As the afternoon slides by and the sun finally begins its descent, giving the sky to the moon, I head to my room. My crew will be back before sunrise. I'm not worried about them. I'm sure half of them are already passed out, face down on some sticky tavern table and drooling ale-scented slobber onto the floor.

Inside my room, I cross the rug and swing open the door to my balcony. The salt-filled air blows past me, eager to get in my room and chase away the musty scent. I pour myself a glass of rum with water, and lean over the railing, staring out to sea. Glancing down at my wooden hand, I instinctively try to flex my fingers, but the wooden joints stay locked in place.

"Bastard," I hiss under my breath. A moment later, I feel eyes on the back of my head and speak without turning. "Would you like a drink? Or do you prefer to hide in the shadows?"

Tsu comes to stand at my side, the gold stitching on her mask glowing in the dying sun. She keeps her catlike eyes forward but shakes her head in answer. Tsu isn't much for indulging in… well, anything. I don't pressure her because I know it will only be a waste of my energy. Instead, I angle toward her, keeping my tone light and quiet as I always do with her. "What do you think of Caspian?"

She thinks for a moment, then does a quick series of movements with her hands. My eyes read her words carefully. *He's brave and kind. He's smart, quick on his feet, and doesn't give up without a fight.*

I smirk, taking a sip of my drink as she continues. Tsu turns toward me more, her eyes growing serious. *Now, why don't you tell me the* real *reason we're here?*

Dammit. I should've known Tsu would figure out that something was up. Nothing gets by her. "I will," I promise. "I just… I need more time."

She crosses her arms, raising a thin black brow to that.

A deep sigh caves in my chest. "Tsu, everything is fine, all right? I'd tell you if it wasn't."

We're going to the Constellations? she signs.

"Yes."

A muscle in her jaw ticks, tightening under her mask as if she's chewing her lip. Then she asks, *This isn't about Rani—*

"No," I interrupt before she can sign her name. Even seeing it spelled out would be like a stab to my heart. "It's not about her, Tsu, so quit prying and just drop it. I'll tell you when you need to know." My tone comes out sharper than I meant. There's an apology on my lips, but Tsu is already breezing through my room. "Tsu, wait—"

She closes my door quietly behind her.

"Fuck." I drain the rest of my rum and retreat inside. Pulling the string from around my neck, I remove the two pieces of the map and set them on my table. I stare at them for a long time, drinking rum until the pieces turn into four. After a while, I shuck off my boots and collapse onto my bed, letting loose a few feathers that drift down to the rug. I fight against sleep for as long as I can, but finally, it claims me, and I'm thrown into a familiar nightmare.

TEN

The next few days pass slowly. The winds aren't in our favor as we sail toward the Constellations, but Jack doesn't seem like he's in a hurry. I haven't tried to ask him again what exactly it is he's up to. I've known Jack for years, and I trust him with my life, so I decide to let it go.

For now.

From my perch above in the crow's nest, I watch the crew below. I like it up here. Sometimes when Hraefn isn't at his post, I'll take over. Of course, I can't shout out any danger. Instead, I ring a bell to warn Jack and the other crew members if I spot a ship or land, or something else.

Caspian is down below, sparring with Ace again while Hraefn stands off to the side with a wide grin on his face. I've noticed him watching Caspian a lot since we left the Helm, and I *know* that look. It isn't one he shows often, but when Hraefn is interested in someone, he can never keep the smile out of his eyes.

"You're getting better, lad!" Ace stands perfectly still as Caspian charges, thrusting his cutlass toward his heart. Slipping out of the way, Ace brings his pommel down on Caspian's shoulder, which earns him a fiery glare. "Well, maybe not *that* much better," Ace teases.

"Oh, like you were any good when you first started," Caspian counters, sitting off to the side next to Hraefn to catch his breath. Ace places a hand over his heart, drawing his brows together.

"You wound me." He lifts his sword in the air and proclaims in a voice not his own, "I am Prince Angus Dragonsbane, son of King Ares of the Tuasian Kingdom! I was born with a sword in my hand."

Caspian and Hraefn exchange a glance, then burst out into a fit of laughter. Ace isn't lying, but he loves theatrics. Ace joined our crew a few years back when he ran away from home. Despite his title and heritage, it seems Ace wasn't all that eager to take the throne, and so he set off on his own adventure. I can't blame him. I know what a hierarchy can do to people.

"Ace, you're such an ass." Hraefn crosses his arms over his chest and smirks at his friend. "You're Ace the loudmouth of Captain Keelhaul Jack's crew. That's it."

"How dare you." He feigns hurt, but there's mirth in his eyes. "You should be bowing to me."

Hraefn snorts. "You're not *my* prince."

Caspian chuckles, glancing back and forth between the two as they bicker. All is normal on the decks, so I turn my sights to the horizon.

Even from up here, I catch Jack's eye from where he stands at the helm with Story. The old man has a thousand stories of all the places he's been and things he's seen since he was a boy. He's the oldest member of our crew by far, and I often enjoy listening to his stories when I grow bored with the silence.

Jack tips his cocked hat up to me, then turns back as Story continues talking. Skye, our translator, walks across the deck, and I notice Caspian's head swivel in her direction while Hraefn's eyes stay locked on the new member of our crew.

I once thought a boy was interested in me back home, but it

turned out he liked my family's money more than he liked me. Thinking of home always gives me a sick feeling in my stomach, yet as we edge closer to the Constellations, the more unwanted memories flood my brain. Hanatsu isn't far off from the crescent-shaped island to which we head. I just hope Jack isn't planning on heading to Hanatsu next.

Hanatsu is a sprawling empire on the east coast of Terrisøl. It sits at the base of a large mountain range that runs from north to south, dropping off the edge of the continent and into the Harpy Sea. Emperor Hitto the Cruel rules there still, and he's also one of the last people who ever heard my voice.

I was fourteen at the time, running along the streets with my older sister, Meng. The cherry blossom trees dropped bright pink petals at our feet as we dashed through the courtyard that led up to our house. It sat on top of a hill, the curled tips of the roof gleaming in the sun as the rays caught the gold. I pushed open the rounded door and smacked right into my father's chest.

"Nami!" he scolded, using my birth name. It was only after Jack found me that he decided to give me the name Tsu, for I couldn't speak my name. "What are you doing? The celebration is in an hour. You and Meng need to change and get ready."

"Yes, Father." I hung my head in a bow until he brushed past me and out the door.

Meng came up and placed a hand on my shoulder. "Come on, Nami. It will be fun!" Celebrating a cruel emperor was *not* my idea of fun, but I knew better than to argue with my sister. She seemed so content with the way things were, and it pained me that she couldn't see the freedom we were missing. Hanatsu was a very strict empire, and only the men ruled there, for they were seen as the more powerful sex.

I allowed my mother to pin up my hair with silver rods and paint my face with blush, powder, and some red stain for my lips. I hated the reflection the mirror showed me, but this was how we were expected to look. The women in Hanatsu had only two jobs—to be a wife and mother. It was forbidden for us to learn how to read or write, and being born into a wealthy family, I was expected to take a husband in the next two years. The thought made my stomach tie itself in a knot. I didn't want to be a wife, a slave of my own home where all I could do was cook, clean, and pump out babies—preferably boys.

I'd voiced my opinions to my mother one night, which earned me a beating from my father the next day. "You must not speak of such things," my mother had warned. "Things are this way for a reason because it works. Why would you try to fix something that doesn't need mending?" I was so hurt at the time that I didn't have words. My mother was brainwashed like most of the other women in the empire, and I knew I'd have to do something drastic to change their minds.

As the celebration started, I stood alongside my sister, back stiff and eyes forward. My father was on the council and would walk with the other members behind the Emperor on the way to the palace. A parade of guards marched by, their curved swords swinging on their hips as they went. Following them, a colorful group of women danced along to the drums and stringed instruments, waving fans in front of their faces.

Meng nudged my shoulder. "Stop fidgeting," she hissed as I tugged on my long robes. The day was hot with the sun beating down on my midnight hair, though I was sweating for another reason.

I stood like a perfect little statue the whole time, my face neutral as the parade went on. Then, finally, Emperor Hitto came into view. He was tall and lean, with a thin black beard that hung down his gold-stitched robe. His narrow eyes were hard as he walked alongside an army of guards. My heart began to thunder against my ribs as he got closer, and a cold sweat broke out all over me, but I was doing this. I'd been silent long enough, and if no one else would stand up to him, then I would.

Stepping closer to the front of the crowd, I left my sister, who didn't notice my absence as her sweetheart came to her side. Meng was to be married in a month, and she seemed happy enough, but I'd never be happy with this life.

I shoved my way to the front, where the cobblestone path was littered with flowers and colorful streamers. People shouted and cheered as their emperor passed, but not me. I couldn't see my father, which was a good thing, because his cold stare might be enough to stop me from doing what I was about to do. The drums echoed through the courtyard and drowned out the pounding in my chest. I could do this.

Emperor Hitto was just ten feet away now, so I jumped into his path. His guards immediately drew their swords and surrounded him, pointing their blades at my throat. The music stopped, and a collective gasp filled the air. Suddenly I forgot how to speak, and I was frozen.

"Move," one guard demanded. "Or I will move you."

"Nami!" my sister shouted for me from the crowd, but I ignored her and found my voice again.

"Emperor Hitto." I bowed low, feeling my whole body tremble as I righted myself. "My name is Nami—"

"Out of the way, girl!" The guard stepped forward and grabbed my arm so hard I thought he'd break it. Panic flooded every inch of my body, but I forced the words from my mouth. They spilled from my lips like a raging river. I voiced my concern for the women here, how they never had a chance to be educated and that if given the opportunity, we could contribute more to our society.

"Enough!" the guard barked, driving the pommel of his sword into my gut. The blow knocked me off balance, and I dropped to my knees, coughing to regain my breath. Shame filled my cheeks as I felt the hundreds of eyes staring at me from both sides, but then the Emperor stepped forward. I kept my head bowed, fear coiling around my ribs and snatching more air from my lungs.

"Stand up, girl."

I did as commanded, not daring to look the Emperor in the eyes.

"Let her speak," he said.

I snapped my head up to look at him out of shock, then quickly lowered it again. Voice trembling, I continued. "Emperor Hitto, I believe women should have the privilege to learn to read and write as men do." I glanced up into his copper eyes, but he said nothing. "Just imagine all that we could do for the empire," I said, with a little more confidence in my voice. "Women could go to work and make a fair wage to bring back to their families. We could work on the council, keep records, and even teach children at the schoolhouses."

My fluttering heart lifted as my hopes and dreams came pouring out of my mouth. All the while, the Emperor listened while his guards eyed me warily. By the time I was done, not a sound could be heard in the courtyard. It was as if everyone held their breath, and the leaves hung limp against the gentle breeze, not daring to make a whisper.

Emperor Hitto gave me a half smirk, tucking his hands behind his back. "You have good ideas and voice them well for someone so young."

I was nearly blown off my feet at the compliment. "Th-thank you, Emperor."

He nodded, then his eyes went dark. "It is a shame you can't read or write. How will you rally other women to follow you?"

I glanced at the guard who hovered by me, then back to the Emperor, feeling my cheeks flush once more. "Well, my father is on the council. Perhaps if I spoke to the other members—"

"Spoke?" he said, shaking his head slightly. "But how will you do that," the Emperor asked, leaning his tall figure down to meet my eye, "without your tongue?"

"What?"

Before I could fully register the pure terror forming in my

gut, two guards latched down on my shoulders. The Emperor stepped back, a look of pure disgust on his face.

"No, please!" I begged, bucking my legs and trying to kick my way free. One guard came forward and pulled a long dagger from his belt. Tears ran down my cheeks, washing away the powder and paints my mother had carefully applied earlier.

The guard grabbed me by the cheeks while another one pried open my mouth. Adrenaline coursed through my veins as they gripped my tongue with a pair of pliers and yanked it past my teeth. Forced to my knees, I arched my back and threw my head from side to side, but I couldn't get away. I tried to scream, but nothing came out, and then the guard sliced my tongue off.

No one in the crowd looked at me, and none dared to cry out or scream. The only sound was my own gurgled screaming as the guards dropped me to the ground and tossed my severed tongue aside. Blood filled my mouth, the metallic scent making me nauseous and dizzy. The pain was like nothing I'd ever felt, and I fought against blacking out, stumbling up to my knees again. The Emperor stepped closer, careful to avoid the pool of blood. "You'll make the perfect wife." He grinned. "One who can't argue with the man of the house."

With that, he stepped around me like I was some dirty beggar on the street. I'm not sure how long I sat there sobbing, but when I looked up, the crowd was gone, save for one person. My father stood off to the right, and I knew from the cold look on his face that I was no longer his daughter. I'd embarrassed the family, and there was no coming back from that.

I fled the empire that night, not bothering to say goodbye to my mother or Meng. After days of hiking through the mountains, I finally collapsed from exhaustion and woke up sometime later in a temple. It was there I stayed for three years until I turned seventeen. The people of the mountains were a silent people, though that was by choice. They'd fled the empire generations ago and started over, building a new home away from the Emperor and the poisoned people there.

I spent countless hours sitting in silence and meditating or sparring with my teacher. They morphed me into the assassin I am today, and I swore that one day I'd go back and take my revenge on Emperor Hitto.

Now, as the sun begins to set over the sea beyond, I swing down from the crow's nest and land silently on the deck. After Jack found me fighting off a group of men in a tavern, he asked me to join his crew. He spent a long time teaching me to sign my words and how to read and write. It was only then that I could tell him my story. I've been sailing with Jack for four years now, and I know all of his secrets, as he knows mine. We share a special connection that way, and I know he trusts me more than anyone on board. Unable to voice his secrets to anyone, Jack often confides in me, and even though he taught me to write, I'd never betray him. Jack saved me in many ways and gave me a home with a new family.

By now, all of the crew members know I have no tongue, though none know why. I don't think it's important anyway. I'll go seek my revenge eventually. I'm just not ready to go back home yet.

"Tsu!"

Ace waves me over to where he, Caspian, and Hraefn stand. The only one who knows my true name is Jack. After he named me Tsu, I decided to keep it. Nami died seven years ago at the feet of the Emperor while her family watched. I was Tsu now, assassin of the *Chained Maiden* and nothing more.

"Settle something for us, would you, lass?" Ace says as I stroll over. Caspian gives me a sad smile, but I ignore it. I know Hraefn has told him about my missing tongue, but I don't want his pity. I sit atop a barrel and lean back on my hands as Ace continues. "I told young Caspian here—"

"Yeah, I'm only two years younger than you, Ace."

"And Hraefn is three years older than you, as long as we're stating useless facts. Are you done, lad?"

Caspian flips him off, then crosses his arms.

"As I was saying," he continues. "Caspian here is a handsome lad, and I say he should go talk to our beautiful translator."

I keep my eyes neutral but slide them over to Hraefn, who's looking down at his boots.

"I've seen her eyeing you," Ace says. "So what's the problem?"

Caspian's dark skin doesn't allow for much of a blush, but it's written on his expression.

"I didn't say there was a problem… I don't know."

"And Hraefn here"—Ace gestures to his friend— "says to leave it alone and let things happen naturally. So, who's right?"

I've seen Skye eyeing Caspian recently, and he returns her stare, though his eyes rest on someone else as well. Ace taps his foot impatiently as I consider, and Hraefn glances sideways at Caspian, who doesn't notice. Hopping off the barrel, I step up to Caspian, staring into his amber eyes, then point to him.

"What?" Ace throws his arms up. "If there's something good in front of you, you take it, lad!" He jabs his finger into Caspian's chest, then turns and leaves.

I catch Hraefn's eye and wink, which makes him blush and turn his head down. I'm not one to meddle in people's relationships, but I know Hraefn has a hard time being himself, and Ace isn't a great influence. Although he's right about one thing—if you see an opportunity, something good for the taking, then take it.

ELEVEN

CASPIAN

"Land!"

Craning my neck up to the crow's nest, I spot Hraefn. His black hair swirls like mist around his face, and I find myself wondering how soft it would feel through my fingers. As if sensing my gaze, he turns his head down and looks right at me. My head spins away so quickly that I nearly lose my balance, but I'm starting to get my sea legs.

We haven't spoken any more about his past after leaving the Helm, but I can tell he's wary of me now. Hraefn keeps his distance most days, finding things to keep himself busy. I pretend not to notice or look hurt when his eyes glance over me, but I'm not good at hiding how I feel. I'm not even good at *knowing* how I feel. I've always known that I like women, but could it be possible that I didn't *only* like women?

"Have you ever been?"

I spin around at the pretty voice to see Skye standing before me. Her striped pants are cut off at the knee, and her white tunic blows open slightly in the wind.

"No, never," I answer, then clear my throat. Her brown eyes sparkle as she smiles, creasing her amber skin with laughter lines.

"Well…" She steps closer, and my heart begins to thunder. "The Constellations aren't like any land you'll ever go to."

"What do you mean?"

She glances up at the crow's nest and then back at me. I'm sure he's watching, but I don't dare look up. I don't know if I'll see hurt or relief on his face and don't know which I prefer.

"Their ruler, Rana Maryn, is much more relaxed than other rulers. Captain has been selling him Ostium for years now. The Rana only buys the best for his people."

I furrow my brow. "Their ruler drinks that poison?"

She confirms with a nod.

Ace comes up and slings an arm around my neck and moves us over to the gunwale. "There she is, lad." He throws his hand out and gestures to the land in the distance. It's flat, save for a few small hills, and covered in greenery. The Capital sits at the north tip of the crescent-shaped island. As we draw near, I can make out palm trees that line a pale sandy beach. The water here is much different than what I've ever seen. The sharp, vibrant color must be how the Green Sea got its name. The water is crystal blue at the shoreline and clear enough to see the bottom, but as the water gets deeper, so does the color, and the blue fades into a sinister-looking green.

"Is that the Rana's palace?" I ask, pointing to the tallest keep in the tan city. All the buildings are the same shade of tan, with red shingled rooftops.

"That it is." Ace leans his elbows on the gunwale. "Captain will go with Skye, Tsu, and Hraefn to make the sale."

"And what will we do?"

He smiles wickedly. "We'll get a head start on enjoying ourselves. The Constellations have lots of fine taverns and women. I'll show you around."

I instinctively glance up at Hraefn, but he's gone. "But I could help—"

"Nonsense." Ace claps me on the back. "This isn't like the

sale in the Helm. The Rana and Captain Jack go way back, so there's nothing to fear from this place."

"Then why is he taking Hraefn?" I ask dryly. Ace scratches his smooth chin, then snorts. "Good point, lad. Guess you can never be too careful."

We dock the *Chained Maiden* and begin rolling down barrels of Ostium to be carted to the Rana's palace. Hraefn works quickly, rolling two barrels at a time and keeping his eyes down as he passes me. I help Skye load up the cart while Captain Jack speaks quietly with his first mate, Story. The old man nods between words, then marks something down on a roll of paper before tucking it into his breast pocket.

"Listen up!" the captain bellows. He removes his cocked hat to wipe his brow. The air here is thick as mud, and the sun seems to burn like that of a thousand fires. "Story is in charge while I'm gone. You're all free to roam the city or stay on board. Story and Nitelocke will remain here. My business with Rana Maryn won't take long, but I plan to remain in the Constellations for at least a week, so enjoy yourselves."

The crew roars their approval, no doubt eager to get on land and relax after a slow journey. Beside me, Ace stares at the captain for a long moment, and I can see him working out something in his head.

"What is it?"

"A whole week," he says to himself, then shakes the strange look from his face and turns to me. "You hear that, lad? We got a week to drink as much ale as we can and bed as many women as we please."

"I don't think I'll be *bedding* anyone," I say, rolling my eyes.

Ace wags his fingers at me and pouts. "You're no fun."

"Maybe you have too much fun."

"Oh, relax," he says, tapping my chest and gesturing for me to follow. "I only meant for you to enjoy yourself however you want." He leans in so only I can hear. "Or with *whoever* you want."

I stop abruptly and stare at him, but before I can deny anything, he slides his blue eyes over to Skye and gives me a wink. I shove his shoulder. "Has anyone ever told you you're an asshole?"

He cocks his head like he's thinking, but I know he's doing nothing of the sort. "I believe I've heard it once or twice."

A tight laugh escapes through my pursed lips. "Well, you'll hear it a lot more by week's end."

He waves a hand at me. "Your words don't wound me, my friend."

"Then I better sharpen them."

"Ha!" Ace slaps my back as he tilts his head back in laughter. "You're a witty lad, aren't you? I knew I'd like you."

I can't help but smirk. Ace might be annoying at times, but he's a good friend.

Ace and I part from the rest of the crew, and I watch Hraefn's back before he disappears into the crowd. The city is teeming with life—dark-skinned people stroll about, shopping and trading on the streets. They wear similar attire, with the men clad in white silk robes and sandals and the women in colorful linen dresses that drag behind them as they walk. Many wear their dark hair pinned up in intricate knots and braids, decorated with beads and flowers.

Every building is covered in a wall of ivy or flowers that crawl up to the rooftops where they can reach the unrelenting sun. Sandy pink cobblestone streets snake through the city, and the whole time, my head is on a swivel. The Sunken City is so different than here, and I've never seen any place like this.

Ace nudges me in the ribs. "Pretty, isn't it?"

I nod, keeping my eyes on a small shop to the left that sells blown glass in all different shapes. To my right, a two-story bakery entices me with its sweet smells of fresh bread, cinnamon treats, and herbal teas. People happily laugh and chat on the balconies above as Ace leads me further into this strange city.

"Just up here."

I peer past him but can't decipher our destination. "Where are we going?"

He brushes a blond lock of hair from his brow and grins. "A little tavern at the edge of the city. Hraefn will meet us here when he's finished." The promise of Hraefn quickens my pace, and soon we come to a fork in the road. Ace stops.

"So, which way?" I ask.

"The tavern is just down there, lad. Called the Drowned Sailor."

"Sounds… inviting," I say sarcastically.

Ace ignores that and says, "Go on, then. I'll just be a moment." He starts to move away, but I grab his arm.

"Hang on, where are you going?"

He looks at my hand until I remove it from his arm. "Just some personal business. Go on now, get me an ale. I'll be right behind you."

I step back and start down the left fork in the road, while Ace watches me go.

What business could he have that doesn't involve the captain or the crew? I guess it isn't my place to ask. Perhaps he isn't as distant from his family as he leads on and writes to them frequently. Anyway, I know Ace won't stay away from a tavern for long, so I follow the street until I find the Drowned Sailor.

It's a long stone building with windows that have no glass. The laughter and shouting from within greet me as I stand in the street. Stepping inside, I find a table big enough for when Hraefn joins us. I order a flagon of ale and sit back, sipping the sweet-tasting ale as I watch the people around me. Many sit in small groups, heads thrown back in laughter or hunched over in secret. Couples sit closely at the bar, linking legs and smiling over their cups. I wonder what else there is to do here. Surely Ace doesn't actually expect me to sit in a crowded tavern and drink all week?

"There's a good lad." Ace plops down in his chair and kicks his feet up on the table. "What did I miss?"

"Where did you go?" I ask again.

He sips his ale, then sets it down carefully and looks at me with those piercing blue eyes.

"Well…" He leans in, looking around to make sure no one overhears, and I find myself leaning in closer. "The crew doesn't know, but years ago, back when we first sailed here, I found me a lass." He pauses to make sure I'm listening.

"Beautiful creature she was, with hair like midnight and skin like copper. I found myself in her bed one night, and next time we sailed here, I found a bairn in her arms with golden hair."

I narrow my eyes in question, but he continues before I can speak. "I promised the lass I'd take care of them and visit every time we came into port, but then one day I came back, and she was gone, along with the bairn. People say she was so overcome with grief that she sailed to the Harpy Sea and gave up the bairn to the monsters, then jumped overboard. Some think she was a siren who fell for a human man." He takes a quick chug of his ale. "I go and check whenever I'm here, to see if she's come back, but she never has."

Ace is silent for a long moment as he sits back in his chair. I study his eyes, noticing how one flinched ever so slightly as he spun his tale. Picking up my ale, I drink deeply, then set it down loudly on the table. "You're lying."

Ace's lips quirk in an almost smile. As if he can't hold it in. "Am I?"

I lean closer, holding his gaze captive. "Yes."

Ace smirks, then his mask shatters as he bellows in laughter, clutching his stomach as tears roll down his cheeks. Anger flares in my belly, and I smack his ale away.

"Hey!" he cries.

"Dammit! Are you ever serious?"

Ace shoves his chair back and stands up, and I do the same. "Serious?" he repeats. "Is that all you know how to be?"

"You could've just told me *none of your business.* You didn't need to make up some bullshit story."

"I quite like making up stories," he proclaims. "It's one of my specialties."

An exhausted sigh escapes as I sit back down. "Fine, sorry I even asked. It's none of my business where you were."

"You need to relax, lad." He pours himself another glass and points it toward me. "There's no point being so high-strung all the time. You'll get yourself killed that way."

"It's kept me alive so far."

Ace stares at me for a moment, then snaps his fingers. "I've got to check!" He glances under the table, then back at me.

"Check what?" I ask suspiciously.

"Why you're so uptight," he says, leaning closer so I can see the mirth in his blue eyes. "You've got a stick shoved so far up your ass I was wondering whether your feet still touch the ground."

Snarling, I shove back, toppling my chair as anger rises like billowing smoke in my belly, but Ace just laughs. Then I feel a hand clamp down on my shoulder.

"Gods, Ace, you're such an asshole."

Turning, I see it's Hraefn, who instantly douses the raging fire inside me.

Ace chuckles and looks at me. "That's two already, and I've still got a whole week to go." He gets up and heads to the bar for another flagon, still smiling to himself.

Hraefn takes his seat across from me, keeping his eyes on the glass as he pours some ale. The silence between is growing louder than the chaos of the tavern, and I find myself tapping my foot anxiously. After what seems like hours, I clear my throat. Hraefn instantly lifts his crystal eyes to meet mine, and I freeze. The tiniest smile pulls at the corners of his lips.

"So," he drawls, leaning back. "What were you and Ace talking about?" I tell Hraefn that Ace went off on his own before meeting me here at the bar, and I only asked what he was doing, but Ace wouldn't tell me. Hraefn considers that, leaning his elbows on the table. I can't help but lean in closer. "Ace does that wherever we go," he explains with a shrug. I peer over my shoulder and spot the young prince's head of blond hair. He stands out like a star in the night sky.

"But *what* is he doing?"

"Couldn't say." He shrugs again, taking a sip of ale. "But I think he misses home more than he leads on. Maybe he's writing to his father to let him know that he's okay, and telling of all our adventures at sea."

"Doesn't his father expect him to go home eventually? I mean, Ace *is* the heir to the Tuasian Kingdom."

"Ace will never go home." Hraefn's answer is so final that I don't question it, and I don't have time to before Ace rejoins us.

"So, how did things go with the Rana?"

Hraefn glances at me quickly before answering, a fresh blush staining his cheeks. "I don't know. I left."

"Left?"

"The captain can handle things without me," Hraefn states casually. "Besides, I thought Caspian might need some rescuing."

I smile, and Ace feigns hurt. "Rescuing? We were having a swell time. Weren't we lad?"

Hraefn and I exchange a look.

"Oh, fuck off, the both of you." Ace slaps Hraefn upside the head and leans back in his chair.

Hraefn chuckles then gets to his feet and gestures for me to follow. "I don't think Caspian here is used to sitting in taverns all day. Besides, there's much more to see on this island."

"Go on, then." Ace waves a hand. "Abandon your fellow crewmate." Hraefn leans down and musses his friend's hair, and Ace can't help but smile. "But tonight, we're going out!" he calls after us as we leave the tavern.

Hraefn and I walk silently along the streets as the sun crawls higher in the sky. Sweat beads my temples, and I keep tugging at my tunic, which sticks to me like a second skin. Hraefn notices and smirks, then picks up his pace as we head outside the city.

"Where are we going?" I ask.

"Don't you trust me?" He flashes me a wicked grin.

My heart flutters, and the answer comes quickly. "Yes." Through palm trees and up a small hill, we come to a stop at a rocky ledge. Here, the fanned leaves of the trees block out the rays of the sun, though the air still feels sticky all around me. Birds chirp above, and lizards skitter off as Hraefn approaches a tree, unslings his rifle, and begins unlacing his tunic. My whole body goes rigid. "Wh-what are you doing?"

His eyes find mine. A lock of black hair hangs between his brows, and a small crystal of sweat beads at the end before falling and rolling down the side of his nose to his upper lip. Hraefn's eyes travel down my neck, to my chest, then back up. "Aren't you hot?"

Very.

I nod in response as I watch his nimble fingers work at the laces. "Well, come on. You don't want to get your clothes wet."

I'm about to ask what he means, but then he peels off his shirt, and a lump the size of a peach lodges in my throat. My eyes roam all over his pale skin, noting how muscular he is. Hraefn is tall and lean, but standing here without a shirt, he has the body of a warrior. His chest is chiseled muscle, and my eyes travel down the curve of his waist to his toned stomach. He bends down, sliding his pants to the ground, and then he's just standing there in nothing but a thin pair of shorts.

By the gods, he's *beautiful*.

His eyes find mine, and before I can make up some dumb excuse for my lingering stare, he jumps off the ledge. My eyes go wide as I run after him. "What the fuck?" My feet grind to a halt just as Hraefn crashes into a pool of crystal clear water. "Wow." A small waterfall off to the right trickles into the pool, and large flat rocks line the perimeter, where I can see a few lizards sunning themselves.

"Come on!" Hraefn calls up to me with a wide smile on his face.

I tear off my clothes as quickly as I can, leaving on my undershorts. Stepping up to the ledge, I take a deep breath and jump.

The water rushes up to meet me, and a second later, I crash into the cool water, letting myself sink to the bottom before kicking up to the surface. Hraefn smiles at me from a few feet away, but I turn my attention to the surrounding jungle. "How did you find this place?"

I feel waves pushing at my back as he swims closer, but don't dare turn around to look at him. "Well," he says from just behind me, "I found it just last year. It must have been the hottest day of the century. We had crew members passing out right and left, so I decided to head for the jungle. I thought the trees would give me some shade, but then I found this pool and…" He clears his throat, and I finally turn to look at him. His black hair curls over his brow and crystal beads cling to his thick, dark lashes. I have to blink to refocus as he continues. "I kept this place a secret," he finally admits. The nervous grin on his face warms me to my core.

"Then why did you bring me here?"

He shrugs it off like it's nothing special, but I can tell it is for him. "You looked ready to kill Ace, and I was hot, so this seemed like the best option."

"Well, I'm glad you showed me this place. It's beautiful."

Hraefn nods slowly, looking up into the canopy and the surrounding jungle, before his eyes land back on me, and he whispers, "Beautiful."

We spend the afternoon swimming in the pool, chatting casually, and sunning ourselves on the flat stones. My dark skin won't tan anymore, but I welcome the heat anyway, knowing I have somewhere to cool off. As I lay in the sun with my hands tucked under my head, I begin to drift off. I can feel Hraefn's eyes on me, and maybe it's the heat or how comfortable I suddenly feel with him at this moment, but I don't bother to catch him in the act.

Let him look.

I *want* him to see me.

TWELVE

HRAEFN

I can't help but stare.

Caspian shakes out his thick brown hair, now even curlier from the heat. It's beginning to show strands of gold from being in the sun for so long. He shakes out his shirt, his pecks flexing with the movement. Heat pools at my center as my eyes roam over his body, but then he pulls his shirt over his bare chest. I frown to myself as he then straps on his belt with his cutlass. Spending the afternoon with him in my secret hideaway is the best time I've had in a long time. We swam and talked, and I think he flirted with me, but I'm not going to get my hopes up. No one has ever dated a crew member before, and I know it isn't the best idea.

But things between us already feel different.

We're a team and need to trust one another to have our backs should we get into trouble. But can I really keep that space between us and treat him as anyone else on the crew? I don't think so. Somewhere in my heart, I know I won't be able to. It's a place that's been boarded up like an abandoned building, but Caspian is slowly prying the boards away, and already I can feel myself falling.

"You ready?"

I turn to find him fully dressed while I still stand in my undershorts. Embarrassment colors my cheeks, so I quickly dress, grab my rifle, and we start back for the city. Dusk has fallen, finally giving us some relief from the sun and a gentle breeze cools the dense air. Most of the crew will be at the Rana's palace tonight. He always throws a party when Captain Jack comes into town to thank him for the Ostium. I've gone with Ace the past two years, but it isn't my scene—polished, wealthy people drinking Ostium all night and losing themselves. One year, I caught a couple having sex in the hallway and people just walked on by like there was nothing to see. Like that girl's loud moaning didn't reverberate off every polished surface of that place. I don't like the way the alcohol turns people into something they aren't, so this year I decide not to go.

We meet Ace, Tsu, Skye, and a few others at a large tavern on the beach. Ace is already drunk and flapping his hand as we approach. "Where the hell have you been?" He hiccups, then slaps a hand hard on my back. "Doesn't matter. Caspian, lad! Get yourself a drink, grab a girl, and come dance!"

I don't turn to look at Caspian's reaction as he speaks. "Oh, I'm not much of a dance—"

"Nonsense!" Ace grabs his hand and gives me a wink, then leads Caspian away into the crowd. I growl low to myself, knowing Ace is just trying to get a rise out of me, but I won't give him the satisfaction. Instead, I move over to the circular wooden bar and order a drink. I spot Skye across the bar, signing with Tsu, who lifts her mask ever so slightly to sip what looks like water. I'm surprised she's here at all. Tsu isn't one for dancing and drinking, though she's not doing either at the moment. The captain probably sent her to keep an eye on us and make sure we—translation: *Ace*—don't do anything stupid.

I sip my drink, which tastes slightly sour from whatever tropical fruit is in it. Caspian and Ace are across the tavern, chatting with two tall, gorgeous women with dark hair and slate-gray eyes. Ace chuckles, but Caspian seems uncomfortable and keeps shifting on his feet, looking for an escape. I start to move toward him when I feel a delicate hand wrap around my wrist. I turn to a beautiful woman smiling at me. Her hair falls to her ears, her eyes like honey as they twinkle with the light of the lanterns. She wears a deep red dress that plummets between her plump breasts, revealing a flat stomach. "Here alone?" she purrs.

"No," I say a little too quickly. "My friends are—"

She presses a slim finger to my lips, then traces it up my cheek to the shaved side of my head and then into my black hair. "You're very beautiful," she says. "Has anyone ever told you that?"

My cheeks heat from the compliment, then from the truth of my answer. "No."

She removes her finger. "Shame." Stepping back, she runs her honey eyes down the length of me.

I clear my throat. "I should get back."

"But you were standing alone, were you not?"

"Well, yeah… but—"

"Dance with me."

She whisks me away to the middle of the room, where colorful dresses snap and twirl to the rhythm of the music. I'm a lousy dancer, but her manicured fingers dig into my skin. I feel uncomfortable, but I'm not about to cause a scene. The woman pulls me tight to her body, wrapping a hand around the back of my neck while the other traces patterns on my chest. I keep my hands lightly clasped high on her waist, but she gives me an unapproving smirk before lowering my hands down the curve of her hips. "That's better." She presses closer to me, then her hand begins to slide down my front. I desperately want to get away from this woman. I grab her wrist just as her fingers brush against my groin and my body reacts to the sudden contact.

"There you are!"

Fuck!

Caspian glides over the dance floor, the silver buttons of his shirt gleaming in the light. His amber eyes rest on mine for a moment before turning to the woman tangled in my arms. Caspian smiles brilliantly, then bows slightly. "Apologies, miss, but may I cut in?"

She looks down her nose, lifting her chin and narrowing her eyes. "You wish to dance with this handsome creature?"

His smile wavers slightly, turning shy, though I don't think the woman notices. He nods.

"Very well." She turns back to me and lifts my chin with a finger. "He's not as much fun as I'd hoped." With that, she slides away into the crowd.

I let out a sigh of relief. "Thank—"

Caspian bursts out into a fit of laughter, drawing the attention of a few dancers. I stare at him in shock, feeling my neck grow red. "What's so funny?"

"Your face!" he bellows, clutching his stomach as he gasps for air.

My fingers curl into a fist, and I punch him in the shoulder, silencing his laughter.

"Hey!" He steps up to me, the mirth returning to his warm eyes. "I just saved you."

"Then why are you laughing at me?"

His eyes slide to my lips, then back up. "Because you looked like a scared little boy that's never seen a woman before."

I scoff and turn my back, but he grabs my arm to halt me. "Hey, I'm sorry."

"Whatever."

Caspian steps in front of me to block my path, the smile gone. "Hraefn," my name on his tongue sends shivers down my spine. "I'm sorry," he repeats. "I just... know that feeling."

"What feeling?" I ask somewhat defensively.

His head lowers, and the anger leaves me instantly. "Of being confused." When his eyes find mine again, they're raw and serious—open for me to read him completely. I don't know what to say, so I just stand there like an idiot, staring into his eyes and waiting for one of us to say what we're feeling, to confirm that this is real and I'm not just dreaming. The silence stretches thinner and thinner until he finally speaks. "Dance with me."

My head cocks to one side. "You're not serious."

Caspian leans closer. "Unless you want your old partner back." He gestures to the woman, who watches us from the bar. Before I can rattle off a list of excuses, he laces his fingers with mine. The feeling is like jumping off a cliff, and I'm falling again, crashing into my emotions. My pulse is throbbing in my neck as I allow him to lead me further into the crowd. The music picks up, the beat frantic and lively. The whole room bursts to life, people shouting their approval at the song, laughing and swinging their hips. It's addicting.

Caspian clasps both my hands in his and begins bobbing his head to the beat. I stand like a statue, unable to move even with the rhythm moving through my veins. "Come on!" he shouts over the noise. "Like this."

Caspian rocks to the beat with a broad smile that lights up his face as he pushes away and twirls, jumping up and down with the rest of the crowd. People begin to notice me just standing there, and suddenly I feel like an insect under a magnifying glass, burning alive. Caspian must notice the panic in my eyes, because a second later he's right in front of me, so close that I can smell the sweat on his skin and the alcohol on his breath. He places his hands on my hips and starts to move me.

"Don't look at them," he says, getting closer. "Just let go."

Let go.

He removes his hands from my hips and steps back, flashing me a confident smile that I want to stare at all night. I let the music wash over me, feeling the drums in my bones, the melody beginning to sway me. My hips move from right to left, and my foot begins tapping to the beat of the music. Caspian's smile grows even more, and soon I'm jumping up and down, completely lost in the chaos of the dance crowd.

Caspian and I laugh like fools as we bump into one another, throwing our heads back as the music blares throughout the tavern. Everyone else in the room seems to fade away until all I see is him. The word addicting comes to mind again as I watch Caspian. His dark curls bounce as he dances, that smile that seems glued to his lips and the way his cheeks ripple back when he laughs. I let go.

After an hour of dancing, Caspian and I stumble to the bar, laughing and trying to catch our breath. We order drinks and chug them down just to wet our throats before getting another round.

Caspian smacks me playfully. "I thought you couldn't dance?"

"I… thought so too."

That smile again. "Well, you fooled me."

I'm all too aware of the closeness of his body and the hand just inches from mine. My fingers twitch nervously, and I brush my pinky up against his. The sudden contact makes him jump, and I quickly withdraw my hand. He opens his mouth to speak, but a different voice turns our attention.

"Having fun?"

It's Captain Jack.

He stands alongside Tsu, his black hair pulled back to the nape of his neck. His eyes go back and forth between Caspian and me until I answer. "Aye, Captain."

I take a tentative step away from Caspian, but the captain notices.

"Caspian." He tucks his hands behind his back. "Tomorrow we need to careen the ship."

I've done this many times, but by the look on Caspian's face, he doesn't know the first thing about careening. The crew will beach or anchor in the harbor, then attach ropes to all the masts. Men on land will use winches to pull the ship, forcing it to keel over so that the haul can be reached. Barnacles gather along the bottom and need to be scraped away. It can be a dangerous job as the barnacles are sharper than glass. I notice Caspian eyeing the captain's wooden hand.

"I need you at the haul," he continues, and Caspian lifts his eyes back to the captain.

"Most of the crew will be on land while you and a few others clean the bottom of the ship. Be at the beach at first light tomorrow." He glances over at me. "And you'll be down there with him. Show him the way. Understood?"

"Aye, Captain," we both answer.

Then he walks away with Tsu on his tail, likely headed back for the ship. I turn my back, disappointed that this night is ending. "Come on, then. We should get some rest." I chug the rest of my drink and head for the door.

We walk back to the *Chained Maiden*, keeping a good foot of space between us.

Dammit.

This whole evening has gone so well, and now what? After swimming all afternoon and dancing together, I touch his hand, and he locks up on me? Fine, I can take a hint. I guess the drinks and excitement just went to my head. He's only trying to be nice —a good friend.

Crewmate, I remind myself.

We head down to the bunks, Caspian finding his just across from me. Ace still isn't here, though I bet he'll be along soon. There's no way the captain will let him drink himself silly if we have work to do tomorrow. I shuck off my boots, slide my tunic over my head, and collapse back onto my pillow. Caspian moves about, opening the trunk at the end of his bed. The second I close my eyes, I hear the floor creak next to my bed. Cracking a lid, I see him standing over me.

"What?" I snap the word by accident.

He steps back a little, and I sit up.

"I just..." He clears his throat, and I feel an unease twisting in my belly. What is he going to say? I don't think I can handle a verbal rejection, so I cut in.

"Thanks for rescuing me tonight," I say in a deadpan voice. "I can do it myself next time, so you won't need to bother." I barely register the hurt on his face before I lay back down and turn away from him. Caspian says nothing as he walks past my bed and up the steps to the deck.

I don't know why he's acting this way. Surely he was going to explain that tonight was nothing more than some fun between crewmates... right?

I toss and turn for hours. Ace comes stumbling into bed eventually, and Caspian returns to his. Finally, knowing I'll get no sleep, I climb out of bed, grab a shirt, and head up to the deck.

The night is clear, and every star in the sky shines brightly for the world to see. I walk over to the bow and lean over, looking at the figurehead that protrudes from it. The woman's hands are chained behind her back, and her blouse is open, revealing the curve of her breasts. The detail in the woodwork is exquisite, and the pure sorrow on the woman's face strikes a chord in my heart every time I look at it.

After a while, I climb the rigging up to my crow's nest and sit with my legs dangling over the small opening, looking out to the empty sea. I wonder where we're headed next? Maybe we'll go somewhere in Terrisøl or the King's Cloth. I don't care. Suddenly I wish to leave this place. I'm not looking forward to working with Caspian tomorrow, but I'll do what the crew needs me to do.

After all, we're a team.

CHAPTER
THIRTEEN
CASPIAN

The steel tool digs into my palm as I scrape barnacles off the hull of the *Chained Maiden*. Hraefn is cold and distant, standing three people down, next to Skye and a few other crew members. People frequently chastise me when I nick the bottom of the ship with the metal scrapper—this time it's Tetra, the shipwright.

"If you put one more scratch in her, I'll cut your hand off." Her empty threat flies right over my head as I continue to work. Tetra might be big and strong for a woman, but she's a softy at heart. Besides, my mind is momentarily working over a bigger problem.

What the hell am I going to say to Hraefn?

Last night, before he pushed me away, I was ready to confess my feelings for him. It was about to be the most terrifying and probably—*sadly*—bravest thing I've ever done, and he dismissed me before I could even speak.

Grunting in anger, I shove my scraper into the hull, nicking the wood yet again.

"That's it!" Tetra comes stomping over to me and snatches the scraper from my hand. "No more metal for you." She digs around in her work belt and pulls out a flimsy plastic scraper. "Here." I snatch it away and start up again.

Captain Jack is with Story, Nitelocke, and a few other members of the crew. Tommen the tracker paces back and forth in front of Jack, and I wonder what they're discussing. I'm still learning everyone's names. There are so many new faces I see every day, but there's only one I want to see right now.

Pushing that thought away, I squint against the sun. Their figures can be seen onshore as they stand watch over the men working the winches. I couldn't believe my eyes when I first saw the ship begin to tip over to one side as if it were tired and decided to lie on the beach for a nap. Some of the ropes have been tied off to palm trees along the beach, while others are held in place by the winches. The ship groans at the strain, making my heart jump into my throat every time. Tetra assures me that she's never careened this ship and had a problem, but I'm still nervous.

We've been at it for hours now, and the work is almost done. The bottom of the ship looks good as new. Tetra runs a hand down the hull, nodding and smiling approvingly at the smooth wood beneath her palm. "Good work, crew!" she bellows. "Let's get her back in the water where she belongs, shall we?"

The crew shouts and nods in agreement. My arms feel ready to give out, but I harness the pain and let it fuel me. I just want to be done with this so I can get away from everyone.

Stealing a glance at Hraefn, I'm shocked to see that he's watching me in return. I quickly lower my eyes, and he does the same. Ace is up on a winch. I don't know how he managed to worm his way out of this, but I bet he talked the captain's ear off until he finally relented. He's probably too hung over from last night's outing to be sweating down here in the hot sun with us. Well, that's fine with me. I'm not really in the mood for his shit today.

As the captain gives the order to begin righting the ship again, I spot Hraefn's head of black hair as he breezes past and around the corner. My feet instinctively go to follow him, but Skye blocks my path. Her short-cropped hair is stuck to her neck and sweat runs down her face, yet she still manages to look beautiful. "Hey, Caspian, I was wondering—"

Only I don't hear a word she says after that, as Hraefn comes back into view. He shades his blue eyes against the sun, his black hair blowing away from his brow as a sudden breeze comes off the Green Sea. But it's his eyes that draw my attention, blocking out Skye's voice. They're different, something is wrong.

I follow his gaze out to sea where a large black ship with white-and-gold striped sails sits in the green waters. Sliding my eyes back to Hraefn, I find him staring at me, a look of horror forcing his pale skin to grow even whiter. But before I can register what it means or think to open my mouth, a low boom sounds from the sea.

The cannonball tears through Skye like she's a sheet of paper. Blood and wood explode in my face, and I'm thrown off my feet from the sheer force of the impact. A pained gasp is forced past my lips as my back slams into the sand. My ears are ringing, and my vision blurs, but whether from tears or blood, I don't know.

"Caspian!" some distant voice calls to me through the chaos. Everywhere I look, the crew is running, unsheathing swords and calling up to the captain. When Hraefn reaches me, he already has his rifle unslung and offers me a hand. I'm too shocked to even move, so he grabs me up by the collar and shoves me in the direction the crew is running.

We take cover behind the overturned ship as another cannonball tears through the hull, rocking the vessel. I look down at my blood-soaked clothing. My hands are trembling with fear. Skye's blood is sticky on my skin, and I frantically begin wiping my hands on my pants, but it won't come off. Tears form in my eyes and start to roll down my cheeks, dripping pink drops into the sand beneath my feet. My whole body shakes, my mind racing faster than a tsunami headed for land. I can't breathe.

A pair of hands cups my bloody cheeks.

Hraefn tilts my face up to his, worry burning in his pretty blue eyes. "Stay with me!" he shouts, though it sounds like a whisper meant only for my ears. I manage to nod my head, just once, and he takes my hand. We dart from behind the ship with the rest of the crew.

Captain Jack is shouting orders as civilians flee to cover farther up the beach where the cannons can't reach. He takes one look at me and freezes, his copper eyes going wide. Hraefn steps up and speaks a name so softly I barely catch it, but I know.

Skye is dead.

I watched her be torn in half before my eyes. An image that will haunt me for the rest of my life.

When I manage to calm down a bit, and the ringing in my ears finally lets in the full chaos around me, my anger and fear spike. "Who the *fuck* is that?" I demand.

Hraefn and Ace turn to me. "Captain Blacktip," they utter in sync. "He's been after the captain for years." Ace offers, looking out to sea where the ship is.

"But why—"

"Get those ropes cut!" the captain's voice booms over Ace's. The ship strains behind us, groaning as if the cannonballs have injured it. The crew begins hacking away at the ropes, and they snap through the air once set free.

"But, Captain," Tetra pleads, "she's been pierced in the hull."

"She's not in the water," he responds, anger flaring in his eyes. "We need the cannons level with that *ship*." He spits the last word as if it tastes like poison.

Tetra argues no more and starts commanding the men around her.

"Hraefn," Jack yells, "get to the crow's nest." Then deadlier, voice chilled, he adds, "You know what your target is."

Hraefn's face grows two shades whiter, but he nods, steals a glance at me, then takes off for the ship. I watch as he expertly climbs a loose rope that hangs from the mainmast and hoists himself up on the crooked deck.

"You ever fired a cannon?" Ace stands beside me, a look of… something in his eyes. I shake my head. "You will today." He drags me back across the beach, ducking low as sand explodes up from the cannonballs. They can't reach the winches or the rest of the crew, but they don't seem to be aiming for them. They're targeting the ship.

A few crew members help us up. I hoist a shaky foot into the hands of a man named Yonis, and he hurls me up high enough where I can grab a low-hanging rope. Once on board, we head belowdecks and stand ready at the cannons. They're bolted to the floor so they won't move from rough seas or, in this case, when the ship is keeled over. Ace and I stand at the far end as the ship strains against the last of the ropes. "Hang on to something!" he orders.

I grab the barrel of the cannon as the last snap cuts through the air like thunder, and then the ship is free.

The sudden movement lurches my stomach up to my throat as the ship rights itself in the low water of the beach. "Go, now!"

The crew moves at Ace's command, loading the cannons and waiting for his order. The striped sails on the ship creep closer to shore before turning their port side to us once more. "Now!"

I cover my ears as the cannons explode one by one. The force of the one near me rocks back the cannon, almost taking off my foot before Ace shoves me out of the way of the tracks. He loads the cannon again and then instructs me to pull the firing cord. A few cannons strike the target ship while others go crashing into the sea. The feeling is thrilling and terrifying all at once.

"What do they want?"

Ace considers me, a strange look in his eyes, then says, "I don't know."

I shake my head, ready to demand more information, but then I hear the crack of a rifle from above, and my heart plummets.

Hraefn.

Is he up there alone? Another shot answers back, and I hear where it must have struck the gunwale. I take off toward the stairs, but Ace stops me, snagging the back of my tunic.

"Where the hell are you going, lad?"

"Hraefn needs help!" I jerk free, but he grabs me again, his eyes turning serious and voice low as he tells me, "You don't want a part of that fight."

Fear coils in my gut. "What the hell does *that* mean?"

"Captain Blacktip's sharpshooter is the only other person in this world that can outshoot Hraefn." He leans closer. "They don't call him Deadeye Cane for nothin'."

I shake the name from my head and step away. "I'm still going to help him."

Ace chuckles, but it's humorless. "What are you going to do, lad? I don't think you can reach him with your cutlass."

Anger spikes inside me and I grab his collar, drawing his face to mine. "Then give me a gun."

What am I doing?

I stumble up the steps with a rifle in my hands. Another shot echoes through the air, and I duck instinctively, though I have no idea where the bullet lands. Looking up, Hraefn is drawing back the charging handle of his rifle with such force I'm afraid he'll snap the thing off. He's in his element, high above the world with the enemy in his sights. But he isn't safe, and that turns my guts to lead.

"Hraefn!" I shout once he's fired.

When he glances down, there's a look of pure, unwavering *what the fuck are you doing* terror on his face.

"Get the hell out of here, Caspian!"

Shards of wood explode near his face as a bullet whizzes by his head, making my heart lurch to my throat.

Hraefn turns away from me and starts firing again, ducking behind the armored wall of his crow's nest. I edge closer to the gunwale and dare a look over. The ship is much closer now, and I can see small figures running up and down the deck. My hands tremble as I level the rifle with the ship, hold my breath, and fire. The jerking motion pounds at my shoulder, but the noise is what shakes me. I've never fired a rifle before, so what the hell am I doing?

I steal a glance back up at Hraefn as he continues to fire, duck, reload, and fire. A moment later, another shot sounds from the bow of the ship. I crane my neck and spot Tsu, crouched on top of the gunwale, firing off bullets left and right. I guess she has more hidden talents than I knew because when I turn back, figures drop to the deck as her bullets find a new home.

My eyes lift to the enemy crow's nest, where the flash of something catches the sun and blinds me. Then I realize what it was. Their shooter has a scope on his rifle. He has an advantage over Hraefn, and I need to help him.

Seconds creep by at a snail's pace. I have to draw his attention away from Hraefn so he can get a clear shot. Turning back to Tsu, I yell, "Keep them busy!"

She locks eyes with me and cocks her head in question, but I'm already running. Taking the steps two at a time, I run up the aftercastle to where Captain Jack's room is. Throwing open the door, I sprint to the balcony, then toss my rifle up onto the flat roof. Jumping onto the railing, I haul myself up to the roof. My pulse is racing so fast that I think my heart will give out, but I continue anyway. I rip the small flag off the pole that hangs parallel with the water and tie it to the end of my barrel. The bright red will surely stand out and hopefully draw the attention of Deadeye Cane.

Turning back to the ship, I start waving the flag through the air. "Hey!" I shout, ignoring the fear that slips out with that one word. They're close enough that I can see a few crew members pointing at me, and then one opens fire. The bullet whizzes past my head, and I hit the roof so hard that I'm left gasping for air. I check myself for wounds, but Skye's blood is caked on so thick that I can't tell if I've been hit. Would I even know if I had? The adrenaline rush is giving me a numbing sensation throughout my body.

"What the fuck are you doing?"

The anger and fear in Hraefn's voice pulls at my heart, but I get back to my feet anyway and begin shouting again. I keep my eyes on the crow's nest, watching the flash of the shooter's scope as he continues to fire on Hraefn. There's an angry *ting-ting* sound as the bullets bounce off the small armored wall, but then wood explodes near his leg. Hraefn ducks down as he fumbles with a full clip. Even from here, I can see his hands shaking slightly, and that only makes me more nervous. I've seen him shoot before, and his hands never shake.

Realizing I won't draw the shooter by waving a flag, I bend down on one knee to steady my arms and grip the rifle so hard my knuckles go white. Aiming as best I can, I put the shooter in my sights and fire.

The bullet rips through the small flag that flaps above his head, and then the flash of his scope turns on me. Before I can get to my feet, the sound of the shot rushes across the water, and I feel my whole body jerk back. A pained scream tears its way up my throat as the bullet burns through my skin and settles somewhere inside me.

"Caspian!"

I can hear the tears in Hraefn's voice as he calls to me. My vision is slightly blurry as I lift my head from the roof. Raising the rifle and holding it flat against my stomach, I aim again and fire. Snarling in pain, I roll over, catch Hraefn's eye and shout, "Shoot him! *Now!*"

Hraefn stares at me in horror for a split second before he acts. He sinks the butt of his rifle into his shoulder and pulls the trigger with a snarl on his lips the same time Deadeye Cane fires again. I manage to get back on my feet just as the bullet strikes my skull.

My world turns bright white, and stars explode right in front of me. I sway on my feet, stumbling back and dropping the rifle to the roof. My name is being shouted somewhere, but I can't make sense of the fear behind the voice. Everything feels calm and warm, my fingers tingling and my heart slowing. Something warm trickles down my cheek, and gunpowder fills my nose, and then I'm falling off the ship. I land hard on my back, but then the pain stops, and the warm sand wraps me in an embrace. The cool water of the sea pushes at my feet as I lay on the beach, not remembering how I got here, but wishing Hraefn will join me soon.

I close my eyes as his voice calls to me over and over.

FOURTEEN

Trudging along the dirt streets of Ilykos, I clutch my empty stomach as it roars in disapproval at the lack of food. It's been days since my last meal, and the hunger pangs have me keeled over. I need to find something, but I have no money, no family… I also have nothing to lose.

Midsarra is a small island that sits between Vulkan and Terrisøl, floating out in the middle of the sea, alone and forgotten. This is a good place for me.

After a few more hours, the sun starts to set, and I make my way to the marketplace. Vendors are beginning to pack up for the day. They wrap up food, pack away their goods, and discard anything spoiled. I eye a mass of rotting fish heads, though my stomach churns at the smell. I'm not that hungry yet. Moving along, I spot a small group talking with a vendor who sells dried pork, jarred vegetables, and other goods. I've stolen from this man before, and he knows my face, so I don't get too close. Hiding behind a barrel, I watch the vendor talking with a tall man. Of course, everyone is tall to me. At seven years old, I barely come up to a grown man's hips, but that also makes me a good thief.

This man is tall and lean, with a head of blond hair that falls to his shoulders. His tan cocked hat is singed at the front, leaving one tip black. With his long jacket, scuffed leather boots, and cutlass that hangs from his belt, I know that he's a pirate. The pirate hands over a bag of coins as the vendor wraps up a whole pork leg and fills a small sack with jerky. My mouth begins to salivate at the sight, and my stomach grumbles again.

It's only when the pirate turns to leave that I see how young he is. He's just a teenager, with a smooth face, strong jaw, and murky green eyes. Somehow this gives me the confidence to try to steal from him, as if he can't still cut me in half with his cutlass. Deciding my fate, I follow the man and the rest of the pirates with him as they head back to the harbor. The city is growing dark now, shadows lurking where the lanterns won't shine their light. It makes it easy for me to follow the group. They laugh and chat lightly, talking about sailing to a place called the Isle of the Lost. I've never left Midsarra before and have no idea about the world outside of this small island.

As the blond pirate takes a corner, I sprint silently just behind him, reaching and carefully unlooping the bag of jerky from his belt. My heart hammers against my ribs as I catch the bag, then quickly hug the wall and listen to their retreating footsteps. Smiling triumphantly, I dig into the bag, stuffing a handful of the dried meat into my mouth. Sliding down the wall until I'm sitting on the street, I eat the entire bag in a few minutes, temporarily satisfying my hunger. I let myself enjoy my small victory, but it's short-lived.

Echoes of boots stomping through the dirt streets perk my ears. I stand up, peer around the corner, and see the group of pirates doubling back. Panic shoots through me like a gale-force wind as I catch the shine of their cutlasses. I spin around, ready to dart off into the night when I smack into someone and fall back to the ground.

It's the blond pirate. He stands over me with a smirk on his lips, as his green eyes narrow in curiosity. "Well," he says, the deepness of his voice rattling me. "What do we have here?" He slides those green eyes down to the empty bag of jerky, and my heart plummets to my boots. The rest of the pirates come up behind me. "Seems we have a thief," the blond pirate speaks to his friends but keeps his eyes on me.

"What do you want to do with him, Captain?"

Captain?

Oh shit.

The pirate captain eyes me coolly, then flashes a dangerous smile.

"Captain!"

Tetra shakes me violently. The boom of cannon fire and the crack of rifles reverberates on the beach. I expected my heart to race when I saw it—when I saw that ship again, the one that haunts me—but instead, it slowed to that of a dead man.

That's what I am.

A dead man.

A hand comes down hard on my shoulder, enough to make me wince. Tetra steps in front of me. "We have to get back!" she yells over the commotion.

The moment the cannonball struck the *Chained Maiden*, I jumped into action, but now it's as if I am frozen. Reality has set in finally, and I don't know what to do.

"Captain!" Tetra screams in my face, and suddenly my heart starts to beat again. "What are your orders?"

I run my eyes over the beach, over the faces of my crew as they shout for everyone to get back. Civilians run for cover. My crew leads them away from the destruction of the beach. The ship is upright again, and Hraefn is busy up in the crow's nest. The *Chained Maiden* rocks as Ace and Caspian work the cannons below with a handful of crew members. But then…

I shove past Tetra, pointing to my ship. "What the hell is he doing?"

"Oh, you stupid boy," Tetra says quietly.

My eyes widen in horror as Caspian waves a flag through the air while Hraefn continues to fire. I know what he's doing, and he'll only get himself killed. With a curse on my lips, I sprint past Tetra, who shouts for men to follow me. "No!" I scream over my shoulder. "Get everyone off the beach. Now!"

"But—""

"*Now!*" I let the fear fill my voice, knowing Tetra will register the situation for what it is. Her voice fades as I sprint across the beach, jumping over a few bodies—the bodies of my crew, my family.

These are my people to protect, and now their blood stains the pale sand, waiting to be washed away by the tides.

Caspian is firing on the ship, and Hraefn screams at him from the crow's nest. Tsu sits perched on the bow of the ship, too engaged in what she's doing to note Caspian's idiocy. And then he's thrown back onto the roof, his rifle knocked from his hands. I push my legs to run faster, but then the loud whizz of a cannonball screams in my ears. I don't even have time to hit the ground before the cannonball crashes into the sand beside me, throwing me off to the right. I land on my shoulder, and a scream tears from my lips. A shard of a clam shell sticks from my collarbone. Baring my teeth, I take a quick breath and then rip the shell from my flesh. Blood oozes from the wound and stains my shirt red, but I stagger to my feet and keep moving.

My breath comes in uneven gasps. I can see Caspian as he slides the rifle onto his belly and fires again. He then turns and shouts to Hraefn, "Shoot him! Now!"

Hraefn obeys, leveling his barrel with the ship and firing once more. But there's an echo. No, not an echo. Deadeye Cane shoots at the same moment Hraefn does, only his sights aren't on my sharpshooter.

Caspian manages to get back on his feet, and the second he

does, his head snaps back as the bullet strikes his skull. My entire body goes cold and then numb. I can't breathe. My heart feels like it will break through my ribs at any moment. I watch as Caspian stumbles to the edge of the roof and then topples over.

"Caspian!" I scream as I sprint forward. My feet seem to float over the sand as I race to him, completely forgetting about the pain in my collarbone and the warm blood that coats my chest.

Hraefn screams from behind me, which only heightens my panic. Tsu drops down from the ship silently beside Caspian, a look of concern in her eyes. I fall to my knees beside him. There's so much blood. Caspian's eyes are closed and his body is still as I press my fingers to his throat to check for a pulse.

"Caspian!" I say again, shaking his shoulder, but his head just lolls to one side.

When I look over my shoulder, Hraefn is throwing his rifle into the sand and sprinting toward us. He and Caspian have become close since he joined our crew, and I know how being close to someone changes you. I don't need him to see Caspian like this.

I look at Tsu with a silent command. She nods and stands up, grabbing Hraefn around the waist and slamming him to the sand. "Let me go!" he roars, bucking like a rabbit caught in a snare. Tsu clamps down on his arms as Hraefn cries and snarls like an animal. "Caspian!" he keeps yelling.

"Get him out of here," I order Tsu. She helps Hraefn to his feet, who immediately tries to run past her, but Tsu is faster. She twists his arms behind his back and begins to lead him away, though Hraefn digs his feet into the sand.

"No!" he snarls, but his voice sounds defeated. "Let me go! Caspian! *Caspian!*"

Closing my eyes, I force myself to turn away from him, but Hraefn's cries tear through me down to my soul. He screams and cries Caspian's name all the way up the beach before finally breaking into a fit of sobs. My heart aches for him, for my crew that lost their lives… for Skye.

Taking a deep breath, I open my eyes once more and feel for a pulse. Caspian's dark skin seems pale, and it's cold and clammy to the touch. My fingers press against the artery in his throat.

Nothing.

The blond captain twists his lips as he looks down at me, then asks, "What's your name, boy?"

"Jack," I answer.

He motions to his crew. "Get him up." They haul me to my feet then snatch up the empty sack of jerky. My knees quake with fear. I've heard stories of pirates before and what they do to people who wrong them. What will they do to me?

Hang me?

Flog me?

Drown me?

"Jack the thief," the captain drawls. "Where are your parents, Jack the thief?"

A lump forms in my throat, but I don't think lying is a good idea, so I answer honestly. "I don't know."

He cocks his head, the movement somehow calculating. "You don't know?"

I shake my head, and someone behind me chuckles. "He's an orphan, Captain."

Anger rushes through my veins, and I ball my fists and whirl around, striking the man in the gut. The rest of the crew burst into laughter as the man clutches his stomach. "You little shit," he hisses as he backhands me. I fall to my knees, clutching my cheek and staring daggers at him.

"All right, that's enough." The captain pulls me to standing. "An orphan, huh?" He throws up his hands in surrender as I ball my fist once more, but a smile tugs at his lips.

I was raised in an orphanage, then moved around to different families from the time I was four. I ran away from all of them, finding my way back to the orphanage. It was stupid, but at the time, I thought that my mother might come looking for me someday, and how would she find me if I wasn't at the place she left me? So I kept going back until I finally realized no one was coming to claim me. I set off on my own just five months back after I turned seven, and I'd been struggling ever since. There are no handouts or sympathy for me just because I'm a kid. I learned to pickpocket, cling to the shadows, and shoot pigeons out of the air with a slingshot I made.

The captain is staring at me, working his lips and deciding which words will come out. He leans down close, his voice taking on a dangerous tone. "No one steals from me, boy."

If I'm going to die, I'll at least do it with some fire in my belly.

I level my eyes with him and smirk. "I did."

The crew chuckles behind me until the captain shoots them a pointed look, and they shut up. *"Yes."* He smiles, and the sight of it gives me chills. "You did. I'm Captain Blacktip." He holds his hand down to me, but I just stare at it. "It's rude not to shake hands when making introductions, boy."

"Stop calling me *boy*. You're just a kid too."

His crew all turn to one another, and an uneasiness settles between them. Captain Blacktip grins, then chuckles and nods. "You're right. Tell you what." He straightens his jacket and taps a finger on the pommel of his cutlass. "I like you, Jack the thief, so I'll make you a deal. I won't cut off your hand for stealing from me—"

My heart drops.

"—if you join my crew."

My brow furrows in surprise. Is he joking? I look around at the crew, but none of them seem to think it's a joke. "Well?" Captain Blacktip's green eyes tell stories of adventure, but also danger. I'm wary of him, feeling something tied to the end of this offer.

"Why?" I ask.

He leans down, and the scent of saltwater and wet wood washes over me. He flashes a brilliant smile and says, "Do you have somewhere you need to be?"

I don't.

So I join Captain Blacktip's crew.

FIFTEEN

It's been three days.

Three days since Captain Blacktip attacked us on the beaches of the Capital.

Three days since Tetra has been working to repair the damages to the hull of the ship.

Three days since Hraefn has slept more than a few hours.

Three days since Caspian…

My thoughts are interrupted by Ace's angry voice. "You need to tell us!" he roars at the captain.

Jack sits at the head of the table while the rest of us crowd around it. We've taken up an entire tavern while our ship is being worked on. Rana Maryn offered Jack rooms at his palace, but he denied, saying he needed to stay with his crew. He looks beaten and tired. Heavy bags hang under his copper eyes, and his black hair looks unkempt, showing a few extra grays in the mix.

Ace rips a hand through his blond hair as he paces back and forth in the common room. Hraefn sits in the corner, looking pale and haunted. His hair is greasy and mussed, his blue eyes dull as he stares at the floor beneath his boots. "Why did we come here, Captain?" Ace tries again.

I lift my eyes to Jack, wondering the same thing. I know he has an alternate reason to come to the Constellations, but he wouldn't tell me. I tried to ask him that night in his room, but he grew angry at the mention of his lost love. I thought I knew all of Jack's secrets and he mine, but I was wrong.

He finally lifts his eyes to Ace, careful to avoid mine. "It's complicated."

"Uncomplicate it!" Ace snarls.

Jack shoots him a warning glare, but it doesn't douse the anger, just makes it bubble over.

"Skye is *dead*!" Ace shouts.

Jack flinches as if he's been struck. "I know."

"Crew members are dead! And Caspian—"

"*I know!*" Jack throws back his chair and hovers over the table. Ace snaps his mouth shut. "Stop telling me what I already know."

Ace snorts, his lips curling around his next words. "As soon as you start tellin' *us* what the fuck is going on."

Jack glances at me, his eyes hooded. Story sits quietly at Jack's side, not interfering. The old man never gets in the middle of arguments, allowing his captain to maintain control over his crew. He watches Jack now with intent focus. With a sigh, Jack speaks a name, "Captain Armada."

Ace looks from him to me, then back again. Furrowing his brow, he asks, "You mean the legend? That old pirate story? Ha! He's just a *myth*." He spits the word angrily.

"It's not a myth." Jack reaches down his shirt and pulls out a string with a small metal vial attached. He unscrews the lid and slides out a rolled-up piece of paper. "It's a map," he says as he unrolls the pieces and slides them together to create an almost complete map. It shows our world—Terrisøl and the Constellations, the King's Cloth and the Green Sea, but a piece is missing. Vulkan and the eastern part of the world aren't there.

"A map?" Ace asks, doubt in his voice. "Are you saying we came here for, what, a treasure hunt?"

"It's not treasure I'm after."

Ace crosses his arms. "What, then?"

"A ship."

Jack explains the rest of the story. I've heard this tale before—that Captain Armada was unstoppable because of this ship he had. Apparently, it holds some sort of power, like dark magic that protects it from harm. It's impenetrable and unsinkable. Jack explains that he's been hunting down information about this map for years now, and only recently found the first piece and hasn't stopped since then. "I meant to tell you," he addresses the room, meeting everyone's eyes before settling them on the map again. "I just wanted to have all the pieces before I did."

"Why?" Story asks.

"Because I needed to make sure it was real before I asked you to follow me." He grows quiet for a moment. "I put you all in danger by keeping this from you, and I'm sorry. I can never bring back those we lost, and I'll understand if some of you wish to leave."

"Well, that's just great." Ace chuckles, but there's no humor to it. "I'm glad it took the death of crewmates for you to come clean."

Jack slams his fist on the table, knocking over glasses. Ace flinches.

"They were *my* crew, too," Jack snarls. "I handpicked every one of you. So don't sit there and pretend that I don't feel every one of their deaths weighing on my shoulders."

Ace holds his gaze for a long moment, unable to retort. I catch Jack's eye, and the anger leaves him, shoulders slouching as he settles back in his chair.

So where's the missing piece? I sign.

Jack hesitates, running a hand through his hair. "The Isle of the Lost."

"Captain Blacktip will be following us."

"I know." He pulls out a separate map. "That's why we'll have to sail north and then south around the Constellations. I've already asked the Rana to borrow a ship similar to ours. We'll sail our flags on his ship and send it east where Captain Blacktip will be expecting us." He points to the crescent-shaped island, running his finger through the Green Sea.

"More sacrifices," Ace says dryly.

Jack ignores his tone and continues. "The Rana will stock the ship with enough people to get it out to sea, then at night, they'll take a rowboat back home." He lifts his cold eyes to Ace. "No more death."

I lean back in my chair, considering the plan and thinking about what everyone else must be. Jack looks at me, knowing I have something to say, so I sign, *How did he find us in the first place?*

Story turns to Jack. Ace keeps his eyes locked on the map in front of him, and Hraefn still hasn't moved from his seat in the corner.

"I don't know," Jack answers, uncertainty hanging heavily in his voice. "Maybe he paid someone at a port for information. It doesn't matter, he knows where we are now, but he can't know where we're going."

"What if he does?" Ace keeps his eyes down as he addresses the captain.

"Then we'll deal with it. I'll tell the rest of the crew in the morning what's going on and anyone will be free to leave. Understood?"

"Aye," they all respond.

Jack gets to his feet, indicating that the meeting is over. Story pats his shoulder before leaving for his room. "Hraefn." Jack beckons gently. The sharpshooter raises his eyes to the captain but seems to be looking through him. "You need to rest."

His nose flares slightly. "I'm fine."

"That wasn't a suggestion. Get some rest, or I'll have Nitelocke put you under again. Got it?"

"Aye," Hraefn grumbles as he gets to his feet and storms from the room.

I go to follow, but Jack calls my name.

I turn back. "Watch over him? Please."

I nod.

Ace goes off ahead of us, disappearing down the hall where the bar is. Hraefn continues down the hall, past his room to the one at the very end. I follow him, keeping my distance but making no move to conceal myself. I'm sure he knows I'm watching him, he just doesn't care. He raps his knuckles softly on the door, and a moment later, Nitelocke cracks it open. "Hraefn," he sighs. "Get some sleep. There's nothing—"

"Let me in."

Nitelocke twists his lips then spots me down the hall and opens the door fully for us to follow him. Hraefn pushes past the healer and into the room, while Nitelocke holds the door open for me. I stay against the far wall, watching as Hraefn moves over to the bed and sits down at his usual spot in a rocking chair.

Nitelocke makes his excuses. "I'll need more jasmine, poppy…" He lists off things that I'm sure he doesn't need, just to get out of the room. And I can see why. He doesn't want to look at the pain on Hraefn's face—it's heartbreaking.

Caspian lays in the small bed on his back, his head tilted to one side and eyes closed, as they have been for three days. His chest rises and falls steadily, calmly. A new dressing has been applied to his head, and he's been changed into clean clothing after Nitelocke operated on him.

When we got Caspian to the doctor, Nitelocke's face told it all, and yet he got to work trying to save him anyway. The bullet exploded on contact with the skull, raking along the outside before continuing.

"He's lucky," Nitelocke had said. "It's a little more than a graze. He's got a few shards in his scalp, but I think I can get them out." The sides of Caspian's head were already shaved, saving Nitelocke some time. As Nitelocke was removing the metal, Caspian began to seize. We had to strap him down to the bed while Hraefn fought to get into the room. I left him with three crew members in the hallway, but he'd managed to take them all down and burst into the room. We couldn't have him getting in the way. He was frantic, *hysterical*.

So Nitelocke shoved a syringe into his neck, and Hraefn dropped like a rock. He slept for a few hours, and by then, all the pieces of the bullet had been removed from Caspian's head.

Nitelocke allowed Caspian to sleep, dripping water into his mouth to keep him hydrated and medicine for the pain. After today, though, I can tell that Nitelocke is beginning to worry that he won't wake up. He said it was a possibility when he was cleaning and sewing up the wound.

"Head wounds are tricky," he'd said. "You can do everything right, clean and patch the wound, but if the brain swells or is damaged…" He trailed off then as he looked at his patient.

Hraefn now sits like a statue in the chair, staring at Caspian as if he were already gone. He speaks quietly, never taking his eyes from his friend. "Do you think he'll wake up?"

I move silently and stand across the bed from him. Hraefn reaches out and gently sets his hand over Caspian's heart. "He can't die."

The pain in his face tells more than the average eye can see. I put my hand on top of his, making him jump. He finally looks at me. *He will not die,* I sign.

Hraefn watches my hands closely, not as good at reading signing as Jack, but he understands.

"Only the gods know that," he says flatly.

I shake my head and place a hand over my heart. You *know it.*

His blue eyes glisten as they hold mine. I stand up and move to the door. *Come. We both need rest. Caspian will be here in the morning. I promise.*

Hraefn takes one last longing look at Caspian, touches a finger to his cheek, and stands up. I watch him go back to his room, hoping he'll stay there for the night. I set up a chair outside of Caspian's room and lean my head back against the wall. I know Hraefn is worried, so I'll keep guard outside Caspian's room, as I have done for three days now.

Three days since Caspian last opened his eyes.

Three days since we were attacked over a secret that Jack kept from us.

Three days since Skye died.

Three days since someone betrayed us.

I drift off to sleep sometime in the early hours.

Four days.

SIXTEEN

HRAEFN

Standing on the beach, I don't feel the sand under my boots or the wind through my hair.

I feel nothing.

The Rana's ship sails west, flying the flags of the *Chained Maiden*, but I know it won't be enough. Captain Blacktip is no fool, and as soon as he realizes it isn't our ship, he'll be after us again. But this time I won't falter.

Turning my back on the sea, I think about the last time we encountered Captain Blacktip. It was my first year with Captain Jack and the crew, and we were headed for Vulkan. I'd heard some stories of his past with Captain Blacktip but assumed they were all rumors since none ever came from the captain's mouth. He was a private man, and I respected that, so I didn't pry. I was too distracted by the fact that I was sailing home again to pay attention to stories passed around by the crew.

But then he found us.

There was a bad storm off the coast when Blacktip ambushed us. I'd been ordered to get in the crow's nest. Visibility was next to none, yet I climbed. Slipping more than once, I finally made it up, only to nearly be shot down. Blacktip's sharpshooter—who I later learned was named Deadeye Cane—opened fire the second

I unslung my rifle. I remember feeling the force of the bullet slicing the air beside my head. I'd always been an expert with a rifle, but for the first time, my hands shook as I leveled the barrel at my opponent. After our cannons managed to damage Blacktip's ship, and the fighting was over, Captain Jack sat down with his crew.

He only told us what we needed to know—that Blacktip was dangerous and an enemy. After the crew went to bed, the captain pulled me aside and told me about Deadeye Cane. He was said to be the best shooter in the world because he never missed. "But... he didn't shoot me," I'd argued.

The captain only shook his head. "That's because he didn't want to kill you. Not yet, anyway."

"I don't understand."

"Cane is..." He'd paused, twisting his lips and deciding how much truth he'd wind into his words. "He's competitive, but he likes to play. You're more well-known than you think, and word of your skills have been spoken of in ports around the world. When Cane finds a challenge, he wants to make use of it for as long as he can." The captain leaned in, voice cutting like knives. "Make no mistake, Hraefn. Cane *can* kill you, and he will one day. When he grows bored with you, or if you no longer present a challenge. Unless you kill him first."

Since that day, I've been terrified to face the shooter again, but that's not the only reason I feel how I do. I know the captain is telling the truth—that Cane likes to play—it's the same way Ace fights most of the time, like an animal playing with his food. They enjoy fighting, but they also need to drag it out and make it last. It isn't the way I fight or was raised, but I never say anything to Ace about it. He's my best friend, and as long as he gets the job done, I don't care much how he does it.

I walk along the beach as the moon pushes away the sun. The rest of the crew will be back at the tavern, packing their things. We'll be setting sail at midnight and hugging the shore of the Constellations, hopefully throwing off Blacktip for a while.

Up ahead, Tsu and Tetra stand at a small dock where crew members begin loading up. I'm eager to get back on the water, but I have a bad feeling in the pit of my stomach. I try telling myself that it's just hunger pangs or exhaustion, but it isn't. I don't know what I'll do if Caspian doesn't wake up. It's my fault that he's even in this position now, and that fact feels like a cold dagger in my heart.

Maybe if I hadn't taken him to that waterfall days ago or hadn't tried to kiss him that night in Vulkan outside the tavern. I've seen the way he looks at Skye, but I couldn't help myself. I can take his rejection and get over it eventually, and I swear that I will, if only he'd wake up. I can't live with myself if he dies. It's like Captain Jack told me—Deadeye Cane likes to play, and he isn't done with me yet. So Caspian risked his life for nothing. I was never in any danger of dying from Cane's bullet, but Caspian didn't know that, and he risked his life for me. He was there for *me*, and I couldn't help him.

Back in my room, I stuff my clothes into a pack, sling my rifle over my shoulder, and head out the door. I pause, glancing down the hall at Caspian's door, which is slightly ajar. Nitelocke and Captain Jack argued over Caspian's state for hours last night. Nitelocke insisted he stay here with Caspian until he's better or at least wakes up, and after careful consideration, the captain agreed. It's too dangerous, and the Green Sea can be rough this time of year, and he won't risk Caspian again. I tried so hard not to show any emotion at their decision, but leaving him behind was one of the worst pains I've ever felt.

What if I never see him again?

Or what if he wakes up and he isn't Caspian anymore? I lost my mother, and that was the worst day of my life, but she was truly gone. My fear is that Caspian will wake up, and maybe he won't remember me, or he won't be the funny, smart, brave boy I've come to know, and I can't handle that. If I have to leave him here, then I'll at least say my goodbyes to the old Caspian.

Dropping my bag and rifle outside his room, I pause before

pushing open the door. He lays on the bed, just as he has for days now. I sit in the rocking chair, running my eyes over his face. He's starting to grow some stubble along his jawline. My fingers reach out and touch his cheek briefly, but I quickly snap my hand back to my lap.

"Caspian," I whisper, feeling ridiculous because I'm sure he can't hear me anyway. "You have to wake up," I say. "Please. Captain Jack will leave you here if you don't."

His eyes stay shut, and his breathing is calm. Maybe it's the fact that he's asleep, or that I might not ever see him again, but I start to lean closer, placing my hands on the bed before gently slipping my hand under his. It feels warm and safe, but I don't let myself enjoy it too much.

"I didn't think I was going to like you," I admit, staring at his closed eyes. "Ace liked you, but he likes everyone. You were… clever, and I think that made the captain wary of you, but it also earned your spot with us." Caspian's eyes move under the lids like he's seeing it all again.

"That night you confronted Bart about the fake money…" I chuckle lightly, shaking my head. "I thought you were mad. That the captain had made a mistake and you'd get us all killed, but I was wrong. You *saved* us, and you weren't afraid to demand what was owed. I think that's when I knew I could trust you. And then I even started to like you." I give his fingers a gentle squeeze but get nothing in return.

The room is so quiet, the only thing I can hear is our hearts beating—

Wait.

I lean closer, holding my breath as I press my cheek against Caspian's chest.

Thud, thud, thud, thud.

Leaning back to look at him, his eyes are still closed. But Caspian's heart kicked up when I squeezed his hand.

Did he hear me?

I hover over his bed, running my thumb over his hand. "It's me, Caspian. Wake up." I put my other hand against his cheek.

Thud, thud, thud, thud. His heart thumps faster and mine matches his pace. I know I have to do everything I can to get him to wake up, but is that selfish? Caspian needs to heal, but I don't think sleeping for four days is helping. If anything, based on what Nitelocke has said, it's hurting him. The longer he stays asleep, the weaker he'll be when he finally wakes.

No, he needs to wake up now.

"Caspian? Can you hear me?" I cradle his face in my palms, running my thumbs over his cheekbones and praying that his eyes will open. Tears start to well in my eyes. The thought of leaving him here like this is too much, and yet I know that I'll have to if this doesn't work. My frustration and confusion all ball into one and settle in my stomach. His heart keeps a steady pace as I lean in closer, sliding my eyes to his lips.

"It's Hraefn," I whisper so softly I barely hear my own voice. But then the thumping of his heart outpaces my own. His eyes begin moving under the lids, and the corner of his mouth twitches. My eyes grow wide and my hands grow sweaty as I hold his face, but I won't let go. Not yet.

"Wake up, Caspian. Come back..." My voice drifts off as a tear rolls down my cheek. Caspian can hear me, I *know* he can, and my courage falters for a second. Will he remember what I say? It doesn't matter. I place a hand over his beating heart and keep the other cupping his cheek. His pulse pounds against my fingers as his heart leaps out of control at my touch.

Gathering my courage once more, I speak softly and honestly. "Come back to me," I whisper. "I don't want to do this without you, and I can't lose you now. It hasn't been enough time," I rasp. "Our journey can't end here. Not like this. I..." My voice breaks as Caspian's heart begins to slow once again. Maybe he can hear me, and he doesn't feel the same, but what if he does? "Caspian, I... I..."

The words refuse to leave my lips, so instead, I lean in and kiss him. My lips press ever so gently to the corner of his mouth, barely a kiss at all, then I back away. His eyes remain closed. I take a deep breath, let out a sigh, and get up. Standing at the door, I take one last look at Caspian, then turn my back and leave. The crew will be ready to sail soon, and right now, all I want to do is get up in my crow's nest and forget.

Forget the way his beating heart feels under my fingers. Or the way his skin feels against my lips, but mostly I want to forget why Caspian is lying in that bed in the first place. Maybe it was a mistake for Captain Jack to allow him to join the crew. Getting close to someone like that will only bring trouble. It made me lose focus and got Caspian shot.

Tonight, under the moon, I swear to the gods that if Caspian wakes up, I won't pursue him any further. It's for his own good, and no matter how much it will crush me, I can't allow myself to fall any more than I already have. We're a crew, and I can't put Caspian's safety above anyone else.

I sink to the floor once in my crow's nest, cradling my rifle in my lap and muttering to myself, "He's not more important than the rest of the crew. He's not special. The captain's life comes first, then my own. I will not pursue Caspian. I will treat him as I do the rest of the crew." Over and over, I lie to myself under the watchful eyes of the gods until I begin to drift off to sleep.

SEVENTEEN

CASPIAN

I can feel him.

As sure as there's still blood in my veins and air in my lungs, I can feel him.

"Come back to me," he said, and then his lips brushed mine.

My eyes crack open, and I'm assaulted by darkness. Panic tears through me as I start to blink away the blurred edges of my world, only to realize I'm in a dark room. I let out a sigh of relief that I still have my sight, then do a mental check of the rest of my body. My head throbs and feels as heavy as a bag of wet sand. When I try to roll over, a wave of nausea crashes over me. My vision is blurry, my stomach churning, and sweat starts to bead on my temple. But I need to get up and find Hraefn.

Psyching myself up, I swing my legs over the edge of the bed and immediately flop back to my pillows. My head is swimming with flashes of the battle—cannonballs, screaming, blood, and then…

Skye.

She was right there in front of me. Beautiful and real, and then she was gone. I look down at my hands, wondering who scrubbed her blood from beneath my fingernails. I can still feel it coating my skin now, like the ink that once covered her arm.

Though it isn't my fault she died, I know I'll carry her ghost with me forever.

Trying to get up again, I start to remember bits and pieces of what Hraefn said to me. Was that a dream, or was he truly here? I can't tell, everything is still fuzzy and jumbled up. How long has it been since I was shot?

As my feet touch the floor, I stand up, only to stumble back. I catch myself on the bedpost, sending a wave of pain to my other wound. The gunshot wound to my shoulder throbs madly as my muscles flex to keep me upright.

Growling through my clenched teeth, I slowly move toward the table where a mirror hangs on the wall, showing me the stubble on my jaw and bags under my eyes. I swallow, then pull down the collar of my shirt to look. The wound has been sewn and dressed, so I move on to my head, pulling away the dressing as gently as I can.

Stitches line the entire side of my skull, back to the nape of my neck. I touch it gently, feeling the skin that's still raised and the thread that winds through my skin. Suddenly I feel sick to my stomach. Grabbing the nearest bowl, my body lurches as I throw up. Dropping to my knees, I sway, feeling lightheaded and weak. The strained movement makes my wound throb like crazy, making me too dizzy to stand up. I drop the bowl and get on all fours, trying to focus my eyes, but then I hear a voice.

"Caspian?"

Lifting my eyes, I find Nitelocke running down the hall toward me. His gray eyes are wide with worry, then they crinkle in the corners as he drops to his knees with a smile on his face.

"You're awake!" he bellows too loudly, making me wince. Nitelocke grabs my shoulders and chuckles nervously. "What the hell were you thinking?" he scolds, looping my arm around his shoulder and lifting me to standing.

"Hraefn," I rasp, wiping my mouth.

"Come on," he says. "Back to bed. The crew will be off soon—"

My feet grind to a halt, and I whirl on him. "Off? What do you mean *off*?"

"They're setting sail soon. We're to stay here until you're better."

All the blood in my face drains.

Hraefn.

He's going to leave me behind.

I have too many emotions rushing me in a matter of seconds —pain, anger, regret, sadness, and finally confidence.

I lock eyes with Nitelocke. "No."

He raises his brows, his lips quirking. *"No?"* He lets go, and I sway slightly on my feet. He smirks as if to prove his point.

"I won't be left behind."

"You're too weak," he says gently. "You need time to heal—"

"I'm going," I snarl. "With or without your help."

He stares at me for a long moment, deciding whether to obey his captain's orders or help a crewmate. Nitelocke lets out a deep sigh, his shoulders dropping. "Fine, but we need to hurry." Nitelocke turns and begins packing up his things, but I'm already moving out the door. I can't wait for him. "Caspian!" he yells, dropping a bottle as he frantically packs. The glass shatters on the wooden floor, a curse leaving his lips.

My legs feel like they're made of jelly as I stumble down the empty hall of the tavern, splaying my hand out on the wall for balance. The stitches in my head hammer at my skull, but I keep my feet moving. Once outside, and after waving off patrons who try to assist me, I head for the docks.

The silver moon slowly crawls across the sky, lighting my path back to my crew. I've become so close with them in such a short period, and I can't understand why they'd leave me. Am I not as important as the others? Do they still not see me as part of their family? The thoughts pain me, but I keep them alive anyway. If I expect everything, then I'll never be disappointed. But that's just a sad lie.

Through the darkness, I spot the *Chained Maiden* still docked, but her new sails are unrolled and ready to catch the wind. My heart feels like a panicked bird trying to escape a cage. I can see figures moving in the distance and people already aboard the ship. No one notices me as I wobble down the narrow dock, weaving around crates and barrels. I crane my neck up to the crow's nest, desperately searching for Hraefn when I get hit by a wave of dizziness.

Dropping to my knees, I clutch my head as the world begins to tilt on me. My body slams down to the dock, and I'm fighting to stay conscious, but I can feel the world slipping. Hurried footsteps come my way, and I think I hear my name being yelled just before I black out.

"What the hell did I tell you?"

"I'm sorry. He insisted—"

"I don't give a shit! I gave you an order."

Silence.

A deep sigh. "Just get out. It doesn't matter now. Let him sleep."

I wake up in a strange bed. The room is dimly lit by a lantern that swings in the corner. The smell of jasmine and herbs hit my nose and the sound of the sea perks my ears. Am I here? Did I make it?

"Caspian."

The voice startles me. Turning, I see Hraefn sitting in a chair on the opposite side of the room. His black hair is slicked neatly, blue eyes like shards of glass in the candlelight.

He's beautiful.

Hraefn gets up, crossing his arms over his chest, and comes toward me but stops a few feet from my bed. I struggle to sit up, but Hraefn makes no move to help me. Finally, propping myself up against the pillows, I asked what happened.

His tone is casual. "You passed out on the docks. Nitelocke

yelled to us for help. I... saw you coming from the crow's nest." He averts his eyes, finding his boots much more interesting than me. Did I imagine the things he said to me while I was asleep? Perhaps it *was* just a dream, but... there's something different about him.

His demeanor is almost cold. I can feel every inch of space between us like a frigid breeze off the sea. He tells me how long I've been out, the ceremony they had for all those we lost. Skye's face flashes before my eyes, and I turn away, not wanting Hraefn to see my pain, but he isn't even looking at me.

"Where are we?"

His eyes meet mine briefly. "Still at the tip of the Capital. We were a little late setting sail." He gives me a pointed look, but that's not what's bothering him.

"What's wrong?" I ask, feeling my palms grow sweaty.

Hraefn snorts, but there's no humor behind his smile. "What's wrong?" he repeats. "We were attacked," he snarls. "And you decide what? Play the hero and almost get yourself killed?"

Shame heats my cheeks, but anger coils tight around my heart like a viper. Hraefn begins pacing the room. I sit up, slinging my legs over the side of the bed. "Hraefn—"

"I didn't need your help!" he explodes, eyes cutting right through me like icy daggers and pinning me to the bed. "You should've stayed belowdecks with Ace! But no, you had to come to my rescue and get yourself shot. *Twice!*" He laughs, ripping a hand through his midnight hair. "I mean, gods, Caspian. What the *fuck* did you think, huh? That you would kill the most famous sharpshooter in the world with your first shot? Or did you think the gods would perform some kind of miracle and strike him down? *Well?*"

My mouth hangs open, but no words come out. I've never seen Hraefn this angry, but I also know some of it is fear. He's afraid for me, whether he admits it or not. I push myself to my feet, fighting off another wave of dizziness. "I wasn't thinking," I say gently. "Not about the gods or getting shot or dying. I was only thinking of you... it's always you."

My mouth snaps shut at the confession. The anger melts off of Hraefn, and his face softens, but only for a second before he builds up the wall again. "Yeah, well, don't. I don't need your help. I need you to follow the orders that the captain gives you and stay the hell out of my way before you really get yourself killed."

Hraefn turns his back on me, and something in me snaps.

"Fuck you, Hraefn!" He pauses. "I got shot in the head trying to help someone I thought was my friend."

He whirls on me so fast that I almost lose my balance. Inches away, he jabs his finger in my chest. "You're a crew member. Same as anyone else. You're not special or different, Caspian. You're just a hazard."

My heart drops to my boots. I see a flash of regret on his face, but I'm too furious and hurt to care. "What kind of crew leaves one of their members behind?"

He doesn't have an answer for that, so he just stands there staring at me.

"You're right," I curl the words into a snarl and step closer, ignoring the way his breath on my lips makes my heart pound. "I shouldn't have come on deck. I shouldn't have helped someone who doesn't give a shit about me. But I did."

His gaze is shattering me, and he falters for the right words. Then he scoffs and angles away from me, but I grab his arm. Hraefn's eyes grow wide, and his lips part slightly as he seems to force the words past his lips. "Let go."

I don't.

"If you don't care about me, then why are you here?"

His pulse is racing through his wrist as my fingers hold on for dear life. I step even closer. "Why were you sitting here in this room, waiting for me to wake up if you don't care about me?"

His blue eyes shimmer in the low light, and his voice is

nothing but a whisper. "I..." But he doesn't finish. Instead, he shakes his head, then yanks his arm from my grasp. "I have to get above decks. We need a lookout."

He leaves me standing there at the edge of my bed, at the edge of everything. As he closes the door, I sink back down to the bed and cradle my head in my hands. Tears well in my eyes, and that only frustrates me more. How can he say that to me? What did I do? Or maybe I was being stupid, and Hraefn never felt anything for me, but I can't let go of that sliver of hope that I'm wrong. Of all the possibilities I've run through my head, this wasn't one of them, and the disappointment breaks me.

I shoot to my feet, grab a bottle off a shelf, and throw it at the wall. "Fuck!" I scream as the glass explodes. Leaning against the wall, I try to ignore the pounding headache as I slide to the floor, hugging my knees to my chest. A moment later, someone knocks at the door. "Fuck off."

The door opens anyway, and a head of blond hair comes into view. "Is that any way to talk to a friend, lad?" Ace steps into the room and strolls over to me before sitting down.

"What do you want?"

He cocks his head, picking nonexistent lint from his blue jacket. "I came to see you. Hraefn said you were awake."

Hraefn.

I block out the image of him.

"Didn't intend to get my head bitten off," Ace continues and tries a smile while handing me a flask. "Mind putting your fangs away?"

I snatch the flask from him and drink deeply, closing my eyes and leaning back on the wall. Ace whistles low, gesturing to my head. "That's going to be one hell of a scar, lad. It'll drive the women crazy."

I glare at him, and he throws his hands up, taking back his drink.

"I'm sorry," I say. "I'm just..."

"No need, lad. I'd be a bit grumpy too if I got shot in the head."

My lips force themselves into a smile. "Yeah."

Ace snaps his fingers. "I ken what you need. A nickname." He leans in and winks. "A true pirate name."

"Such as?"

He sips from the flask again, tapping his chin. "I got it! How about Lead Head Caspian."

I snort and shake my head. "No."

He waves the name away. "Fine, how about... Bullet Stopper."

I just stare at him, brows raised.

"You're awfully picky for someone who nearly died."

"Ace."

"Oh!" He claps his hands. "The Bullet Crusher. No! Caspian the Undead."

"Ace..."

"You're right. Doesn't exactly roll off the tongue, does it?"

"Would you shut up?" I snatch the flask away and down the rest. "You're horrible at coming up with names."

Ace raises a brow to me but a grin lifts the corner of his mouth. "That hurts."

"Good."

I get to my feet, using the wall for support, and head out the door. I need to find food. Ace follows me and offers his arm, which I take because the hall starts to tilt.

"Does it hurt?" He gestures to my head.

"About as much as it does to hear you talk."

Ace throws his head back and cackles, wiping tears from his eyes, and I find myself smiling too. I need this right now, and Ace might be a pain in the ass, but I like him.

"Here we are." He leaves me at the door to the kitchen, saying Bas will be happy to make me something since I missed dinner.

"Thanks."

"Well, I'll leave you to it then. Eat your fill. You look half dead."

I narrow my eyes and open my mouth, but he holds up a hand. "No need to retort, lad. I'll assume it was something clever." Ace walks down the hall, then pauses and looks back at me with a sly grin. "Clever Caspian." He smiles at the name. "That's who you are."

The name sits on the surface of my skin for a moment and then begins to sink in as Ace turns to leave.

Clever Caspian.

Is that who I am?

EIGHTEEN

We sail east, heading far from the Constellations, and out into the Harpy Sea. Captain Blacktip and his crew are nowhere in sight, but that only heightens my nerves. His absence is only temporary, and I know the longer we go without hearing from him, the closer he lurks.

We left the island two days ago now, with Caspian back on board, though he seems more miserable than ever. I don't pry or ask, though the crew whispers of a fight between him and Hraefn. My eyes run up the mainmast to my sharpshooter, where he sits in the crow's nest, his attention turned west. I trust Hraefn to do his job, so I don't interfere with whatever he has going on with Caspian. We can't afford to lose sight of our mission. We can't lose any more crew members.

When I told my crew what I was hunting and they all decided to stay with me, I was shocked. I'd sat them all down and explained the hunt for the map, the island, and the ship. And even though we lost people when Captain Blacktip attacked, even though we were likely to lose more, they all stayed anyway. I didn't understand it at first. Here they are, risking their lives for me, not because I ordered it, or even asked, but because they're loyal. I don't deserve it, but I'm not about to argue either. After all, they're free to leave whenever they want, and they know that.

"Captain?"

Story comes to my side as I stand at the helm, watching my crew from above.

"What is it?" I ask.

The old man grins, showing a mouthful of yellow teeth and creating a whole murder of crow's feet around his eyes. "I just thought you'd like company."

Hiding my annoyance behind a pleasant smile, I say, "You were wrong."

Story levels his eyes with mine and cocks his head slightly. We both smirk before I turn my eyes back to the crew. Caspian is down at the bow, sparring with Ace while Tsu sits off to the side and watches with a keen eye.

"You know what they'll want in return, yes?" My attention is pulled back to Story, whose face has gone serious. I know who he means—the people of the Isle of the Lost. Gold and jewels don't interest them. What they want is something people don't want to give up—they trade in secrets and information.

"I know what they want," I respond dryly.

"And are you prepared to let it go?"

My fingers grip the wooden railing until my knuckles go white. "*Yes.*" The word slides from my mouth in a hiss. "And I don't need you questioning my commitment."

"No one is questioning your commitment." Story jerks his chin toward the crew below. "They simply need to know that you're not leading them on some wild goose chase."

I turn to face him fully. "They could've left. I gave them an opportunity, so are you telling me they're having doubts, or did you just come to piss me off?"

He scratches his gray mustache while his brown eyes search mine. Story is a valuable member of my crew, and without him, I wouldn't have this ship.

It was on the Isle of the Lost that I found the old man

wandering and traveling the world alone in a schooner. I try to bargain with the natives to buy this ship, but they won't take my gold.

Finally, Story interrupts us and explains what the people want. At first, I'm not willing to give them anything. My life isn't an easy one, and I prefer to keep my burdens tucked away, letting people think what they will. I've heard more rumors about myself over the years, but I never confirm or deny them. After I trade a secret with the people, I get the ship, and Story is the first member of my crew. He's been sailing since he was just a boy, and though I was young, he joined me anyway. I needed someone experienced.

Since then, we've been sailing the world, picking up more members for the crew, and avoiding Captain Blacktip as much as we could. Story likes to think he knows everything about me, but that's not true. Only one person knows all of my secrets, and yet I kept this from her. My eyes find Tsu. As if she senses my regret, she lifts her green eyes to mine.

"I didn't mean to upset you," Story answers, drawing my attention back to him.

Letting go of a sigh, I shake my head. "You didn't. I'm just…"

My words leave me, and Story places a hand on my shoulder. "I know," he says gently. "But if what you say about this map is real, then you'll have to give the people something more. Something bigger than the last time."

I try to avoid going to that island, but the people there are my best customers for Ostium, and I can't afford to lose them. There's no trading of secrets or information for the alcohol, they simply pay what is owed, and I leave as soon as I can. I've only traded with them twice before—once for the ship, and once when I sailed with Captain Blacktip.

"I'll give them something valuable," I reply, turning to face Story. "Something no one knows."

After sailing with Captain Blacktip for four years, I've come to see his crew as my family. The young captain musses my hair as he strolls by, talking with his sharpshooter, Deadeye Cane. The man is tall and lanky, with messy brown hair and eyes the color of the dying sun. He winks as he walks by, chewing on a matchstick with his yellow teeth. He's younger than Blacktip by a few years, though he doesn't look it. Blacktip, whose true name is Marlyn, still looks boyish with his head of blond hair and smooth jawline.

"Jack!" he calls over his shoulder. "Come here."

"Yes, Captain?"

Blacktip casts me a tight smile, then waves Deadeye Cane away. He hangs his arm around my shoulders, which now come to his chest. "We're going somewhere special," he explains as we walk the deck. "These people are much different than any others we've traded with."

As we come to the bow of the ship, I see the island. The beach is rocky and dark and leads up to a forest of palm trees and thick brush. High cliffs frame the beach, sharp rocks protruding from the waters like shark fins, but the rest of the land looks flat as far as the eye can see.

"The Isle of the Lost," the captain whispers in my ear, as if the land can hear us talking about it. "We're going to make a trade with these people."

"Trade what?" I turn to look at him. There's an odd gleam in his eye.

"Well, they have no use for the things a normal man might want."

I furrow my brow, so he specifies. He tells me that they don't want gold, coins, or even jewels, but information. I don't believe him at first, thinking he's just messing with me, but I'm wrong.

As we walk over the rocky beach, people emerge from the brush until about twenty stand before us. The crew around me is armed to the teeth, and I have a large whalebone knife on my belt, but no one draws their weapons. The native people gesture for us to follow, not even exchanging greetings with the captain. Their skin is so dark it almost looks like charcoal, and their hair is braided in intricate knots or shaved to the scalp. They all wear similar plain attire, cotton robes for the men and long skirts for the women, leaving their breasts bare. My cheeks flush, though I try to avoid staring. The captain notices and nudges me.

"Beautiful, aren't they?"

I just nod in response.

We follow the people down a dirt path to a village. The huts are small and dot the land that has been cleared away. At the center is a large stone temple with odd-looking stone creatures that sit perched on the roof. Women watch us go by, balancing babies on their hips or baskets on their heads. Men with spears guard the temple, their cold eyes never straying in our direction. An uneasy feeling settles over me but I follow my crew up the steps anyway.

The captain stops at the door and locks eyes with me. "The rest of you go find something to do. Jack and I will handle this one." The crew turns around and heads off into the village, and I follow Blacktip inside.

The structure looks much larger than it does from the outside. As if the building inhaled us, expanding its walls to make room for more bodies. To my right, a small group of women sit on plush pillows, sipping drinks and chatting in hushed tones. We walk down a few stone steps to the center of the temple, where a beautiful woman sits on a throne of bones. She's terrifying and enchanting at the same time. Blacktip inclines his head, and I do the same, finding it difficult to take my eyes from her.

"Come, child." She beckons me closer. I look at my captain for assurance, and he nods. Her hair is like a hundred black snakes that fall to her hips. Woven in her braids are colorful feathers, seashells, and tiny bells that jingle as she leans closer to me. The woman has gray-blue eyes, like the color of the sea before a storm hits. When I get close enough, she grips my chin between her long fingernails and turns me from side to side. Tsking, she addresses Blacktip. "He is too young."

"Madame Kiera, I assure you he isn't."

She scoffs and releases me, sitting back and tapping a finger to a rib bone on her throne.

"Did you tell the boy what he must give?" Blacktip doesn't answer. "I didn't think so. It will be you, and we'll be done with this."

"Madame Kiera," Blacktip says, taking a step forward before she can dismiss him. "Jack here has been sailing with me for four years. He's proven himself a valuable member of my crew." He steps closer, but Kiera shoots him a warning glare, and he backs away. "Every member of my crew has given to you. Now it's his turn." He looks down at me. "That is, if Jack truly wants to be part of this crew."

There's silence in the temple. Deafening, uncomfortable silence. I don't even breathe for fear of making a sound. Madame Kiera observes the captain closely, her stormy eyes calculating. Finally, she inclines her head in agreement.

Blacktip blows out a sigh of relief. "Thank you."

"Wait outside." She wags her fingers in the captain's general direction. A dismissal.

My heart pounds madly as I watch my captain leave me with this strange woman. Is she a witch? And why does she want information instead of gold or coins? It doesn't make any sense to me.

Madame Kiera beckons me to sit on a pillow in front of her. "Tell me, child. Why do you want to be part of Captain Blacktip's crew?"

I have a sense that she'll know if I lie, so I tell the truth. "I have nowhere else to go."

"Hmm." She slides down to the pillow with me and takes my palms in hers. Her hands are covered in black markings that swirl up her arms and under the collar of her top. "Tell me something about you, Jack. Something that no one else knows.

Tell me a thing that lurks deep in your heart. Tell me a secret that's trapped inside your mind. Tell me, and the trade is complete."

Her hands turn icy cold in mine despite the humid conditions. I try to move away, but she holds tight. My pulse spikes.

"What does the captain want from you?" I ask, avoiding her request.

Madame Kiera twists her lips and considers me. "We have an abundance of iron on the island from which we make steel. Your captain wishes to trade for this steel. Our steel is the strongest in the world." Her gray-blue eyes settle on my lips, eager to hear them form words. "Now, *tell me.*"

I think for a moment, considering what I should tell her. What if she doesn't like what I tell her? Will she refuse to give the captain what he wants? I can't let that happen. I'm a part of the crew now, and I won't let my captain down.

"I'm an orphan," I start. Captain Blacktip and the crew already know this about me, but I never talk about my past much. It's an odd thing being only eleven years old and feeling as though I've lived a lifetime already. Madame Kiera narrows her beautiful eyes and waits for me to continue. I swallow a lump in my throat and push on. "My mother gave me up when I was born. I was raised in the Sacred Souls Orphanage on Midsarra."

"And your father?"

"The women who raised me said that he was a bad man. They said he used to beat my mother, and that..." I clear my throat and try to take my hands from hers again, but her nails dig in. "They said... that I was a mistake. That I'd bring nothing to the world but pain and misery for those closest to me."

"And that bothered you?" It sounds like more of a statement than a question. Probably because she already knows the answer.

My head nods in response.

"So, what did you do about it?"

I tell Madame Kiera that I ran away when I was five years old. "I wanted to find her," I explain. "I wanted to show my mother that my father was wrong." Tears start to burn my eyes, and shame stains my cheeks crimson. I've hunted for my mother for years, hoping that one day I'd find her, but I never did. Eventually, I gave up, feeling embarrassed and ashamed of who I was. I tell Madame Kiera all of this, and she sits patiently, drinking up my words. When I'm done, she lets go of my hands and shakes her head, disappointed.

"That is information anyone could get if they only sought out the orphanage where you were raised." She leans in close until all I can see is the storm in her eyes. "You're not telling me everything."

Shrinking back, I stumble over my words. "I... I didn't lie."

"No." She sits back too. "You just left out something. Tell me, how do you feel about your captain?"

I blink at her in confusion. "What?"

"*Tell me.*" Her tone comes out sharp, making me flinch.

Sweat beads my temples, and I shift uncomfortably on the pillow. "Captain Blacktip is... a good man." She sits in silence until I get so uncomfortable that I start rambling. "He's taken care of me and protected me. The captain trusts me, he's like family to me."

Something sparks in her eyes as I continue. "I never had a family. Those women who raised me"—I wave a hand, dismissing their existence with a flick of my fingers—"they were awful! Always punishing me for running away. They never hugged me or tucked me in at night. Never said anything remotely affectionate. But the captain..." Tears stream down my cheeks now. "He's been like... like a father to me."

As the words leave my lips, I feel a sense of calm wash over me, like releasing a bird after you nurse it back to health and watch it fly free. I know my words are true, but I've never let myself think too much about how I feel for fear of being let down again. I've been alone in this world from the start, and now that I have a family of my own, I'll do anything to keep it.

"A father," Madame Kiera repeats.

"I know he's young," I say defensively. "But he *is* like a father to me. At least what I imagine one would be like. He cares about me."

Her stare is cold. "Does he?"

My tears freeze on my cheeks, and I ball my fists. "Of course he does," I snarl.

"And you've never told him that? How you see him?"

I shake my head, casting my eyes down as I wipe away my tears. I won't tell the captain that I see him as a father figure. I might still be a kid, but I know that's a delicate relationship, and I don't want anything to change between the crew and me. It's my only secret, and I just gave it away for my captain.

Madame Kiera cups my cheek, leans in, and kisses me gently. I feel a shudder go through my body as she backs away, her eyes sparkling in the dimly lit room. "Thank you, young Jack. I shall keep your secret forever."

"So… that's it? You'll give the captain the steel?"

She inclines her head. "I am a woman of my word. The trade is done." She looks past me to a guard who I hadn't noticed before and tilts her head. He leaves the temple, and I get up to follow, but Madame Kiera stops me. "Your captain cares about you, yes?"

I turn back to face her. "Yes."

She twists her lips and stands up, towering over me. "He has an odd way of showing it."

"What does that mean?"

She shrugs her slender shoulders. "People who care for one another don't take advantage." She leans down and whispers in my ear, "He *used* you."

My head snaps back, and I stare daggers at her. "What are you talking about? The captain said this was the only way, the rest of the crew has done it, and it was my turn."

"A lie."

I stumble, blinking at her like she's crazy.

"I've never traded with his crew before, only him. And only once."

My stomach plummets. "You're lying."

She chuckles lightly, twisting one of her braids around her finger. "And what would I have to gain by lying?"

Faltering, I rack my brain for an answer, but there isn't one. "Well… then, why would you tell me that?"

She's silent for a long moment, which only heightens my nerves with every passing second. "I know things about the captain that you don't. I just urge you to be careful and guard your heart. It's the easiest thing to be broken."

Anger and fear bubble in my veins as I step up to her. "What did the captain trade with you? What did he tell you?"

"Oh, child." She places a hand on the crown of my head. "I can never speak of the things exchanged within this temple. Go now. Your captain will be waiting." With that, she turns her back and sits on her throne of bones.

I storm out of the temple and into the thick humid air of the island. What the hell does she know? The captain cares about me; I *know* he does. Maybe she's only trying to get a rise out of me, but why?

No.

I refuse to believe her. But doubt is like a heavy lead weight in my stomach.

Captain Blacktip and Deadeye Cane are posted up on a palm tree, talking and laughing. When the captain looks at me, his smile fades, and his eyes turn cold. He must have read the expression on my face, for he pushes away and walks briskly toward me. "What happened?" He grabs my sleeve and pulls me off to the side. "Is the trade done?"

"It's done."

"Oh." His shoulders relax and he lets go, running a hand through his blond hair. "Then what's wrong?"

My eyes are on the sand below my feet. "I just… I didn't like that."

"I know," he says, placing his hands on my shoulders and getting eye level with me. "But the entire crew has done it before, and now that you have, you're officially one of us." He smiles, and I concentrate on it, focusing until I see the crack. There, just as the lie passes his lips, he glances down ever so slightly. Am I imagining it? I have to be sure, so I ask another question I already know the answer to.

"You've traded with Madame Kiera before?"

"Of course I have."

He doesn't look away from my eyes once. The truth is staring straight at me, and it slides effortlessly from his lips. He smiles and stands up straight, calling to his crew. We head back to the ship with wagons of steel.

I sit on the dock, swinging my feet over the side as the crew loads the ship with some help from the natives. The sun is beginning to set, lighting the waves on fire as the moon claims its rightful spot for the night.

Captain Blacktip comes to get me once everything is set. "You ready to go?"

I get to my feet and nod, faking a smile.

"Good. We're off to Vulkan…" His words trail off as my thoughts take over, blocking out everything around me. I stand there, summoning my courage. The captain stops and turns back. "What is it?" He strolls back to me, concern wrinkling his brow, but is it fake? I swallow my fears and keep my tears back as I speak.

"I'm part of the crew, right?"

His head cocks in confusion. "Of course, Jack."

"And… you care about your crew?" I look up to the ship, and the captain follows my gaze. A smile plays on his lips as he watches them unroll the sails and Deadeye Cane climbs to his perch.

"I do care about them," he says, not the slightest hesitation in his voice.

My heart pounds through my shirt, and my palms grow slick. I lock eyes with him and ask, "Do you care about me?"

I wait a heartbeat. Then two.

His eyes stay pinned on mine as he smiles, parting his lips, and lying through his teeth. "I care about you, Jack," he says, as his eyes glance down for a split second, not noticeable if you've been drinking in the pretty lies that slip from his mouth. That's what I've been doing—drinking them up.

My heart plummets to my boots, and I can't stop the tears that come pouring down my cheeks. It's all a lie. These last four years I've been sailing with a man who I thought cared about me, could be a *father* to me. The idea enrages me now, and I feel my heart shatter with the realization.

Captain Blacktip takes my tears for happiness, cups the back of my head, and pulls me into his chest. "Shh, it's all right," he coos. "You're our family now, Jack. *My* family and I'd never let anything happen to you."

Though I can't see his eyes, I know they hold nothing but more lies. My tears come faster and harder the longer he holds me because I know in my heart that I'll never have a father. I've never had affection before I joined his crew. I recall the first time he ruffled my hair or clasped a hand on my shoulder—I thought they were loving, but now I only see them as condescending.

I pull away from him, wiping my tears and keeping my eyes on my boots. The captain touches my shoulder, and rage shoots through me and down to my core, but I keep my face neutral.

"Come on," he says gently. "Our crew is waiting."

Our crew.

These people aren't *my* anything.

As we walk back to the ship, I swear that one day I'll have my own crew and captain my own ship. As soon as I'm old enough and have enough money saved, I'll leave Captain Blacktip and never look back. I'll be Captain Jack one day, and that thought keeps me going.

NINETEEN

The ring of steel assaults my ears.

Caspian and Ace spar at the bow of the ship, the latter landing blow after blow, each more forceful than the last. Caspian growls through clenched teeth, ducking under the dull blade as Ace swings for his head.

"Watch it!"

Ace just cackles madly and swings again.

I can tell by the way he moves that Caspian is still feeling the effects of his gunshot wounds. He's slower to dodge, not quite fast enough to block every blow, and Ace takes advantage of that. He pursues Caspian, backing him up farther and farther until his back is at the gunwale.

"Come on, lad!" Ace jabs his sword forward, but Caspian moves in time. "At least make it a challenge for me. A straw dummy moves faster than you."

"Do you ever shut up?" Caspian breathes, swinging his sword at Ace's head.

Ace ducks under Caspian's sword and then taps a finger on his chin. "I don't know." He turns his head up to the crow's nest. "Hraefn, lad! Do I ever shut up?"

Hraefn doesn't take his eyes from the sea as he calls back

down. "Not since you clawed your way from your mother's womb."

Ace turns back to Caspian with a smug grin. "Well, then. There you have it."

Caspian growls and lunges again.

The sky clouds over with the promise of rain. As the wind picks up my short hair and swirls it about, Ace and Caspian end their training. "I'd say good job, but… well."

Caspian snarls and punches at Ace's shoulder, but the prince slides away, laughing his way belowdecks. I catch Caspian's eye and beckon him over. The skin along his skull still protrudes, laced with neat stitching courtesy of Nitelocke. He says nothing as he joins me along the gunwale, watching the clouds roll in from the north. I nudge his shoulder, then gesture up to the crow's nest. A question.

Caspian glances in Hraefn's direction, eyes hooded and hurt. "That's not your concern," he says quietly.

I roll my eyes.

He sighs, and it's too deep and hurt for someone his age. "It's fine, Tsu. Don't worry about my shit." His tone sounds more defeated than angry. You don't need to have a keen eye to see that Hraefn has grown close to Caspian. I know the pain in Caspian's eyes now, but I also know that Hraefn is shutting him out on purpose.

I reach out to him, but then the wind picks up and brings with it the smell of rotting fish. Hair pricks up on my skin as I turn my gaze out to the sea. Thick black clouds loom above, pushing down the first drops of rain. The wind snaps madly at the sails, drawing my attention up. Hraefn is leaning over the edge with a spyglass to his eye.

Caspian looks at me curiously, then follows my gaze. "What does he see?"

Turning my head, I spot Jack and Story up on the aftercastle. We exchange a worried glance.

"Tsu?" Caspian urges. "What is it?"

My hands fumble in the many pockets of my jacket before I find it. Caspian's eyes grow with concern as he reads my expression. I show him the two small pieces of wax, then gesture to his ears. "I don't—"

Before he can finish, I shove the pieces in his ears and sprint across the deck toward Jack. He's shouting orders to the crew, all of whom panic and begin running about. I collide with Tetra, who wields a long ax and holds murder in her eyes. We're of the handful of women aboard, and the last hope for our crew if things go wrong.

Gale-force winds rock the ship now, and lightning crackles up in the sky, announcing the arrival of thunder. It claps so loud that I feel the deck vibrate beneath my thin boots. Ace comes tearing up the steps, cutlass drawn and wax already in his ears. I look to my right, where the Harpy Sea opens up to the east. There, some three hundred yards out…

"Sirens!" Hraefn bellows from the crow's nest.

I tilt my head up to him just as a shrill cry echoes over the boom of thunder. All eyes turn to the sky, hands blocking out the rain that seems to stop compared to the speed of the diving harpies.

Caspian gasps, backing up and almost colliding with Ace. "What the fuck is—"

"Move, lad!" Ace shoves him aside, pulling his cutlass for him. "I hope you've had enough practice."

The look of pure terror in Caspian's eyes spikes my own. We're surrounded.

"Get to the gunwales!" Jack shouts. "Nothing gets on this ship! Understood?"

"Aye!"

I draw the two short swords from the back of my belt. Pulse racing, I run to the bow and watch as the first sirens begin to emerge from the sea. They're nothing like the harpies that scream above. Their skin is like copper, shining even in the dark storm. Hair of every color flows behind them as they breach the surface, leaping out of the water and singing to the crew. The melody sounds like nails on stone to my ears, but I know if the men remove the wax, they'll sound like goddesses. A fiery red-haired siren stops at the bow of the ship and smirks up at me. The water begins to circle around her until her torso lifts from the sea, and the rushing water creates a cyclone that encircles her tail fin.

She clicks her tongue at me. "Move aside, girl. We don't want to have to kill you." Her voice is like that of ten, all woven into one. It makes me shiver and cringe beneath my mask. I know if they board the ship, it will be difficult to fight off both them and the harpies. They scream as they descend upon the ship, pointed teeth bared and beady eyes locked on.

"Very well." The siren flicks her wrists, and the sea obeys, swirling her higher and higher until we're at eye level. She lets out a devilish scream and launches herself from her sea throne and onto the deck of the ship. I whirl around as the sky lights up my killing floor. Slicing my twin blades over one another, I lop off the siren's head effortlessly. Another slams into me from behind, knocking one of the blades from my hand. The shouts of my crew fighting off harpies claw at my back, but I need to focus.

The siren begins to transform her tail fin into legs. Her fingernails grow as long as daggers, and I know they are sharper than any steel. I move before she can, thrusting my sword forward and slicing her newly formed leg. She yelps in pain and slashes at me, but I move just in time to see a lock of my black hair fall to the soaked deck. With a snarl on my lips, I attack, slicing and ducking as the siren tries to claim my life.

From the corner of my eye, a harpy comes into view as it falls from the sky after a shot fired from above. Hraefn is defending the ship as best he can, shooting down harpies, but more come to fill their place. It's common for sirens and harpies to work together—the sirens will claim the men they want, but the harpies only want meat, and they don't discriminate.

The creature is haunting to look at. Their upper bodies look human, with thick black scales that cover every inch and wiry arms too long for their torso. Eyes like rubies in the sun and teeth like a shark. Their waists taper off into long tails, with sharp fins running down their spines and featherless wings that grow from their backs. They're a thing of nightmares.

I slice through siren after siren as they fling themselves on the deck. Jack is down on the main deck, fighting alongside Ace and Caspian, who struggle to pierce a harpy that flaps above them. I watch as a siren manages to drag a crew member from the ship and down below the surface. He's lost. Another is pierced from behind by a siren, but a harpy moves in to steal the kill, clutching the dying man between its long teeth. Another comes at the smell of blood, and I cringe as the two harpies pull the man in half and fly away. More crew members fall by the minute.

Caspian swings his sword fiercely, missing the tail of a harpy as it lunges for Jack. The captain ducks out of the way and whirls around, driving his cutlass into the creature's gut. It lets out a shriek that drowns out the thunder above. Falling to the deck, the harpy begins clawing its way toward the gunwale, but Jack pierces his sword through its wing, while Ace walks up and cuts the beast's head from its body.

Crack.

Hraefn's rifle fires off another shot, killing a harpy in midair. The sirens no longer hurl themselves on deck, preferring to fight from the safety of the water. I run to Caspian, who is losing his battle with a harpy that still hovers above. Its tail lashes out, snapping into the main mast and just barely missing Caspian's head. He's winded already and should've gone belowdecks before this started. I leap onto a barrel of Ostium and sail through the air, driving my sword down into the harpy's back. The creature bucks and screams, but I hold firm, squeezing my thighs around its torso.

"Tsu!" Jack screams to me from below, but I'm lost in my bloodlust.

The harpy flies higher and higher, flapping its wings madly to get away. I twist the sword, trying to force the creature back down, but that only heightens its panic. Adrenaline and fear explode through me as the ship grows smaller.

Hraefn comes into view, and when he sees me on the harpy's back, his jaw drops. I grit my teeth, shifting so that Hraefn can get a clear shot.

Shoot it, I sign.

Hraefn shakes his head, and I sign again, urging him to do it, then steal a glance to the sky above—the harpies are retreating, but I won't let this one get away.

SHOOT IT!

The shot tears through the air so quick that I don't have time to brace against the harpy's back. We fall with the rain, twirling through the air toward the sea. I put my boots flat against its back and pull on my sword, but it's deep in the flesh. One last yank and it comes free, just as my body hits the water.

Tiny bubbles float past me, breaking against the waves. My eyes sting from the salt, but I force them open anyway, kicking my feet to the surface, but I'm not alone.

The lightning above illuminates the world below the sea surface, showing me a grouping of sirens that surround me. I curse silently in my head and kick my feet, but a hand latches on to my ankle. Sword still in hand, I drive it down without even looking, and somehow their screams are magnified below the water. I almost drop my sword to cover my ears, but I need to get out of here. I need air.

I swim upward, using my sword like a spear to fend off the sirens, but this is their world now. Here, they're in their element, shooting through the water faster than dolphins. They're just a blur in my peripheral as I kick up and up while my lungs scream at me. I can hear my pulse slowing in my ears, but then I breach the surface. My cold fingers pull my mask down as I gasp in a lungful of air. The storm still rages above, rain beating down on my head and thunder rolling across the sky.

"Tsu!" someone shouts at me, but I'm disoriented. Turning in a full circle, I come face-to-face with a siren with hair like gold.

"Hello, little one," she purrs, then pouts. "You killed my sisters."

My heart pounds through my shirt, but my hands move instinctively. I pierce the siren through the heart, my blade concealed under the water. Her green eyes grow wide as she coughs up blood, then screams for her sisters. Quickly, I shove her away, fear burrowing deeper into my stomach as I kick like mad through the sea.

"Tsu!"

It's Jack, and his voice is closer now, but I don't dare look up. Something splashes down in front of me—a rope.

All I have to do is reach it.

A siren digs her nails into my calf, and I scream.

Another splash just in front of me, this one larger. I whirl around, punching a siren in the face and stabbing my sword forward. She catches my wrist, and I have no choice but to let go of my sword and snatch my hand back before she can take it. She smiles and lunges at me, grabbing my shoulders and forcing my head below water. I buck and thrash, but her nails sink into my flesh yet again. A scream bubbles from my lips, and I watch the last of my air leave my lungs. Managing to flip around, I drive my elbow into her gut, then kick my feet until I find purchase on her. I kick off from the siren and swim for my life, the sea clouding red.

A pair of hands latch down on my shoulders, and I immediately throw a punch, but it hits nothing but water. A hand gently slides down to my wrists, then begins pulling me to the surface. Jack and I burst through the water, coughing and gasping as he hooks the rope around my torso.

"Pull!" he shouts to the crew above.

The sirens scream, enraged, and come torpedoing through

the water. I grab Jack's collar, and he hauls himself up, looping his good hand around the rope. His wooden hand hangs limp, useless. A siren launches herself at us, and Jack's foot shoots out so quickly that I nearly miss it. The siren's jaw snaps to the left with a sickening crack.

I'm pulled up over the deck and flop down to my back, breathing heavily as Jack comes to my side. "You're hurt."

I can feel my wounds still seeping blood, though the cuts aren't deep enough to kill, and I don't think they nicked an artery.

I'm fine, I tell Jack, picking myself up with his support.

The fight isn't over. Crew members still run around the ship, defending it from the few sirens that still lurk.

And then I hear a shrill scream from above.

A lone harpy.

Hraefn falling.

No, not falling, he's *jumping.*

Their alluring song doesn't reach my ears.

The pieces of wax keep out the voices, the ones that will coerce me into the sea and to my grave. My heart drums against my ribs as I fire, bullets tearing through the falling rain and striking the hearts of the flying beasts. The harpies scream as they fall, crashing down beside the sirens as the storm rages on above me.

We've encountered sirens once before, and harpies another time, but never like this. They're working together, scooping up crew members from the deck and tearing them apart like they're made of cotton. The sirens throw themselves on the deck below, risking death for the prize of a man.

One crawls toward Caspian. Her back fin begins to split, forming two human-looking legs. She stands up and launches herself at him just as I fire, dropping the siren at Caspian's back before turning back toward the sky. A harpy flaps its massive wings just ahead, snarling through its shark teeth. Below me, the muffled screams of my crew push past the rain to reach my ears. I steal a glance down—Ace is fending them off left and right, his blade a blur. And then I see Tsu on the back of a harpy, her sword buried deep in its flesh.

Shoot it! she signs to me frantically, but I don't. I stare in horror as the beast thrashes, trying to knock Tsu from its back. *SHOOT IT!* she signs again, this time more frantic. I don't allow myself to falter again. I shoot it.

The beast plummets toward the sea with Tsu on its back.

What have I done?

I strain my eyes against the rain, looking for Tsu in the swarm of sirens. She doesn't resurface. A crack of thunder startles me, and I look back up just as a harpy dives for me. Gritting my teeth, I whirl my rifle and take aim, but the tail of the beast lashes out before I can pull the trigger. I'm knocked to the floor of the crow's nest, hitting my head on the railing and almost losing my rifle. It screams, the sound shrill and primal, flapping its wings and swirling the rain in the air. I aim again and fire, blowing through its left wing.

Just as I get back to my feet, the harpy rams the crow's nest. The mast shakes, and I tumble out of the opening, losing my rifle. My hands scramble to catch the rigging. The ropes burn my skin as I grip them, yanking myself to a stop. My shoulder pops, and I scream, snapping my eyes shut at the sudden knife of pain.

I look down at my crew, but they're occupied. I can't let them down, but I've lost my rifle. It now lays on the deck below, and I'm unarmed except for a dagger I keep in my boot. My fingers reach for the blade, and I pull it out, clenching it between my teeth as I start to climb. The harpy shrieks and roars, whirling around and sending its massive tail into the rigging just above my head. I duck, spin around, and put my back flat against the ropes. Looping my left arm through the rope, I hold the dagger in my right hand and challenge the beast.

"Come on!" I bellow.

The harpy eyes me with its red gaze, then lashes out again. I grunt as I shove my blade into its tail. It whips up, catching me in the jaw, and suddenly the sky is filled with stars. I have to make it back to my nest. With shaky hands, I haul myself up through the opening of the crow's nest and crouch down, peering over the edge. The harpy is in a fury, thrashing and snarling. I brave a look over the edge to see Tsu and the captain being pulled back on board. Relief floods me, but it's short-lived. That split second costs me.

The bleeding harpy claps its wings together, sending a gale-force wind straight at me, and I feel a piece of wax leave my ear. Panicked, I dive to the ground and fumble around for the wax, but the storm makes it difficult to see, and then I hear them.

A chill coats my body, and I feel myself standing up. The melody of their song caresses my ear, and I pull out the other piece of wax so that I can better hear it. I've never heard anything so beautiful in my life. Their voices weave together like silk, notes high and low, perfectly in sync. My shoulders relax, and my heartbeat slows its panicked rhythm. A tingling sensation moves throughout my entire body, and tears roll away from my eyes, but the rain washes them away.

I look over the side of my nest. There is a whole pod of them, beautiful women waiting for me—*calling* to me. With the harpy forgotten, I stand up on the edge of my nest and dive.

I don't feel the fall or the rain whipping at my face, not the water as I crash down, I only see them. The song is amplified under the sea. I didn't think it possible for the melody to sound even more beautiful, but it does.

A siren swims to me, her hair black like mine and eyes like burning embers. She parts her plump lips and speaks. "Hello, beautiful boy."

My lungs begin to constrict, but I don't understand why. I feel like I'm meant to be here, with these sirens under the sea.

She runs a long finger down my cheek, sending sparks of fire to my heart. I wrap my hands around her slim waist and pull her to me, pressing my lips to hers. They're salty and warm, devastatingly soft. She pulls back and smiles. "You'll be a fun one."

Others begin to swarm us, raking their fingers through my

hair and squeezing and groping me. There are so many, smiling at me and kissing my skin.

Something pulls at the back of my mind. I take note of my lungs again and the lack of air in them. I open my lips to breathe, but then a voice shoots through the water and pierces my ears. I know that voice. It's a boy. But why is he calling to me? Can't he just let me stay here and be happy?

Lightning flashes above, and when I tilt my head back, water erupts around me. The sirens hiss and begin their song again, scattering as more bodies drop into the water. The black-haired beauty holds my wrist firmly and begins to pull me down farther. I kick my legs to help her along, but then someone grabs my ankle. I spin in the water to see a dark-skinned boy with amber eyes yanking at me.

Confused, I try to kick him away, but the siren lets me go and swims to him. They collide, twirling in the water as they fight over a dagger the boy wields. Confusion floods my brain, and when I look around, I see more men fighting with the sirens. They slash knives through the water, cutting them and creating a fog of blood.

"Stop!" I try to yell, but water fills my mouth, and then my vision begins to waver. The dark-skinned boy plunges his knife through the heart of the siren, and my blood runs cold as I watch her body sink to the bottom of the sea.

They sing louder and scream for their fallen. Beside me, a siren skewers a man, then sinks her teeth into his neck and drags him down below, disappearing into the abyss. There are hands on me now. The dark-skinned boy turns me around. His eyes seem sad as he looks at me.

My body starts convulsing, and I realize I'm out of air. He keeps one hand on my arm while the other searches his pockets. I yank my arm, trying to fight him off, but my vision is starting to turn the world black and my muscles are spasming.

Finally, he shoves something soft into my ears, blocking out the beautiful song of the sirens. My body goes cold, then numb, arms going slack. The boy grabs the back of my head and pulls me in, pressing his lips to mine. My heart explodes, and the veil of fog lifts.

It's Caspian.

He forces air between our joined lips, but it isn't enough. When his lips break away, I feel myself fading. Caspian turns me around, pressing his chest to my back and holding me tight as he kicks for the surface. Below, the bodies of sirens and crew members sink to the bottom of the sea. My lungs scream at me, and I unwillingly open my mouth to breathe. Seawater rushes in, burning my throat, and then the world goes black.

Voices.

"Hurry!"

"Move aside!"

"Get those sails back up!"

"Hraefn!"

Chaos.

Lips to mine, breathing life, then a pounding on my chest. Water rushes up my throat, and my eyes shoot open. I cough up water, rolling to my side and hacking, gasping for air.

"He's fine," I hear Nitelocke say. "Back up!"

My whole body trembles and the frigid rain feels like icicles on my side. Rolling back, I cringe, remembering my dislocated shoulder, then someone tackles me, wrapping their arms around my neck.

"You're all right," Caspian whispers, though it sounds like he's convincing himself. I can't even manage to hug him back. My limbs are like bags of wet sand, and my head feels as though it's been caved in. I lay back on the deck as Caspian releases me, then I pass out.

I wake in a warm bed, tangled in blankets. I know from the shelves lined with glass bottles that it's Nitelocke's room. The strong smell of salve burns my nose. Sitting up, I notice the wrap on my shoulder. Nitelocke must have popped it back into place when I was out cold. It's still stiff, but I can move it with little pain now. I look over my shoulder to the small circular window. It's dark outside.

"Just a day."

The voice startles me, and I slowly turn back around to see Caspian. He's been sitting in the dark corner of the room. As he comes closer, I can see a fresh cut on his neck and a few on his face. He's dressed in a long blue jacket and high-waisted pants tucked into his black boots. He doesn't limp and seems fine otherwise.

A flush crawls up my neck as I realize I'm shirtless, but Caspian's eyes don't waver from mine. "How many?" I ask, averting my gaze.

Caspian looks down at the floor. "Seven," his voice is quiet and raspy like he's been screaming or crying. I can't tell which.

Seven.

All those crew members lost their lives, some of them for me.

The guilt crashes down on me, heavy and suffocating.

"You shouldn't have done that," I say, looking down at the blanket covering me.

Caspian steps closer, leaning his hands on the edge of the mattress. My eyes lift to his, and there's a fire burning in his gaze. "Are we really going to do this again?"

I wince at the sharpness of his voice.

"You would've died, Hraefn. I did what anyone else would've done. I'm not special," he says with a sneer, throwing my words back at me, "just a member of the crew. Same as you."

Shame heats my cheeks, but I can't look away from him. Those things I said to Caspian… they aren't true. I didn't mean any of it; I was only trying to protect my heart. Caspian stares at me then turns and heads for the door. My stomach flips, and my heart drops as I scooch to the edge of the bed. "Wait."

He pauses.

I stand up, ignoring the wave of dizziness as my legs stretch out.

"Thank you."

He doesn't even turn around to look at me. "You're welcome."

My feet carry me closer, and I grab his arm, turning him around before he can reach the doorknob. "Caspian…" When he finally faces me, his amber eyes are shiny with tears. It breaks me more than I expect it to. "I… I'm sorry." I let go of his sleeve. "I didn't mean—"

"I think you did," he interrupts, stabbing his words at my heart. Caspian chuckles, humorless, running a hand through his dark hair. He walks past me and begins pacing the room.

"I understand why you said those shitty things to me." I wince but don't interrupt. "I'm not stupid, Hraefn. I know you care about me." He stalks closer, eyes burning. "But *you* decided to push me away. *You* chose to hurt me. So don't apologize for something if you don't mean it."

My throat closes, and my palms grow sweaty. There's so much I want to say to him, but I've never been good at this. Caspian is an open book, and he isn't good at hiding his feelings. Even now, as he stands before me with rage in his eyes, I can see warmth behind them, affection.

"I *am* sorry, Caspian. But you're right, I chose to push you away." I shake my head. "But, I was wrong."

His eyes lose some of the fire.

"I thought that maybe you liked Skye."

Caspian blinks at the mention of her name.

"That maybe you didn't see me as I saw you." My cheeks catch fire as the words pass my lips, but he needs to know how I feel. We both almost died, and maybe that's what boosts my confidence now. I don't want to be alone forever, and if I'm going to die on this mission, I want to spend as much time as I can with Caspian. "I'm sorry for hurting you," I say quietly, my voice barely a whisper. "I was just scared."

"Of what?"

"Of losing you." I cup his cheek, and he freezes. "I knew if I allowed myself to get close, to *care*, that I'd get lost. But I don't want to lose you now."

Seconds tick by, and Caspian doesn't move or say a word. My heart slams to a stop in my chest. Is he going to reject me? Am I wrong about how he feels? His lips part, and he whispers, "You aren't going to lose me, Hraefn."

My stomach flutters with nervous energy, but I gather all my courage, lean in, and kiss him.

Something inside me explodes, cracking open from my core and allowing me to take my first free breath in what seems like a lifetime. Caspian returns the kiss, moving his lips methodically over mine. I slide my fingers around the back of his head, brushing my thumb along his scar as I do. His pulse rages against my fingers where my other hand lightly rests at the base of his neck. It lights my skin on fire, and each kiss burns hotter than the last. I never want this feeling to end, so I kiss him like it's the last time. Both hands cup his face now, and I tilt his head back, drinking him in as his hand comes to rest on my bare chest. The sudden contact chills me, and a sigh of pleasure pushes past our joined lips.

A second later, Caspian's lips are suddenly still, and he leans away from me slightly. I pursue his lips, but then he whispers my name, and his tone is sorrowful. "Hraefn…"

My heart turns to lead in my chest and drops to my stomach. Leaning back, I stare at him, but he avoids eye contact, looking at the floor between us instead. I take a full step back, embarrassed and hurt. "I thought—"

"I do," he says hurriedly, stepping back up to me, but he doesn't touch me. "I mean…" He sighs and shakes his head. "I'm just confused, Hraefn. I *do* care about you, I just…"

He trails off, and I throw up my protective walls yet again, blocking him out. My throat constricts making it hard to breathe, but I won't let him see the disappointment on my face.

"What we're doing," Caspian continues, "it's dangerous. That captain will find us again, and when he does, we need to be ready." His eyes finally find mine, and it breaks me even more to see that they're sad. "I just think it's better if we… wait. We don't know what will happen, and it's like you said, we can't be distracted when the time comes. The crew needs us. The *captain* needs us."

I can't speak. I stare back at Caspian, not fully hearing his words as blood rushes through my temples. Is that just an excuse to reject me? I'm an idiot for kissing him or thinking that it will ever work out.

"Hraefn?"

"I heard you," I snap, walking around him.

Caspian grabs my hand in his. "Hraefn, wait—"

"I get it, Caspian." I yank my hand free. "I'm not a child. No need to soften the blow."

He recoils, and the pain returns to his face. I can't handle his presence right now. It's too painful. "I should get some rest," I say, forcing myself to look away from him, to face my bed.

"Right." I hear his boots walk across the room, then pause briefly at the door before leaving.

I collapse into the pillows, wishing the mattress would swallow me whole. I don't know whether to believe what he said or not. He does have a point—this mission is dangerous, and I doubt that we've lost the last of our crew members. More will die or get hurt, and Caspian might be one of them.

But even if he tries to keep space between us, I can't ignore how I feel about him. I know in my heart that I'll be destroyed if he dies. Frustration and anger consume me like a plague. I'm already in too deep, and I don't think I'll have the strength to climb back out of the hole I find myself in.

Rolling over, I close my eyes and try to sleep, but Caspian's face keeps me up. The feel of his lips against mine and the way it makes my heart rush. He felt it too, I *know* he did. I could feel it in his pulse, the way it rushed and raged with excitement, but he still pushed back.

Maybe I deserve this for what I said to him, for trying to push him away in the first place. What would be different now if I hadn't? No, I can't fall into that trap. It doesn't matter anyway, the past is dead and gone, and I need to focus on the future. We'll reach the Isle of the Lost soon enough and get the last piece of the map. After the captain gets his ship, I'll revisit my feelings for Caspian, and decide what to do then.

For now, I shove away thoughts of him and sleep.

TWENTY-ONE

I stand at the bow of the ship, watching the waning moon slide across the starry night. We'll reach the Isle of the Lost in the morning, and so far, there's been no sign of Captain Blacktip. The crew is on edge, posting more guards throughout the night, and Hraefn lives in the crow's nest now. I resist the urge to look at him, though I feel eyes at my back.

Captain Jack is at the helm alongside Tsu, signing to one another. Even from here, I can make out the urgency behind their fingers and feel the captain's unease like a thick fog that lingers on the decks. He's nervous, and though he tries to hide it for the sake of his crew, he isn't a great actor.

"Evening, lad."

Ace sidles up behind me, clapping a hand on my shoulder. The sea winds ruffle his golden hair as he hands me a flask. "I'm on guard duty," I say, pushing it away. "I have to stay sharp."

"Psh," Ace shoves the flask back into my hands. "Sharp as a wad of cotton, you are."

My glare pierces his.

"A joke. Gods, you're all so tense lately. You need to loosen up."

"And how the hell are you so calm?" I ask, taking a sip from the flask. My face scrunches as the rum passes my lips.

"I'm always calm." He takes it back and drinks.

I cock my head. "You're not afraid Captain Blacktip will find us? Or that we'll be attacked in the night?"

His answer is sure and quick. "Nope."

I turn back to the outstretched sea. "You're naïve."

Ace snorts. "I ken we won't be attacked in the night. So, Clever Caspian, do you want to stay here all night or go below and have some fun?"

His smile is broad and confident as I turn to look at him. It's hard not to like Ace, even if he is an asshole sometimes. He always knows how to have a good time and make people laugh. Maybe I have to take a page from his book. After all, we could all die tomorrow. So do I really want to spend my last night up here alone, with Hraefn's eyes burrowing into my spine?

Down in the galley, a row of tables has been set up to form a square. Members of the crew sit along benches, drinking flagons of ale and chatting loudly. Their laughter rattles my bones as Ace and I step into the room. The cook, Bas, and our navigator, Sundance, stand at the center of the square, sizing one another up. Ace pulls me in closer, shoving the flask into my hands. "What are they doing?"

Sundance pushes his glasses higher on his nose, drawing his brows together in concentration.

Ace leans in. "The point of the game is to catch someone in a lie. If you lie, you drink. Easy."

"So how do you win?"

"*Win?*" Ace chuckles. "You don't win, lad. You just don't lose."

Bas crosses his thick arms atop his big belly. The game seems odd to me, but I soon realize that it's just a fun excuse to drink.

The two simply have a conversation, asking general questions, and if you manage to sneak in a lie without the other person catching it, then they drink. Sundance snickers and gestures to Bas's cup. "Drink."

"What? Which part did you lie about?"

Sundance smirks. "You truly think my mother named me *Sundance*?"

The crowd starts to chuckle, and Bas's cheeks turn red. "Fine, then what is your name?"

"Howard."

"Drink," Ace calls, with a knowing smirk on his face. He pushes through the crowd to stand in the square with the two players. "Howard, huh? I said drink." His blue eyes sharpen on Sundance, but he only laughs and tips back his cup.

"I can never beat you, Ace."

"No one can!" someone calls from the back.

Bas and Sundance clear the floor, and Ace turns to me. "Come on, lad. It's fun." Someone hands me a cup of ale as I step into the square. Ace eyes me coolly, pacing the floor in his polished boots like a lurking shark. "Tell me, Caspian." He tucks his hands behind his back. "How many siblings do you have?"

It's a simple question, one he probably already knows the answer to. He's trying to feel me out, looking for signs in my body language for when I lie. I'm not a good liar. "Five," I answer, then try to lie. "Four brothers and one sister."

Ace doesn't miss a beat. "Drink."

"What about you?" I ask, taking a sip and wiping my lip. "Only child?"

"That's right, lad. And heir to my father's kingdom."

"A kingdom you don't want," I state. Ace has told us over and over that he left home for a reason. He doesn't want to be king, he wants to explore and see the world.

Ace grins devilishly as he answers, "A kingdom I don't want." Just as he says it, his left eye flinches ever so slightly, and it makes me pause. I rack my brain, trying to remember when I'd seen him do that, but before I can call him a liar, he continues talking. "You joined our crew out of the blue," he says, looking to the crowd and then back at me. "Do you regret it?"

The question knocks me off balance.

Regret?

I've been beaten and mocked, almost killed, cut, and more confused than I've ever been in my life, but I'd do it all again. I lift my chin and say, "No. Best decision I ever made."

"Really?" Ace sounds genuinely surprised. "And why is that?"

There are so many reasons, I just start listing them all. "Because I'm free to be who I am here, finally stepping out of the shadow of my brothers. I've seen more in these last few weeks than I have in my entire life."

The crew mumbles, some nodding their heads as they listen. I tell the truth, not because I'm afraid of lying and losing the game, but because it feels good. I haven't really thought of home or my father since I left or what my life would've been like had I stayed because it doesn't matter. I'm here now, with my crew, having the adventure of my life, and I wouldn't trade a moment of it.

Being here is the last little shove I needed to break out of my shell. It isn't as if I'm a shy person back home, it's more of a shell that my father built around me. After my mother died, he was always so cold and hateful, and at the time, I chalked it up to grief, but it's just the man he is. I know now that if I'd stayed, I never would have left the Sunken City or my father's shop. I would've been stuck, locked into a life I never wanted, and forced to watch as the world went by.

Ace nods as I finish, then plasters a wicked smile on his face. Stepping closer, he leans in, his blue eyes wide. "And what about Hraefn?"

I don't want to play anymore.

My heart does a flip inside my chest.

I clear my throat. "What about him?" I ask, ignoring the eyes on me. I suddenly feel like an ant under an eyeglass, catching fire as the sun beats down on me.

He shrugs. "Are you sure it's not *him* that comes to mind when you think about joining our crew as the best decision you ever made?"

My nostrils flare in anger. Ace knows how I feel about Hraefn. He's too smart not to have picked up on it, but still, I don't think the whole crew knows about it, and it's no one's business besides Hraefn and me.

I level my gaze with him, trying to keep my face passive as I answer, "No. Hraefn isn't the reason." The words feel like ash on my tongue, but then I realize it's because they're true. I care about Hraefn deeply, but he isn't why this new life of mine is great. It's just as I told Captain Jack the day he found me aboard —I have nowhere else to go, and I just want to be free, and now I am.

Ace seems disappointed, hoping to catch me in a lie. He laughs at himself and takes a swig of rum, waving a hand for me to continue with the game. Ace always seems very open, like nothing bothers him, but I'm starting to think it's a mask.

I try my luck. "You're hiding something."

The crowd hushes, and Ace whirls on me, eyes on fire. "You'll need to be more specific." The uncertainty in his eyes gives me pause. I'm just fishing, but am I right? Is Ace hiding something under that mask?

"You use humor to numb your pain," I speak the words slowly and calmly, watching his eyes for that flinch. "I think you miss your family more than you let on."

Ace lets out a sigh, sounding a little too relieved, then he clinks his flask to my cup and drinks. "You got me," he bellows, throwing his arms out and earning a laugh from the crew.

"Just because I don't want to rule…"

There. A flinch.

"… doesn't mean I don't miss my family."

I hurry to continue before he can speak. "And why is it that you don't want the crown?"

His smile falters, and he walks his way around the question. "Would you want to sit on a throne all day, listening to petty complaints? Or be told when you can leave the kingdom, how to dress, and what not to say?" Ace clicks his tongue. "Of course you wouldn't. You came here for freedom, after all."

Then I remember where I've seen Ace do that before.

It was the day we arrived on the Constellations, and he brought me to a tavern. I asked Ace where he went before the tavern. He wove some story about having a secret lover who was a siren, and his eye twitched ever so slightly. I nearly missed it, but when I called him out on the lie, he cackled and admitted to it, but he never said where he'd gone.

Ace deems the game over and chugs the rest of his rum. Someone starts singing in the back, and the few guys begin tapping their boots to the song. I stand in the middle of the square, confused as I watch Ace loop an arm around a pretty young girl. I set my cup down and leave the party, deciding to go back to my post for the night. I doubt I'll get sleep anyway.

As I stand at the bow once more, I run over the game again. *A kingdom you don't want,* I'd said, but Ace lied. I saw it in his eye when he agreed that he doesn't want the kingdom. But that doesn't make any sense. Why would he lie about something like that? It isn't as if Ace can't go back home and take his spot on the throne. Right? An uneasy feeling settles over me, though I try to push it away. Ace is always playing games with people, whether they play along in return. He isn't a very serious person on the surface, though I was right about him using humor to cover pain, but what pain?

Ace admitted that he missed his family, which Hraefn and I had suspected before, but I can't help but feel like there's more to it. Leaning over the gunwale, I let out a deep sigh as the wind ruffles my hair. I'm overthinking a stupid drinking game. Besides, we all have secrets, so who am I to judge Ace on his?

He's a good friend and a valuable part of the crew, and that's all that matters.

As the moon paints the sky, I begin to drift off. I sit on a crate with my hand supporting my head. My fingers run over the stitches on the side of my skull, where the bullet left its mark. My shoulder wound no longer bothers me, though it's still a little tight when I swing my cutlass. I've been practicing with Ace just in case we have to face Captain Blacktip again. I tell myself that I'll watch my own back and not focus on Hraefn, no matter what. But that's a lie, and even saying it in my head feels wrong. I know Hraefn is afraid to face Deadeye Cane again, and I'm nervous for him, but I have a feeling it's inevitable.

My eyes find their way to the crow's nest high on the mainmast. Though I can't see Hraefn, I know he's in there, probably curled down on the floor with his rifle in his lap. I can't help but replay our kiss in my mind. I was surprised at the moment—not for the fact that he kissed me, but because I liked it. I still remember the feel of his lips on mine, the saltiness of them from having been in the sea.

And yet I pushed away this time, not him. I know it's the right decision, no matter how much it hurts. Hraefn and I just can't be together—at least not now. There's too much that can happen between now and a future where we might be free to be together. I've known for a while that I'm attracted to Hraefn, but after he kissed me, that affection grew. It spread and consumed me until all I knew was that I didn't want anyone else but him.

Turning away from the crow's nest, I lean back against the gunwale and let my eyes droop with sleep. I'll only get lost if I let my mind linger on Hraefn, and that is the exact reason I pushed him away. We both need to be at our best, and then maybe one day, we can let our guards down for good. Whether it's tomorrow, two weeks from now, or a year, I'll wait. I just hope I don't lose him before then. I can't.

TWENTY-TWO

The Isle of the Lost.

It appears on the horizon just as the sun slides to the center of the sky. Jack's voice comes from behind me, shouting orders to his crew and commanding Hraefn to stay put until we dock. He's paranoid about Captain Blacktip following us, though there has been no sign of him so far. As we approach the lush green island, I wonder what secret Jack will trade for the last piece of the map. He's traded with these people before, but I have a feeling this time the price will be higher.

Someone whistles beside me. "Beautiful, isn't it, lass?"

I don't look at Ace, keeping my trained eyes ahead.

"So, Tsu." He turns around and leans his elbows back on the gunwale. "You ken all the captain's secrets, right?"

I don't answer.

"Ah, come on, lass. Which do you think he'll tell, hmm? Perhaps the story of how he lost his hand?" Ace wags his fingers in front of me.

I slide my eyes to him, and he grins.

"Now that's got to be a good story."

Shut up, I sign.

Ace lowers his hand, rolling his eyes. "Don't you think it's a little unfair that we, his loyal crew, can't be let in on his secret?"

No.

"Ah, you're only saying that because you already know."

Ace flicks a lock of my black hair, and I grab his hand, twisting the wrist until pain floods his eyes.

You're an asshole.

I let go, Ace rubs his wrist then snorts. "Says you and everyone else, lass. You could at least have an original insult."

We step off the *Chained Maiden* and onto the rocky beach scattered with dark-skinned people and children. Jack walks with a purpose toward an elderly man with large gold hoops hanging from his sagging earlobes.

As they exchange words, I steal a look to my left where Caspian stands, his eyes cast downward. He looks tired, but not from a lack of sleep, more like something is eating at him from the inside. His golden eyes hold no spark, even in the relenting light of the sun above. Turning to my right, I spot Hraefn chatting with Ace, though I can tell he isn't listening. He has his rifle slung across his back and arms crossed protectively over his chest. I know something happened between him and Caspian— nearly the whole crew knows it. Whatever it was, now they won't even look at each other.

Jack waves for us to follow, and I fall in step with Caspian. He offers a half-hearted smile in greeting. He doesn't read sign as well as the others, but I've seen him watching carefully anytime I speak with a member of the crew. Ace's nickname doesn't do justice to just how clever Caspian is. His eyes slide to my hands as I ask, *Are you okay?* I can see his brain working, dissecting the quick movements of my fingers to reveal the message behind them.

He frowns. "I'm fine, Tsu."

I grind to a halt, catching him by the arm.

"What the hell?"

You're not a good liar.

"I know," he growls, not even denying the lie he just tried to sell me. Caspian yanks his arm away, and I let go. I glance over my shoulder, staring pointedly at Hraefn, then back to Caspian. He huffs. "What do you want me to say, huh?"

I just cross my arms and wait.

Caspian shakes his head, but I can see words forming on his lips. "Look, Tsu, I appreciate your concern, but I'm fine. There's nothing to tell. Hraefn and I—" He cuts himself off as if the name chokes him, then tries again. "We're all part of the same team, and it wouldn't be wise to mix work and… and pleasure. We have a job to do."

I cock my head, raising a brow to him.

"What?" he demands, cheeks flushing slightly.

Pleasure?

He curses under his breath. "You know what I mean," he snaps, then recoils, the anger leaving him, replaced by sadness. Caspian hangs his head, ripping a hand through his wavy brown hair as his lips move with unspoken words. Finally, he looks at me, his mouth a thin line.

I'm sorry, I sign before he can speak. *I know you and Hraefn care for each other, but I think you're right. Now isn't the time.*

He snorts at that. "Yeah, well, try telling him that."

I follow his gaze. Hraefn has been watching us, turning away at the last second to rejoin Ace and the others.

The longing look behind Caspian's eyes pains me, but he's right in his decision. Hraefn will just have to accept that. We catch up to the rest of the crew—only a handful are here, the others stayed aboard to watch out for Captain Blacktip should he show up. Caspian and I walk in silence through the village, where small huts leak smoke up into the air and people go about their daily chores. Children run alongside our crew, laughing and chatting. Sitting at the center of the village is what appears to be a temple. It's the only structure made of stone in the whole village, and as I crane my neck up, I spot small stone creatures perched above, as if guarding the temple.

A flash of an image comes to mind. Back in Hanatsu, the emperor's palace had large stone dragons that guarded the place, meant to ward off evil that would harm the ruler. I shake the thought from my head. I need to focus and stay alert.

Jack beckons me over. "Stay here and keep your ears open." He looks back toward the beach where our ship sits. "If the crew spots sails, they'll blow the horn. If that happens, don't wait for me. Get back to the ship and get her ready for battle, got it?"

I nod.

He glances over his shoulder to where the older man is waiting for him. "I shouldn't be long. I know how Madame Kiera works. We should have the missing piece of the map and be out of here in no time."

Jack... I pause as I try to think of the right words. His copper eyes are searching, but words fail me, so I just squeeze his arm lightly and nod. He smiles, covering my hand with his, before turning and heading into the temple

After an hour of standing in the sun, the crew is becoming restless. Some of the guys post up under the shade of trees, their wide leaves casting enough shadows to shield them. I lean my back up against the trunk of a tree, arms crossed and ears open. Beside me, crouched on a rock, Caspian absentmindedly tosses a smooth stone in his hand, running his thumb over every inch.

"Good gods." Ace yawns. "What the hell is taking so long? I thought the captain had done this before."

He looks at me for an answer. I don't have one. Hraefn pipes up from where he stands beside his friend, his rifle acting as a cane at his side. "He *has* done this before, so shut up and be patient."

Ace's lips pull into a smug grin. "You're awfully grumpy today."

"I'm just not in the mood to hear you yap," Hraefn retorts, digging dirt from under his fingernails.

Ace gets to his feet. "Is that so?"

Caspian shifts beside me. Hraefn pushes off the tree, coming to stand in front of Ace. They wage war between their blue eyes, though Ace's hold more mirth than fight.

"That's right," Hraefn says with a cocky smile.

"Is that all I do?" Ace asks. "Yap?"

"And drink."

I turn at Caspian's input and watch a tight smile spread across his lips. He locks eyes with Hraefn for half a second, but it's enough to go through a list of emotions—amusement, happiness, longing, sadness, and regret. They both look away, and Ace barks out a sharp laugh, strolling toward Caspian with his hands behind his back. "Yap and drink." Ace chuckles. "Can't argue with that, lad. Tell me, Clever Caspian, how are your gunshot wounds?"

Hraefn flinches like he's been struck, but Caspian doesn't even blink. "Fine. Like it never happened."

"Oh, really?" Ace moves about like a cat, running his eyes along the scar left by the bullet. Caspian crosses his arms, waiting for Ace to get to the point and finish his little game. Some of the other crew members now watch from where they hide in the shadows. Everyone is tired and hot, and Ace is the best hope for entertainment.

He stops in front of Caspian. "Do you wager you can take me in a fight now? If you *are* all healed as you say."

"Ace," Hraefn warns, stepping closer but keeping distance between him and Caspian. "Quit being an ass and just sit down."

Ace smiles and then morphs his face into genuine confusion as he turns to Hraefn. "Who's being an ass, lad? All I did was ask a simple question."

Behind him, Caspian answers. "I'm healed."

That challenging smile slides back into place. "Excellent."

Before Caspian can blink, Ace shoots out his right foot, catching Caspian in the shin. He drops to one knee, just barely able to block the second kick with his forearm. Ace spins around, swinging for Caspian's head, who ducks and rolls out of the way.

"Ace!"

Hraefn's voice echoes through the village. Crew members begin hooting their approval, and villagers gather around, exchanging hushed words and confused looks. I lean back against my tree and watch. If they want to fight, then let them. I'm done being their babysitter.

Caspian stumbles back as Ace's fist just misses his jaw. He moves fluidly, one moment weaving and striking out faster than Caspian can move, the next, he's a cat, prowling and calculating his movements as if he runs every possible outcome through his head before attacking. I'll give him this: Ace is a great fighter.

"Come on, lad!" Ace ducks under a punch and drives his elbow into Caspian's ribs, who wheezes, doubling over as the air leaves his lungs. "I taught you better than that."

Caspian growls, widening his stance and waiting.

Ace stops and cocks his head, nodding. "That's better." Then he attacks. The punches come fast, catching Caspian all up his side, drawing Ace closer to him. Then…

He grabs Ace by the back of his jacket and, using his momentum as he swings a punch, throws Ace to the ground. He jumps on top of Ace, and suddenly the fight is nothing more than two boys struggling to pin one another, rolling around like pigs in shit. Ace cackles, and Caspian scowls, twisting and bucking to throw Ace off. He latches down on Caspian's wrists, pinning him to the sand and squeezing his thighs around his ribs. "Yield," he commands.

Caspian struggles harder, kneeing Ace in the side, but he doesn't budge.

"Oh come on, lad. Yield and I'll—"

Hraefn tackles Ace from behind, throwing them both off to the side. Caspian sits up quickly as Ace shoves his friend away. "What the hell? That's cheating."

"I didn't realize you were playing by any rules." Hraefn gets up, dusts the sand from his pants, then walks over to Caspian and holds out his hand. Electricity sparks between them, igniting a blue fire in Hraefn's eyes.

Caspian hesitates, then finally takes his hand, and Hraefn pulls him to his feet. "Thanks," he breathes, snatching his hand back to his side.

Hraefn shrugs one shoulder. "I was getting bored watching you two struggle like a couple of little boys."

Caspian holds his gaze as Ace comes and slaps a hand on his shoulder, breaking their eyes apart.

"Little boys?" Ace snorts. "You want a turn, Hraefn?"

"No, thanks."

"Ah, come on!" Ace ruffles Caspian's hair. "We both ken who was going to win—"

Caspian drives his elbow back straight into Ace's gut, dropping him. Hraefn chuckles, earning a blushing smile from Caspian.

"What the hell is going on?"

Their smiles die on their lips as Jack steps out of the temple. The rest of the crew all get to their feet, mouths sealed and eyes down. Ace gets back to his feet, clutching his stomach and spitting in the sand. "Lucky shot, lad." He steps closer, almost nose to nose with Caspian. "It'll never happen again," he hisses.

"Hey!" Jack storms toward them, fists balled and eyes narrowed. Caspian's lip is cut, and I'm sure he'll have fresh bruises in the morning. Jack stops before Ace, who smiles sheepishly. Something hangs over Jack, like a heavy cloud lingering above his head, ready to burst. He lets out a deep breath and drops his shoulders, unclenching his fists. I push myself off the trunk as he addresses the crew.

"There's been a… change."

The crew gathers around, and the group of villagers that had watched the fight now slide away, back to their chores. Jack scratches his beard, eyes darting back to the temple, where the elderly man watches from the doorway.

I touch his arm. *What is it?*

The lines around his eyes seem to deepen. "The price for the map was more than I can give her," he says.

Ace snorts humorlessly. "Does the lass even have it?"

"She has it," Jack says. "But she wants more before she's willing to give it up."

"What does she want?" Caspian smooths his hair back, where Ace's fingers had tangled it.

Jack hesitates, looking at me with eyes that hold more than I can read in a quick exchange.

"Madame Kiera collects information," he says. "Secrets rather than coins."

"Yes." Ace waves a hand. "We're aware, Captain."

"She requires everyone from the crew to participate."

Ace laughs, shaking his head as he sits down on a large rock. The crew begins mumbling among themselves, casting wary looks at the temple behind Jack.

"I know this isn't what you expected." He holds his hands up as if they're all about to flee. "But we will not get the map unless we give her what she wants."

"Some old crone wants me to confess to her like a child?" Ace scoffs, picking the sand from under his fingernails.

"She's not an *old crone*, and if you won't do it…" Jack steps closer, putting some bite behind his words. "… then you're no longer a part of this crew."

Ace freezes, that smug grin slipping from his face. Jack needs everyone to participate to get what we came here for. I can tell by his tone that he's serious. He's hunted this map around the world and lost crew members along the way, and he won't stop now. He's too close.

Jack peels his eyes away from Ace and softens them a bit. "That goes for everyone," he announces. "If you're unwilling to give Madame Kiera what she wants, then leave now. Every single member of the crew must participate, and if you don't..." He sighs, casting a look at me for support. "Then I have no choice but to banish you from the *Chained Maiden* and her crew."

A hush falls over the courtyard, and I see a few men and women actually turn away and head back toward the beach. Jack lets them go. He won't argue or beg them to stay. They've been through a lot just to get here, so Jack won't blame them for leaving.

Caspian is the first to step up, lifting his chin. "I'll go first."

Jack quirks his mouth into an almost smile but shakes his head and looks right at me. "She wants you first, Tsu."

I look around as all eyes turn toward me. I'm not frightened by some woman who harbors secrets, but I am nervous. I nod and follow Jack into the temple, glancing back once to see Hraefn, Caspian, and Ace gathered to watch me go. My heart kicks up as I step into the temple, and the door closes, shutting out the sun.

"Tsu," Jack says my name so gently it hurts. "I know this might be hard—"

I hold up a hand to stop him. *It's what needs to be done. I'll be fine.*

He touches my cheek, a sort of fatherly love passing to my eyes.

As I'm guided down the steps of the temple toward the center, I start thinking about what I'll say. My hands begin to sweat, my pulse spiking as memories rush through my head. My home, my sister married off to some man she thought she loved. My father and his cruel eyes, my mother so fragile and weak, like a baby bird. I know what I'll tell Madame Kiera—though just thinking about it makes my stomach churn.

After I left Hanatsu and Jack found me, I felt like I could breathe again. Like some massive burden had been lifted from my shoulders the moment I boarded the *Chained Maiden* and became part of a new family. I try not to think about my family back home, or the emperor who took my voice because it only brings pain and regret. But now all those suppressed feelings are tearing their way to the surface, and I can't stop them.

The guilt crashes down on me like a falling star. I might not have changed anything for the women back home, but my words scared the emperor because he knows I'm right. Women deserve as much freedom as men, and what did I do? The second I was beaten, I ran away, abandoning my home and family and all the girls who needed a voice. I could've been there for them, silently leading them to reform, but here I am, about to tell a stranger how guilty I've felt all these years. But I'll make it right, one way or another.

I sit down before Madame Kiera and spill my heart out for the crew. For *Jack*.

TWENTY-THREE

One by one, the crew makes their way to the temple, ready to give Madame Kiera what she requires. It's been a couple of hours now, and the sun has started to slink away. Many members of the crew actually come back out looking… relieved. At first, I think it's strange, that maybe they were acting so we won't see the hurt or unease on their face.

But the relaxed way in which they stroll from the temple tells me all I need to know. I suppose it makes sense—we all have secrets, and perhaps it feels good to finally tell someone who you know will keep it locked away for you.

But not me. As time crawls on, I become more and more nervous.

Tsu was the first one to go. Captain Jack told us that he hasn't even taken his turn yet and that the first hour he spent in the temple had been arguing with Madame Kiera about the new requirements. I wonder what the captain will give the woman, and if he'll feel relieved afterward, or haunted.

When Tsu emerged from the temple, I could tell by her eyes that she'd been crying, and Tsu never cries. I can guess what she told Madame Kiera, though I don't pry. Her past is difficult, and I know that she feels sorry for leaving Hanatsu, not having helped other young women, but it isn't her fault that their way of life is wrong.

Ace, being the raging idiot that he is, went up to Tsu and started grilling her about what it was like. He shot her question after question, growing more eager with every passing word until Tsu snapped. She'd grabbed Ace's wrist, twisted it behind his back, and kicked him to the ground, burying his face in the sand with the back of her boot. Some crew members cackled, and others just looked away, not wishing to be next.

Now, Ace sits off by himself, being uncharacteristically quiet. I tap my foot anxiously, casting a worried glance at the entrance of the temple and waiting to see those beautiful copper eyes. Caspian has been inside for some time now, and I can't help but worry. After I kissed him, I thought that that was it—that we'd finally stop this silly dance of ours and just... be. But I was wrong, and he rejected me. It hurt more than I care to admit, and we haven't spoken much since then.

I wonder what he's telling Madame Kiera right now. Is he talking about us? Confessing something to her that he can't bring himself to tell me? The thought makes my heart kick up more, and a second later, I spring to my feet as Caspian emerges.

Ace glances up from where he sits under the shade of a palm tree, but he doesn't approach. Tsu has been sitting alone as well, not even sparing a look in Caspian's direction. My nerves get the better of me, and I walk right up to him. His eyes are cast down as if the sand under his feet is a puzzle he can't piece together.

"Caspian," I say gently, startling him from a trance.

His eyes find mine, and I freeze.

They're rimmed red, the bright spark usually shining in his golden eyes snuffed out. He turns away quickly, but I follow him over to a gathering of rocks. Caspian sits down with a sigh, twisting his hands in his lap.

"Caspian," I try again, coming to sit beside him. I'm all too aware of the danger of being this close to him, but I ignore it for now. "What happened?"

He stays silent.

I angle toward him, lowering my voice. "You can tell me." He sniffs, but his face remains hard, a muscle in his jawline twitching. Finally, he glances at me, eyes searching and unraveling all the pain he's likely just endured. I want to reach out and touch his cheek or hold his hand, but I stay still. Caspian shakes his head, knocking loose a brown curl that hangs over his brow.

"I... I didn't think it would be like that," he says, turning his eyes back to his lap. "It's like she knew what I was trying to say before I did, and she worked it out of me."

My brow furrows. "What do you mean?"

His eyes find mine again. "I tried to give her something that I thought was a secret, but she wouldn't accept."

My heart slams to a stop.

Is he talking about us?

"She kept prying," he continues. "Until I told her what she was after all along."

"I'm sorry," I say while trying to keep my panic at bay. If Madame Kiera somehow already knows what secret she wants, then I'm screwed.

We sit in silence for a moment, then Caspian leans back, brushing his fingers against mine. He doesn't seem to notice as he retreats further into thought, but it sets every inch of me on fire. "My mother," he says so quietly that I almost miss it. "I think..." His lips twist as he works out the words in his head. "I just worry that she'd be... disappointed."

"Why would you think that?"

He keeps talking as if he hasn't heard me. "Before she died, my mother told me to find my own adventure, but I don't think she meant this." He gestures toward the crew members. "If there is a place we go after death, then... I just..." He sighs deeply around the next words. "I'm afraid to face her."

"You've done nothing wrong, Caspian."

"You don't understand." He draws his knees into his chest,

shielding his heart. "My family is well known in the city and the second wealthiest among them. There are certain… traditions that I'm expected to uphold."

"What are you talking about?" I lean in closer.

"There was always a lot expected from my brothers and me. An image for the public eye, and my father has always been well aware of that. He's conservative, and though he's traveled a lot, he doesn't exactly understand other people's way of life."

"Caspian, what are you trying to say?"

"My mother was my best friend," he continues. "I think she knew all the secrets I had, even the ones I didn't know about yet, but I'm afraid to face her again because I don't want her to see my shame."

He turns to face me fully, leaning in closer. His eyes are serious, latching onto mine and refusing to let go. "The more time I spent with you, the more I started to realize that…" He smiles sweetly. "That I *like* you."

And then the smile dies. "And I'm ashamed to admit that it made me nervous. Not because it was something new, but… because of my family name. I was worried about what people might think of me, what they might think of my father and my brothers. So you see, I *have* done something wrong because if my mother knew for one second that I was ashamed to be happy with someone, she'd be disappointed in me."

I don't know what to say. He holds my gaze for a long moment, eyes growing more worried the longer I stay silent. Caspian is ashamed of me? To have feelings for me? I can feel my neck growing hot and a redness filling my cheeks.

"Hraefn…"

"I get it," I say a little too quickly. "Images are important for important people."

Caspian shakes his head hurriedly, reaching out to take my hand, but I move it at the last second.

"You don't understand," he says quickly. "Yes, I *was* ashamed about how I felt and what that might mean for my father, but

Hraefn…" He touches his fingers to mine where they sit between us. It's fire and ice coming together.

"Hraefn!"

My head snaps up as Yonis emerges from the temple and beckons to me. "It's your turn," he calls.

My heart skips a beat, then plummets to my stomach. I stand up, but Caspian jumps in my path.

"Hraefn wait—"

"I have to go." I move around him, but he grabs hold of my wrist.

"I'm not ashamed anymore," he rasps, then more confidently, "I'm not ashamed to be with you."

I stare into his eyes, choking on the words as they slide past my lips. "Then why did you push me away?"

Caspian lets go of my wrist like I burned him, and his face crumbles. I force myself to turn away and head for the temple before he can try to lie to me.

The smell of scented candles dances around my nose as I sit down before Madame Kiera. She's stunning, but the sharp angles of her face also make her terrifying. She slides from her throne of bones to sit beside me on the pillow. I rub my sweaty palms over my pants.

"Hraefn," she coos. "What a beautiful name for a beautiful boy." She grips my chin between her long fingernails and turns me from side to side. "Your eyes," she whispers. "Stunning."

I lean away from her. "Can we just get this over with?"

She smiles and leans back as well. "Straight to the point. I like it. Very well, tell me, beautiful boy, what secret do you have for me?"

There will be no dance with her, no lying or skirting my way around the question. She was able to pull something from Caspian that he kept locked down deep. I close my eyes at the thought, that Caspian has been ashamed to give in to his feelings. But… he said he isn't anymore, so why did he push me away after I kissed him? Can it be as he said? That this mission is too dangerous, and he doesn't want to lose me? But how can you lose something that you've never had? The more I think about it, the more frustrated I become because a part of me knows he's right.

Suddenly I feel bad about our talk just a minute ago and wish to flee the temple and tell him that it's all right. I need to tell him that I understand and won't pursue him anymore. No matter what Caspian might have thought about his feelings, I know that he cares about me. Maybe one day, when things are easier, we'll be free to be together. Whether it takes a week or years, it doesn't matter because—

"I'm waiting." Madame Kiera clicks her long fingernails against her tattooed arm.

I take in a deep breath and lock eyes with her, finishing my thought with words. "I'm in love with Caspian."

A pleased grin spreads across her lips. "The boy with eyes of gold."

"Yes."

She chuckles lightly, and my cheeks flare with anger. "Look, I know what he told you."

Madame Kiera's eyes narrow as she looks at me. "He told you his secret? *You?*"

"He did."

"Hmm." She twists her lips. "An honest boy, he is. Couldn't hide the spark in his eyes from a blind man." She leans in. "Especially when he mentioned you."

"But… he's ashamed to have feelings for me. He worried what it might do to his family, and what his mother would think."

Madame Kiera considers this, smiling as she leans back against her throne. "Tell me, Hraefn. Have you ever been ashamed of something? Or perhaps regretted a decision afterward?"

"Of course." The memory of kissing Caspian comes to mind but then vanishes like fog in the wind.

"And you feel that way because you overthink it. You wonder how others might see you, or how this thing that you regret might change your life, and that scares you." I stare at her, brows drawn together, and she continues. "Perhaps that shame or regret you think you feel is all in your head."

"I don't understand."

"I think you do." Her smile is as charming as a snake. "You regret something because someone *else* told you it was wrong. You feel ashamed because society tells you they're right and you're wrong. Don't you think it would feel good to step out from others' expectations and just be who you are?"

My mother's final words run through my head, so similar to Madame Kiera's now. Bells jingle in her hair as she leans closer. "Do you regret kissing that boy?"

How does she know that?

She smiles, and I think my blushing cheeks confirm her suspicion.

"Yes," I answer.

Madame Kiera knows I'm not lying, but admitting it out loud hurts. I do regret it in a way. She twirls a lock of corded hair between her nails. "Why?"

"Because he turned me down. I thought…" I huff a laugh. "I thought that we'd be together."

"So you regret your choice because of the outcome, but tell me, did it feel good?"

My skin tingles with warmth at the memory. "Yes."

"And if given a chance, would you do it again?"

I told myself that I won't pursue Caspian any longer, but I can lie to myself all I want, not to Madame Kiera. "In a heartbeat."

"So then why regret it?"

I open my mouth to answer, but she covers my lips with hers. It feels as if something inside me breaks away with her lips. "Thank you, beautiful Hraefn. I shall keep your secret forever." With that, she waves me off and asks me to fetch the next crew member. I walk from the temple in a fog, my brain raking over her words again and again.

Why regret it?

Is she trying to say that Caspian never truly felt ashamed? That it's the pressure of different ideals that fill his head with the sense that his feelings are somehow wrong? I shake my head as I step out into the cool air, taking a deep breath.

The sun has set, and the villagers begin stoking fires to roast whole pigs on a spit. Crew members flock to them, graciously taking the food they offer. I feel drunk—too much information and feelings rattle through my head, making me dizzy.

Caspian catches my eye and starts heading my way, but I veer right toward Ace. He gets to his feet, an unreadable look on his face. "You all right then, lad?"

I nod. "I think you're up."

He lets out a shaky breath. "Right."

I wait for a snarky comment or something sarcastic to pass his lips, but nothing comes.

"You okay?"

"Fine, lad, just..." He pauses, his eyes averting mine, and instead landing on the group of crew members eating. Ace turns back to me and flashes a smile. "Save me some pig, would you?"

"Sure."

I stand there watching Ace walk into the temple before I turn and head over to where Captain Jack sits with Tsu. I know I should talk to Caspian, maybe even confess what I just told Madame Kiera, but I don't have the energy right now. Instead, I sit down beside Tsu and eat my meal in silence, stealing small glances at the boy I'm in love with.

TWENTY-FOUR

JACK

As the moon slides across the endless expanse of the sky, I stand beneath its face, clutching what I came here for. My crew looks worn out and beaten, though some seem to have taken the experience with Madame Kiera in stride.

My heart won't stop pounding as I slide the last piece of the map into the vial I keep around my neck. We're heading out tonight. I'm too eager to sleep anyway, and I bet more than half my crew are just as eager to get this over with. I haven't put all the pieces together yet, I'm too focused on getting far away from this place. I've told Madame Kiera a lot over the years, but the one thing she's after I've managed to keep hold of. It isn't as scandalizing as one might think; it's just that I don't want to relive that horrible day ever again, though I often have nightmares about it. Instead, I gave her something that might ruin me if it ever gets out.

Sundance approaches me as I board the *Chained Maiden*, his eyes running over me as if I've sustained an actual wound. "All right, captain?"

"Fine. Let's get going."

He twists his lips. "If you say so." Sundance cups his hands over his mouth. "Raise the sails!"

The crew gets to work quickly, unfurling the sails, raising the anchor, and drawing up the ramp. The winds are in our favor tonight, and as I walk up the steps to the aftercastle, I can feel all eyes turn to me. They want to know where we're headed, and so do I.

I open the door to my room to find Tsu, Hraefn, Ace, and Tetra waiting for me. Walking silently to the table, I take out the vial and open it. They all lean in with wide eyes as I begin putting the map together.

"You can trust her, right?"

This comes from Tetra, who sits with her boots on my table, tossing an apple up and down. I answer with a nod, keeping my focus on the map as it comes together. I have a general sense of which way we're heading because the pieces I already acquired only show the eastern and southern parts of our world. My fingers begin to shake as I slide the last piece in, showing northwest, where Vulkan sits, and the sea around it. But then...

Hraefn leans over my shoulder, blue eyes scanning the piece of paper. "There's nothing there."

Tsu eyes me from across the table, and Tetra stands up, towering over me. She runs her finger over Vulkan, to the island where I grew up called Midsarra, and down to a small X in the middle of the sea. She scoffs. "That lying bitch."

"It's just a ship graveyard," Hraefn says, shaking his head and sitting down with a huff.

Ace is silent for once, but that only unnerves me more. His face is hard, eyes dead as they look at the map.

No.

My eyes refuse to believe what they're seeing, but it's true. There's nothing out there but a graveyard. We've sailed over it many times before, though I often avoid that path because the water is shallow, and ships still protrude from the sea.

"Now what?" Tetra asks.

"Just hang on," I growl, feeling my frustration rise like a tidal wave. I move the pieces apart, then back together again, lining them up perfectly, but nothing happens. What did I expect to happen anyway? For some magic light to appear, that will morph the map and show me its secrets?

Snarling, I slam a fist down on the table. Tsu's cat eyes are unreadable, but I know what she's thinking. That this was all just a wild goose chase. Maybe Story was right, and this was nothing but a fantasy. A myth that's passed down from pirate to pirate, but then why is Captain Blacktip following me? He could've fallen into the same trap as me, hunting a fairy tale to the ends of the earth. I've lost crew members because of him, and I won't give up so easily.

I turn to Tetra. "Find Sundance and give him the coordinates. We're headed north."

"But, Captain, there's nothing—"

"I know what the map says," I interrupt. "But I need to see."

Hraefn steps up. "We *have* seen it, Captain. We must have sailed past that stretch a hundred times by now."

Though Tsu can't speak, she agrees with her eyes.

"He's right," Ace says with a shrug of his shoulder. "I think you've been played, Captain."

My frustration boils over. "We're going, and that's that. I won't let their deaths be for nothing."

Everyone turns their heads down, remembering the crew members we've lost. Skye was young, too young, and she didn't deserve to die like that. I can never make it right, or bring them back, but maybe I can still do this.

I level my gaze with Tetra. She shakes her head slightly, then turns her back. "Aye, Captain. We're headed north."

Hraefn's blue eyes look dull as he watches Tetra leave before turning back to the map. He stands up, his chair screeching with the sudden movement. "I hope you're right, Captain." Then he too is gone.

Ace lingers for a moment longer, his eyes locked on the graveyard to which we're sailing. With a bow that holds more mockery than respect, he exits my room. I keep studying the map, but Tsu's eyes are burrowing into me. I sigh and sit down across from her.

"Say it."

She cocks her head.

"Tell me I'm wrong. That this is nothing but a dream, and I'm going to get all of us killed."

Her fingers drum on the armrest, then she begins signing. *I can't do that.*

"Why not?"

Because I don't know if you're wrong yet.

I stay silent, and Tsu gets up and moves around the table, putting a hand on my shoulder. *So what if you are wrong?* she signs, her eyes holding mine hostage. *Then you could stop hunting.*

"But my crew. Skye… she died for—"

For you. They all died for you. Do you know why?

Not trusting myself to speak, I just stare at her.

Because you're not just a captain to us. You're family, and to a lot of us, a savior. Myself included.

"I'm not some hero, Tsu. I'm just a pirate."

If you're just a pirate, then I'm just some homeless girl with no voice. Her eyes turn serious, fingers moving faster with her building frustration. *You think I was happy when you found me? No, but then I joined your crew, and you gave me a family, one that I could never have back in Hanatsu. And what about Hraefn? What would've become of him if you hadn't found him when you did? Or Caspian. Do you think he's happier now?*

My shoulders shrug with uncertainty. I look away, but she grabs my chin and turns me back.

You're right, she signs. *You can't bring back Skye or the others, and maybe their deaths can never be justified in your mind. But Jack…* She pauses, her eyes turning glassy, and my heart snaps at the sight of it, but she continues before I can speak. *We're here because we have nothing to go back to. You gave us a family and hope for a better future. We followed you, not because you're a pirate captain, but because you saved us. All of us, and we're here with you.*

Whether this—she waves a hand at the map—*is real or not, we're with you.*

Tsu steps back and waits for me to speak, but what can I say? My crew all have storied pasts, ones they would probably like to forget, but I don't see myself as their savior. But I know Tsu will never lie to me or say something just to make me feel better, so I have to believe her. I offer a smile, which she returns with her eyes.

"All right," I say, standing up. "Then we're doing this. Go tell Hraefn to take his position and get Ace and a few others to check the cannons. If Captain Blacktip is after this map, let's not make it easy for him."

Tsu nods and turns to leave, but I grab her hand and pull her into my chest, wrapping my arms around her. "Thank you, Tsu." She returns the embrace before pushing away. I'll always have a special relationship with Tsu, and I'm forever grateful for her no-bullshit attitude.

As the night turns into day, the *Chained Maiden* sails over the calm waters of the Green Sea toward the ship graveyard. We're all tired and eager, no one having slept much. I stand at the helm with Story to my right and Sundance off to the left, scanning the clouds. He pulls out his sunstone and begins marking down notes on a sheet of paper. Sundance is an excellent navigator, and I trust him to get us there.

Down below, Ace sits around with Caspian and a few others, playing cards. I can see the snicker on his lips from here as he slaps a card down on the barrel and holds out his hand.

"Pay up, lads."

Caspian throws down his cards with a sigh and hands a few coins to Ace, the others grunting and tossing the coins to the deck. "Sore losers!" he calls at their backs as he counts his money.

Moving down the steps, I sit off to the side under the eave of the aftercastle. As I pull out the pieces of the map again, I feel like my stomach is made of lead. I stayed up all night staring at this stupid piece of paper, begging it to show me its secrets. Ace and Caspian start up a conversation, talking about Madame Kiera and how she lied. This comes from Ace, who seemed uneasy after his visit with Madame Kiera, though he soon snapped back to being the usual pain in the ass. Caspian has been quiet too, not even coming to my room last night to see the missing piece of the map.

When I look at him now, I'm not surprised to find his eyes resting on Hraefn above. I know that look, the longing behind his golden eyes. I wonder what he confessed to Madame Kiera, but I'll never ask because I'm pretty sure I already know.

"Land!"

Ace snorts and lifts his eyes to the crow's nest. "Ha-ha, Hraefn. Very funny."

Hraefn pokes his head over the side, his midnight hair blowing in a sudden wind. "I'm serious. Land ahead!"

I shove back my chair and run to the starboard side of the ship, bracing my hands on the gunwale, and then I see it.

Ace is beside me now. "That's… not possible," he breathes.

"I thought you all said this was a ship graveyard," Caspian says, eyes wide with wonder.

I can't even form words to respond, too shocked at what lies ahead of us.

The island shimmers like a mirage, yet it's real. High red cliffs rise from the sea, pushing at the low-hanging clouds. The top is painted with every shade of green, some trees growing straight out from the rocks and hanging parallel with the water below. No ships protrude from the waters; no ships are docked in the little cove. It's as if this place rose out of the water just for us. I step back and rub my eyes to make sure it's real, and when I open them again, the island is still there.

"Ha!" Ace begins cackling like a madman, shaking his head

as he leans over the gunwale. "By the gods, we did it." He turns to Caspian and begins shaking him by the shoulders. "We did it, lad!"

Other crew members begin hooting and shouting, whistling as we edge closer to the strange island. Caspian's face lights up, which I haven't seen in a long time, but when I turn to look at Hraefn, his eyes are hard and locked straight ahead.

"Get down here!" I call up to him.

"But... shouldn't I keep a look out?"

I throw my arms out to state the obvious. "For who?"

Caspian speaks up. "What about Captain Blacktip?"

A moment later, Hraefn swings down from his perch, rifle slung across his back. I walk over to the map and roll up all the pieces, tucking them away in my jacket. "I think we can only see this place because we have the map." Even as I say it, it sounds ridiculous, but it's the only thing that makes sense.

"A magical map?" Ace snorts. "Whatever you want to call it, Captain. All I ken is that there's an island there when there shouldn't be."

We dock in a small cove shaped like a crescent moon and use the rowboats to get us ashore. Half the crew will need to stay with the ship while I bring the rest with me. I'm still wary of the place, even if it does look abandoned, so I bring our messenger bird along in case I need to get word back to my crew quickly. The pigeon ruffles its feathers, letting loose a few that drift to the bottom of the cage. There's no map of the island, so we'll have to set off if we want to find Captain Armada's ship. I don't know how big the island is or how many little coves lay around the perimeter, but I'll search all night until we find it.

Part of me feels like this is a dream, and I keep expecting to stub my toe or something similar to jerk me awake. We weave our way through the thick jungle, a few men going ahead to chop away brush in our path. We keep the sun to our left, heading north across the island. I figure we can go straight and then split up, one group heading east while the other goes west along the coast.

"Do you hear that?" Caspian whispers.

Behind him, Hraefn unslings his rifle and shakes his head. "No, there's nothing."

We all pause to listen, and he's right. No birds are singing, no crunch of leaves from small critters roaming the forest floor. Not even the croak of a frog—there's no life at all.

"Well, thanks for pointing that out, lad. That's not creepy at all." Ace scans the trees above us as if expecting something to attack.

Hraefn does the same, expecting some sort of trap. "How is that possible?"

Ace snorts. "This island isn't even possible," he says, tapping his foot into the soil. "But it feels pretty real to me."

"Come on," I tell them. "Let's just keep going."

They all fall in line, Tsu ahead of me with her double swords drawn.

Whatever lies in our path better just lie down, or we'll put them down.

I'm not leaving this island without that ship.

We camp for the night in a small clearing. We've been walking all day and still haven't reached the other side of the island. I'm beginning to think there is no other side, and we're destined to walk forever, never finding what we came for.

Captain Jack unrolls the map again, putting the pieces together, but nothing more shows than before. Ace slides his eyes over to it from across the fire. "Ah, put that away, Captain. Lookin' at it isn't going to make the ship magically appear."

I pipe up, only because the captain looks beyond tired, and that map won't show him any more. "He's right, Captain." Captain Jack looks up at me. "It will drive you crazy if you keep staring at it. We'll find it, don't worry."

He considers me for a long moment, but finally rolls it, and tucks the map in his breast pocket. I pull Ace's attention away from the captain, where it's been focused all night. "What do you think it looks like?"

He grins, side-eyeing Hraefn, hoping he'll join in the conversation, but he stays silent. I try to ignore his presence, but he's like a black hole, and I keep getting sucked in.

"I ken she's a beauty."

"You can't know that," I counter, and Ace frowns.

"I can, too." He puffs his chest out. "I ken more than you think, lad."

"Oh yeah?" I ask sarcastically. "Like what?"

Ace leans in, his blond hair lit up in the fire. His blue eyes narrow, and he lowers his voice so that only I can hear. "I ken you're in love."

I choke on my drink, coughing as I spit it up, and Ace cackles like a fool. My cheeks flame up like a bonfire, but I refuse to look anywhere near Hraefn, though I'm sure he's staring at me.

Ace slaps a hand on my back. "You're too easy to get riled up!" He laughs even harder, nearly falling out of his seat when Hraefn slaps him upside the head.

"What the hell was that for?"

"I don't know what you said." Hraefn leans back and pulls a piece of meat off the spit. "But I'm sure it was very *Ace.*"

"And what is that supposed to mean?"

Hraefn smiles, and my heart melts at the sight. "That you're an asshole, and everything that comes out of your mouth is rude, sarcastic, or just plain stupid."

Ace places a hand over his heart. "Aw, thank you, lad."

Hraefn cocks a brow and gives him a look as if to say *see.*

"Hey." He throws his hands in the air. "At least I don't have a stick up my ass." He gives me a sideways look.

I set my drink down and glare at him. "I know you're not talking about me."

"I'm lookin' at you, aren't I?"

I know by now not to take what Ace says so seriously, that getting angry only fuels his fuckery. "You know, your behavior is not very princely."

His eyes narrow to slits. "Careful, lad."

I shrug off his threat. "I mean, you *are* a prince, right? Prince Angus Dragonsbane," I proclaim in a deep voice, and Hraefn chuckles.

Ace gulps his drink. "Fuck you."

I rearrange my features into a submissive frown and bow my head. "Yes, Your Highness."

Hraefn smirks, seeing the annoyance on Ace's face, and follows suit, bowing his head and saying, "Forgive us, Your Highness."

"May I refill your drink, Your Highness?" I gesture to his cup.

Ace growls.

Hraefn kneels before him. "Might I rub your feet, Your Highness?"

"Oh, piss off." Ace throws his empty cup at Hraefn's shoulder, then gets up. "You're lucky I don't have you executed for mocking a prince."

Hraefn and I burst into a fit of laughter. Ace gives us a dangerous smile before leaving the fire. When our laughter settles, I catch Hraefn's eye, and his smile falters.

The silence between us is more painful than the bullets that not so long ago tore through me. I have a million things I want to say to him, but for some reason, my tongue feels like a swollen piece of cotton. He shifts on the log, dropping his hand next to mine and staring into the flames. Around us, the crew starts to crawl into their sleeping mats for the night. Captain Jack settles down too, tucking his hands under his head and staring up at the stars. A log pops, and I slide my eyes back to Hraefn, only to find him staring at me. His lips twitch with words unspoken, then finally I can't take it anymore.

I edge my body toward him, but he speaks before I can. "This is almost over," he says wistfully, but there's a question in his eyes. I know what he wants me to say—what I've said before about being together after this is all done. But the words won't come.

Hraefn shakes his head and turns away, his face hard yet again. "Did you even mean what you said?"

"What?" I ask, even though I know where this is going.

He looks at the crackling fire, his voice is soft with sadness. "That you were ashamed of your feelings."

My heart plummets, but I won't lie. "Yes."

Hraefn nods slowly, never taking his eyes away from the dancing flames.

"Hraefn…" His back goes rigid as his name passes my lips. I finally find my words, and they come pouring out of me. "I'm sorry if I hurt you. I did mean what I said, but I thought about it a lot and…"

His foot bounces with anticipation, brows creased with worry. "And what?"

I can't ignore the hopeful tone of his voice. "I told you I was wrong. When I joined the crew, I felt more at home than I ever did in my real home after my mother died. It was like I got a piece of what was missing back, and you were a big part of that." I try to catch his eye, but he refuses to look at me. Sliding my hand along the log, I brush my fingers up against his. Hraefn snaps his head down to his hand, but he doesn't move, and I hurry on. "I was confused for a little while, but when I left my brothers and father, I gave up my name."

Finally, he slides those crystal blue eyes up to me.

"A name is just a name," I whisper. "If it keeps me from being happy, then I don't want it."

His eyes dance back and forth between mine, then he moves his hand away. "But you still don't want to be with me."

"I think I do—"

"You *think*?" He huffs a humorless laugh. I can see him recoiling from me, building up that protective wall that shields his heart.

I break through it. "I *do* want to be with you, Hraefn. It's just… like you said, this is almost over, and neither of us can afford to lose focus. Not now."

Hraefn glances back at me, his eyes soft before he nods. "I know. It's just… difficult to be around you."

"Oh."

The silence creeps back in, encircling us in a bubble. I know what Hraefn means because I feel the same way. Being around him and not being *with* him is exhausting emotionally, but I can't imagine not being around him at all. Who knows how this will end or if we'll even make it out of here? So what the hell are we doing? We've sort of had this unspoken thing between us, and then I had to go and open my big mouth. Hraefn is right—that first night he tried to kiss me, he told me that I don't know when to keep my mouth shut. I just want to enjoy this simple moment with him, because it could be the last.

I gather my courage and reach out to take his hand. The touch is like an electric shock through my body, and my heart starts pounding madly against my ribs. Hraefn stares at me in shock as I thread my fingers with his. "Is this okay?"

"I thought you said—"

"I know what I said." I turn to face him fully. "I don't want this to be complicated, I just want to enjoy this moment right now. With you."

Hraefn smiles, and it takes everything in me not to lean in and kiss him.

"All right, then." He gives my hand a light squeeze, and I feel my cheeks flare. "Maybe someday it won't be complicated."

"Someday," I agree.

We sit like that for a long time, holding hands on the log and listening to the crackling fire. Hraefn tells me a few stories from back home, and I cling to every word like a lifeline. I offer a few in return, earning low chuckles and side smirks. As the moon moves across the sky, we sink to the ground, leaning our heads back on the log and watching the stars. I fall asleep with Hraefn's hand in mine.

And wake up to a scream.

"Wake up!"

"What happened?"

"Is she dead?"

The camp is in chaos. I let go of Hraefn's hand and touch the hilt of my cutlass. The fires have long gone out, though ours still smokes in front of us. Captain Jack's face is tight with too many emotions to fit. Tetra roars in a fury, and other crew members scramble about, drawing weapons or running off into the brush to check for intruders.

"What's going on?" I ask.

Hraefn walks over to the captain, then stops dead and drops to his knees. I run up behind him, my heart pounding a mile a minute, but it stops beating when I see her.

"No…"

Hraefn reaches out to touch the captain's shoulder, "Captain—"

Captain Jack whirls on him, shoving Hraefn to the ground. Tears streak down his face and disappear into his beard. His eyes are so shattered and broken that it hurts to look at him. I help Hraefn off the ground, but my knees buckle when I look back at her. Hraefn is there to hold me up.

Tsu lies with her head to one side, eyes still wide with shock. Her neck has been cut ear to ear, and the blood runs down her throat in rivulets. It hasn't congealed yet, which means that this happened recently. I choke down my tears and force myself to look away. No one sneaks up on Tsu ever, so how did this happen? And who killed her?

The captain draws his sword, and with a scream of rage, slashes at a nearby tree. The bark chips off, and the metal on the wood creates sparks in the air. He hacks away at it, yelling and grunting as more tears run down his cheeks. No one says a word, just turn their heads down so as not to see his pain. I look away, and that's when I notice that we're missing people. I nudge Hraefn, who follows my gaze and lands on something that makes his eyes go wide.

He runs over to the edge of the camp and bends down, picking up a cutlass. "Ace," he breathes. The sword belongs to Ace, and beside it is a large pool of blood. Beside that the birdcage is overturned and empty. Hraefn grips the handle so tight his knuckles crack. "They have Ace," he snarls.

Tetra comes up behind us, armed with a large hammer in one hand. "Who?"

"Who do you think?" he roars. "Captain Blacktip!"

Captain Jack stops his hacking when he hears the name. He turns around slowly, letting his arms hang at his sides. Tetra scans the crew. "We're missing two more," she says. "Gilly and Yonis aren't here either."

I shake my head, trying to make sense of this. "So what? They…" I choke on the words, refusing to look at our dead crewmate. "Killed Tsu and took the others as hostages?"

"Why would they do that?" Hraefn asks.

Tetra twists her lips. "In case we catch up to him," she offers. "Maybe he'll use their lives as a bargaining tool to get away."

That's when I realize something else. I turn to the captain, but his eyes are glazed over and unfocused. "Where's the map?"

Captain Jack reaches into his breast pocket and pulls out the pieces of paper, though his eyes don't watch what his fingers are doing. It's like he's in a trance, his eyes haunted. Tetra lets out a relieved sigh, but that only complicates things more. "How the fuck did he find us if he doesn't have the map?" Hraefn slides Ace's cutlass through his belt.

No one has an answer.

The captain sinks to the sand, clutching his head between his palms and mumbling to himself. He's being torn apart, every second another thread unraveled. We have to keep him together until we find out what to do.

Calming my breathing, I look to see what crew we do have left. My eyes land on a burly man with a red beard: the tracker. "Tommen." I beckon to him. He straightens up and nods. "What do you see?"

"I already scanned the surrounding woods." He jerks his chin east. "They went that way."

"How many?"

He shakes his head. "Hard to tell. Looks like they tried to cover their tracks."

I turn back to Hraefn and grab his hand, not caring who sees. "We have to go after them. Be ready."

His eyes lock on mine, and he nods numbly, squeezing my fingers before we break apart. Tetra goes over to Captain Jack and offers a hand. Everyone else forms up, weapons at the ready. As we go to leave, Captain Jack jerks away from Tetra and falls on his knees in front of Tsu. "We can't leave her."

I wave Tetra away and kneel in front of my captain. His eyes are so filled with tears that I wonder how he can see at all. "Captain…" I say gently. He doesn't respond, so I reach out tentatively and touch his wrist. "Jack."

His copper eyes lift to mine as he blinks away the tears that have built up.

"We have to leave, but I promise we'll come back for her."

He still doesn't move.

"Please, Jack." I've never called him by name without using Captain in front of it, but right now he isn't a captain. He's a broken man who needs a nudge. "We can't let them hurt Ace and the others too. We have to find him and end this."

Jack shakes his head but gets to his feet anyway, taking one last long look at Tsu, and then his face changes. It morphs into something deadly.

We trek through the brush, following the footprints left in the soft soil. They head east, weaving through the thinnest of brush, likely so we didn't hear them. The sun beats down on us, coating my skin in sweat, but we push on. Captain Blacktip has a head start on us, and if we're to have any chance of getting our crew members back, we need to hurry.

Beside me, Hraefn keeps his rifle at the ready, eyes on a constant swivel, landing on me every so often to make sure I'm all right. But how can I be? None of this is okay, but I won't even let myself think about what will happen if we're too late.

Minutes pass like hours, and the sun seems to stay in place in the sky, mocking us and telling us we'll never make it. Finally, we break free of the jungle and onto a beach. It's a small cove similar to the one we docked the *Chained Maiden* in. At that thought, I turn to Tetra.

"The rest of the crew."

She nods in realization. "I'll go back with—"

"No, we'll need you." I've seen Tetra fight before, and she's stronger than most of the men on the crew. I turn to another crew member. A small framed man who's quick on his feet. "Remmie, go back to the ship. Warn them of what's happened."

Remmie looks from me to Jack, then back again. "Should I bring more men?"

Jack doesn't answer, his eyes down.

I step up. "No." I look back at Hraefn and Tetra, the rest of our small group, and wonder how many of us will make it. I pinch my eyes shut and turn back to Remmie. "Don't come back for us. If we don't make it back by nightfall, leave."

He shakes his head. "But… I can't leave the captain—"

"You'll do as he says," Jack interrupts, meeting Remmie's eyes. "Leave at nightfall."

Remmie nods and then takes off back through the forest.

With one crew member down, and only eight of us left out here, I don't like our odds much. We keep on along the beach, climbing up a rocky pathway and down into another cove. Hraefn's fingers keep twitching at any sound, and I have to reach out to him many times to calm his nerves. I know Ace is his best friend, but I'm betting it isn't that thought that has him so nervous. Ace can handle himself a lot better than most of the crew. What bothers Hraefn is the fact that he'll have to face Deadeye Cane again. I can tell by the way his eyes grow wild at the rustle of leaves above, or how his whole body goes stiff when we clear another corner.

The afternoon slides by, and we stop for water in a nearby brook that runs down from the rocky cliffs. Hraefn fills a skin, and I crouch down beside him, taking a sip when he offers.

"We can do this," I tell him, trying to convince myself at the same time.

"I can't lose anyone else." His voice is quiet and pained.

I place my hand on his arm. "I know."

He covers my hand with his. "No, I don't think you do." When his eyes meet mine, they're sharper than a knife. Serious and open for me to see into his soul. I drink in that sight, the way the light reflects off the dark specks of blue, how they shimmer when he looks at me. I lock it away, deep inside, hoping I'll never need that memory.

"Caspian…" My name passing his lips gives me chills. "I need to tell you something."

"What is it?"

Hraefn takes in a shaky breath, and my heart skips a beat. He locks eyes with me and smiles shyly, "Caspian, I—"

The crack of rifle fire tears through the air, then the thud of a body as it hits the ground.

Tommen is dead before his body even hits the ground.

I shove away from Caspian, swallowing the words I was about to say to him. Now isn't the time, and I don't know what I was thinking. He just told me last night that he doesn't want things to be complicated. Well, telling someone that you're in love with them isn't exactly easy.

I level the iron sight to my eye, scanning the jungle in the direction the bullet came from, but I don't see anything. My hands are sweating so bad I have to keep readjusting my grip. I know he's out there, watching me like I'm prey. He's a cat and I'm the mouse—he'll play with me until I'm too bloody and beaten to fight back, then get bored and kill me.

Focus, Hraefn!

Another crack, this time followed by a cry of pain. I whirl around to see Tetra clutching her upper arm where the bullet skimmed her. "I'm fine," she says before anyone can ask. She tears a strip of cloth with her teeth and begins wrapping her wound.

"We have to move!" Caspian shouts. We take off running toward the gunfire, though my legs want to go in the opposite direction. Jack runs beside us, no longer looking broken, but insane. His eyes are wild with rage, teeth bared like he plans to rip out their throats, and I wouldn't put it past him. They've taken something precious to him—*someone* precious—and he'll never forgive that.

Just past a gathering of trees, another large cove opens up to us. My eyes land on Captain Blacktip's ship in the distance, but there, sitting on the beach, is another ship. *The* ship. Captain Armada's ship from the stories. It's real, and Blacktip's crew is boarding her.

"No!" Jack snarls and sprints forward.

"Jack, wait!"

I grind to a halt, aim, and fire, dropping a man in front of Jack and giving him a clear path. Tetra pulls an ax from her belt and takes off left. Caspian stays by my side. I can see Captain Blacktip standing below the beached ship, and I don't have to be close to see that he's smiling. We're vastly outnumbered, and he knows it. I scan the faces for Ace and the others, while also trying not to die. Deadeye Cane fires off another round, just missing Caspian's foot. I instinctively grab him around the waist and push him behind me while I aim at Deadeye and fire.

The bullet rips through another member of their crew as Deadeye takes cover behind a large boulder. Blacktip's crew comes at us, screaming, swords at the ready. Caspian takes off before I can grab him, so I perch on a nearby rock, taking in the scene as it unfolds.

The beach is wide since the tide is out, but it won't last forever, and the afternoon is quickly slipping into evening. Our crew fights like animals, slashing and dodging the swords that try to slice them. My eyes find Caspian as he parries blow after blow, then dodges the downward arc of a sword and pierces his attacker through the gut. The man drops to his knees, and Tetra runs by and takes his head with her ax. I have to trust that she'll watch after Caspian.

I turn my focus back on Deadeye, only he isn't there

anymore. I fire instead on Blacktip's crew, taking down more as they pour out of the ship. The constant bump of the rifle to my shoulder calms me, and I take down a grouping of men before they even get close to my crew. That's when I hear someone approach from behind. I whip around with my finger on the trigger but stop when I see Ace standing there.

Blood coats his blue jacket and crusts on his pale face. "Ace," I breathe. "You're all right." I look past him. "Where's Gilly and Yonis?"

Ace flashes his usual smile, but it's misplaced here. "Worried about them more than me, lad?"

I shake my head. "Ace, we have to get out of here. They killed—" I choke on her name, snapping my mouth shut. He waits patiently until I calm myself. "They killed Tsu."

He doesn't even blink. "Did they?"

My eyes lower to his hands, which are crusted in blood. I step closer. "Ace." His blue eyes are dull as they meet mine. "Where's Gilly and Yonis?"

He just shrugs. "Dead."

The look in his eyes makes me sick to my stomach.

Behind me, men and women are dying. We have to get Jack and get out of here. Screw the ship—there will be no one to captain it if we all die. But I know Jack isn't here for the ship anymore—he's here for Blacktip. I turn back to find Caspian, but there are so many bodies moving further away down the beach that I can't see him.

"Lookin' for your lover boy, lad?"

Something in Ace's tone chills me down to my core. I turn back slowly, my finger hovering over the trigger.

"I'm sure he's fine." Ace waves a hand, then notices the blood and begins flaking it off.

"Ace… whose blood is that?"

"Oh, this?" He smiles devilishly, then sighs. "It's too bad, really."

My pulse skyrockets, veins thumping in my neck so hard it blurs my vision.

"I didn't want to," he goes on. "But you know Tsu." His voice is like a snake slipping past my ear. "No one could beat her in hand to hand. So, I had to take out the threat immediately."

Breathing is impossible. My whole world comes crumbling down around me. I stare at Ace, no longer seeing my best friend, but a stranger. I don't know this man at all. Time slows, and Ace's lips slowly slide into a confident grin. His blue eyes look like shards of ice that freeze my finger on the trigger. "Hraefn," he coos. "You were my friend—"

I level the barrel to his chest and fire. Ace is thrown back, slamming against a rock and sliding down to the sand. My heart feels like it's going to explode at any minute as I stumble away from him. I can't breathe, can't fucking *think*, and anytime I try, my throat closes up. My legs shake as I stumble away from him. The distant figures on the beach are fuzzy. I try to blink my world into focus, but I'm panicking. A sob escapes as I drop to my knees.

Ace…

No, I don't want to believe it. Ace wouldn't betray us—he's one of *us*!

In the distance, I hear someone shouting my name, but I keel over as my stomach threatens to empty. Dropping my rifle into the sand, I clutch my stomach as I dry heave. My body feels like it's tearing itself apart, like my brain is turning into mush inside my skull.

"Hraefn!"

I blink up to see Caspian running toward me, Jack just ahead of him, fighting his way to Blacktip. Caspian screams at me to move, but I don't think I can, and then I see the shadow beside me. Just as the barrel levels with the back of my head, I gasp, throwing my head to the right as Deadeye Cane fires.

The world erupts, and then everything is silent save for a

loud buzzing sound. I drop to the sand. I think I'm screaming, but I can't hear myself. Slapping my hands over my ears, I dig my forehead into the sand and grind my teeth so hard I'm surprised they don't break. There's a whoosh of air as someone rushes past me, then I feel the thump in the sand as a body hits the ground. I force myself to my knees, pulling my hands away from my ears. One is coated in blood. As I stumble to my feet, I grab my rifle at the last second, then I see Deadeye and Caspian struggling behind me.

Snarling, I swing my rifle and crack Deadeye in the head. He isn't what I was expecting. I've only ever seen him from afar, but I always pictured someone who looked insane. He looks like a normal man, just a few years older than the captain with a head of messy brown hair. His eyes burn like fire, and when he gets back to his feet, I can see just how tall and skinny he is.

I pull Caspian up to his feet. The look on his face is one of pure terror. Deadeye makes a break for his rifle, and I lunge, tackling him to the ground as my hearing starts to come back. He grunts, trying to grab my throat, but I punch him in the nose. Blood spurts over his face, and I punch the inside of his arm as he reaches for his rifle again.

"Get Ace!" I direct to Caspian. He's behind me but comes to stand in front of me, cocking his head to one side.

"Ace?"

"Ah, he doesn't know?" Deadeye muses.

My fingers grip his throat, and I squeeze as he writhes beneath me. Deadeye claws and kicks, so I squeeze harder. "Over there." I jerk my chin to where I'd shot Ace, and Caspian takes off without another word. A wave of dizziness hits me, and I let go of Deadeye, who's now unconscious.

Getting to my feet, I see that Blacktip's crew is retreating. Not because we're winning, but because the ship is now pulling in the tide.

It's *pulling in the tide.*

I lift my head to the sky. The tide shouldn't be coming back in for a while, yet it draws closer and closer. Blacktip boards his new ship, pulling up the ropes as the last of his crew haul themselves up. I see Tetra nursing her right arm where blood pools down into the sand. Two of our men lay in the sand unmoving, and the others are bleeding from various wounds.

Caspian comes back a moment later, panting and wide-eyed. "He wasn't there."

I look down at the sharpshooter, swallowing the bile in my throat as I turn back to Caspian. "I shot him."

His face falls. "You *what*?"

My eyes snap shut, and I shake my head. "He's a traitor, Cas. He killed Tsu."

Caspian only stares at me, looking as numb as I feel. "No, no, Ace is an asshole, but he wouldn't—""

"He did!" I snap, letting a few tears roll away. "He betrayed us, killed Tsu, and now Blacktip has the ship."

Caspian snaps his head to the sea, eyes growing even wider when he sees the waves now lapping up against the starboard side.

"We have to stop him." He tries to walk past me, but I grab his arm.

"It's done. *We're* done. We failed. We should leave while we can."

He pulls away from me. "No..." But then he can't speak anymore. I watch his eyes as he goes through denial, then realization, then rage, defeat. "No!" he screams, slamming his fist into the sand as he drops to a knee. "Tsu..."

Hearing her name lights a fire in my belly. I grab up my rifle and head for the boat.

"Hraefn, where are you going?"

Stomping past Tetra and the others, I slam a new clip into my rifle and pull back the charging handle. "Hraefn!" Tetra grabs for me, but I shove a hand into her shoulder and keep going. Jack is standing before the ship as the waves grow higher. The ship groans and creaks as she touches the water again, as if she's coming to life. I spot Ace's head of blond hair, and Jack must see him at the same time because he just barely breathes his name before I fire.

The bullet hits the gunwale. I pull back the handle and fire again, stepping closer and pulling the trigger as hard as I can, as if that will add extra force to my bullet. I unleash them all as tears stream down my cheeks and hurt weighs me down like a lead blanket.

I fill the ship with hole after hole, but then it groans louder than ever, and I pause. Before I can blink, a wave comes crashing into me, throwing me onto the beach. I land hard on my back, the air knocked from my lungs. Jack's eyes hold wonder at the ship's powers, but also sorrow and rage.

Blacktip leans over the edge and catches Jack's eye. Locks of blond hair ruffle in the breeze from under his cocked hat, and his face splits into a smile. "Jack, my boy. Is that you?"

Jack snarls.

"She's beautiful, isn't she?" He looks around his new ship, running his hand along the smooth stained railing as if she were a cat that wants pets. "You're welcome to try and take her from me, but if that's only the tip of the iceberg"—he gestures to the phantom wave now rolling away from me—"I don't think you want to see what's underneath."

Jack is too enraged to form any words, so he stands there as the magical ship carries herself out into the bay. A sudden wind fills her sails, and then she's off, with Ace aboard instead of down here with us.

An hour passes after we watch the ship slide away from the island. Tetra tends to her wounds before helping the rest of the crew. A few able men went back for Tsu's body, which now lies on a stack of logs and sticks. The sun is setting, and we don't have much time to get back to the *Chained Maiden* before our crew leaves us here.

There's eerie silence all around us. No one speaks as Jack lights the torch and lowers it to the sticks below her. No one so much as blinks as five of our crew members go up in flames. We found Gilly's and Yoni's bodies in the forest after the fighting was over. And now they burn alongside Tsu. I refuse to shed a tear, not allowing myself all the feelings that will come with it.

Jack's face is pale and haunted as the flames engulf Tsu, snapping as her hair catches. Her double swords lay crossed over her chest, and her mask has been removed. She looks peaceful, almost like she's asleep and will wake any moment, stretching like a cat, but her eyes will never open again.

Caspian stands at my side. His presence is comforting—it's welcoming and cracks something inside of me open but I feel like an empty hole, a void that will never be filled again. Images of Ace flash through my mind, images of all the time we spent together. I told him about my mother and my past, I drank with him until he couldn't function. We've shared so many laughs and tears, memories that were meant to never be tainted, but now they're coated in blood. How could I have been so stupid?

I can't take it anymore. I walk away toward the water and let the sea lap up against my feet, fixing my tired gaze on the horizon. "Hraefn?"

I don't look at him as Caspian comes to stand beside me. What does this mean for us? He said that after this was over, maybe we could be together, but this is just the start. I silently curse myself for even thinking about Caspian and me right now while Tsu's body still burns at our backs.

"It all makes sense now."

I turn to face him. His eyes are trained ahead, deep in thought. "What makes sense?"

"Ace." He lets the name fall from his lips. "In the Constellations, Ace and I went to a tavern, but before that, he went off on his own. When I asked him about it later, he gave me some fake story, but I could tell he was lying."

I remember that night, but we both just assumed Ace was writing home. Caspian continues. "And then we were attacked by Blacktip." He shakes his head and breathes out a laugh. "And when we played a drinking game belowdecks, Ace lied about not wanting the throne." Caspian turns to face me fully. "Why would he lie about that?"

"I don't know."

"I still don't understand how…" Caspian trails off, then his eyes go wide.

My hand lands on his shoulder. "What is it?"

"The map."

"Yeah… the captain—"

He cuts me off. "Last night, Ace urged him to put it away. Said it would drive the captain crazy."

I raise a brow, not following.

Caspian grabs me by the shoulders. "Ace took the map." I open my mouth to speak, but Caspian takes off back toward the crew. "Jack!" he calls.

The captain turns around with a blank expression on his face.

"Give me the map."

I come up beside Caspian as Captain Jack reaches in his pocket and hands it over. Caspian scans the pieces, putting them together, and when the image is complete, the captain's eyes burn with rage once more.

It's almost a perfect copy of the map, but right where the ship graveyard sits, Ace signed his name.

Prince Angus Dragonsbane of the Tuasian Kingdom.

Captain Jack's reaches out and snags the map. His hands shake so bad that he rips the paper until it falls like ash to the sand. "He switched the maps," he growls. "I didn't even look at it after we found Tsu… it's my fault."

Tetra steps up beside him. "No, Captain. It isn't."

"I… I should've stayed awake. I knew how risky this was, and now seven of us are dead."

I stare at the sand beneath my boots, then turn to regard Caspian. He meets my eyes and raises a brow in question. "Clever Caspian." I breathe the name in a hushed voice, and Caspian cringes at the name now.

We say a quiet goodbye to our silent friend and crewmates before heading south toward our ship. We're all a little too broken to have things figured out right now. All we can do is put one foot in front of the other and hope we end up somewhere that's better. We came here not believing the legend that Jack did, but after seeing the ship in person and the look on the captain's face, I know he won't rest until he hunts Blacktip to the ends of the earth.

The sun finally sets, and we pick up our pace, afraid of missing our ride off this horrible island. As we crest the hill, the *Chained Maiden* comes into view, and relief washes over me. I should've known that they'd never leave us behind. The crew comes to the gunwale as we approach, taking in the blood that coats our faces as we board.

"What happened?" Story asks, going straight for the captain.

Tetra takes the old man by the elbow and begins speaking softly to him. She leads him back to the ship, Story casting sorrowful looks over his shoulder as Tetra tells our story.

I pause at the gunwale, looking back as if Ace were hiding in the shadows, ready to bury another dagger in my back. Caspian's hand on my shoulder startles me.

"Sorry," he says gently. He steps back, twisting his hands in front of him. "Hraefn," he chokes on my name, and my heart snaps. I don't want him to tell me how sorry he is, or that everything will be okay. I just need him right now. Before he can break me more, I pull him in by the back of the head and wrap my arms around him.

Caspian melts into me, pressing his cheek against mine and rubbing his hands up and down my back. I close my eyes and take in a long breath, my lungs finally opening up. It's like his touch calms my entire being and sets me off at the same time. I hug him tighter, allowing myself this small sliver of peace after the horrors of today.

Caspian doesn't speak or pull away, he stays pressed into my chest, and I realize that he fits in my arms perfectly, like he was always meant to be there. We stay entwined like that for a few long moments, savoring the comfortable silence between us.

After we set sail, the crew gets back to their usual duties, almost like this is normal. We don't know where we're going yet, but we all trust the captain. He stands at the bow, arms behind his back and eyes forward. I go to his side, following his gaze to a pod of dolphins that breach the surface. I can feel Caspian's eyes on me, but I don't look back. We still have a lot to figure out between us, but that can wait.

"Do you know that Captain Armada never named his ship?" he asks, his gaze still on the dolphins.

"No, Captain."

He blinks and turns to look at me. "Don't call me that." I meet his gaze with a questioned look. "Just call me, Jack." He turns back to the sea and continues. "The ship never had a name. The legend says that Captain Armada left her stranded there on that island, waiting for the right person to come along. A person who was deserving of the ship. Only then would she be given a name."

"Then clearly the ship doesn't know the difference between a good man and a bad one."

Jack scoffs. "And you're so sure I'm a good man?"

I don't answer. After a pause, I ask, "What would you have named the ship?"

A sad smile tugs on Jack's lips, and when he turns to me, his whole being seems calm as he speaks a name. "Ellka."

The name sounds familiar to me. I run it through my head but come up blank. The wind picks up, ruffling Jack's head of black hair, now streaked with silver strands. His face is stained with a smile, but it looks somewhat sad now. I shift to face him. "Who's Ellka?"

Jack lowers his head and looks down at his wooden hand. There's longing in the way his eyes run over the permanent curve of his fingers. "Ellka was my wife," he says so quietly I almost miss it. "Rani Ellka, first of her name and ruler of the Constellations."

A Rani?

They're kings and queens on their land, and Jack *married* one? A million questions are flooding my brain, but none come out.

Jack turns to me before I can speak. "Get some sleep," he says, casting a look at the crow's nest. "No one is hunting us now."

He leaves me at the bow, retreating to the aftercastle where Story stands at the helm. Jack touches the old man's arm, then goes into his room and closes the door. I turn back to the open sea ahead of us, closing my eyes and taking a deep breath of the briny air. The cool wind rakes their fingers through my dark hair, blowing it back across my scalp. A moment later, I feel a presence at my back and turn to see Caspian.

He wears an easy smile that lights up his entire face. As he approaches, my heart beats faster just for him. I'm beyond exhausted and want nothing more than to crawl into bed and sleep for days, but I won't miss a stolen moment with Caspian. He leans his elbows on the gunwale, and I run my eyes over his brown curls and golden eyes, down to his full lips.

He catches me staring and smirks. "See something you like, sharpshooter?"

Surprised by his playful tone, I chuckle and lean back against the gunwale. "Maybe, *thief*."

Caspian snarls, but he's smiling, and I know what he's doing. He's trying to make me feel better, to comfort or distract me in some small way. The gesture melts my heart.

"I'm not a thief," he says with feigned disgust.

I lean my elbows back against the gunwale and shrug. "That's what we hired you for."

"Just because I can sneak past you lot, doesn't mean I'm a thief." He jabs a finger in my chest, but I catch it and pull him closer.

"Semantics, Clever Caspian." He loses his smile some, and I let go of his finger. "Sorry."

"No, I'm going to keep it. I think the name is fitting, no matter who it came from." I nod, crossing my arms over my chest. Caspian's grin turns devilish.

"What?"

He flashes a shy smile. "Back on the beach, you called me Cas."

"Oh. So?"

He lowers his head. "My mother used to call me that."

My eyes flit down to the deck. "I won't call you that anymore."

"No," he says a little too quickly, then blushes when I look at him. "I mean… you can. I like it."

My smile comes easily. "All right, then."

Caspian cocks his head, observing me.

"What are you doing?"

"You need a nickname too. How about Hrae?"

I snort, brushing a lock of hair from my brow. "I like Hraefn just fine, thanks."

Caspian smiles, his eyes running down my body, then back up. "Yeah, me too."

We lock eyes, and his smile grows soft. My heart thumps against my ribs when he looks at me like that. Like he's deciding whether to kiss me or punch me in the shoulder, brush off his feelings and stick me in the friend zone. Caspian parts his lips slightly and steps closer, eyes drifting down to my mouth. I know my face blushes bright red, but I can't help it. Everything is a mess right now, but the one thing I'm sure about is my feelings for Caspian. He came to us so suddenly and was more of a hazard at first, but we've come to accept him. And if not for Caspian, we would've been in trouble more than a few times, and I might be dead. Deadeye Cane now sits in the brig belowdecks. I know we'll have to question him eventually, but not now.

He lifts a finger to my ear, and I cringe at the pain. Deadeye missed my brain thanks to Caspian's warning, but the bullet tore through the top of my ear. "Does it hurt?"

I swat his hand away. "It does if you touch it."

His fingers drop to my cheek, and his skin is like fire against mine. My back goes rigid, and my breaths come up short. His smile is everything as he leans in closer, just a shared breath away...

"Cas—"

He presses his lips to mine, hard at first, but I part my lips in an instant, and his kiss turns soft and tender. He presses his chest to mine, backing me up against the gunwale while one hand caresses my cheek, and the other holds my hip. I feel it the moment I let go, and my heart opens up completely—whether we'll be together in the future or not, right now I'm his, and he's mine.

I grab his face and straighten up, tilting his head back. Caspian's lips slide over mine in perfect rhythm, just light and tender enough to make me crave more. My tongue brushes against his teeth slightly, and Caspian makes a groaning sound low in his throat. My entire body flushes at the sound. A second later, I feel him smiling against my lips and pull back a little to look into his eyes. "Why are you smiling?" I ask, running my thumb over his plump bottom lip.

"Aren't I allowed to smile?"

My eyes drift to his lips, then back to his beautiful eyes. "As often as possible, please."

"I'll try my best," he whispers. His breath across my lips makes me shiver before he leans back in and kisses me.

Caspian is right. We don't need to complicate things. Not

when we have so much going on right now. But someday we'll be together. Perhaps today is one of those days, and maybe tomorrow won't be, but I'll hold on to that hope with everything I have.

Someday can't come soon enough, and when it does, I know Caspian will be by my side and a part of this family aboard the *Chained Maiden*.

CHAPTER
TWENTY-SEVEN

JACK

Captain Blacktip docks his ship, *The Flying Tide*, in the port of the Constellations. The Rani waits for us in the Capital, where the captain will trade rare furs and jewels. I'm to meet with Rani Ellka to discuss payment, and so I set off by myself toward the palace while the captain goes off in search of a tavern.

As I approach her throne room, two guards flank me, then pat me down for weapons. They lift my cocked hat, pat down my torso and waist, and make me empty my pockets. The Rani doesn't allow weapons inside her palace, save for the guards who have curved swords swinging from their hips.

"You're good," one tells me, handing me back my hat. I snatch it away and enter the room.

As always, my breath falters when I see her, high atop her throne. Ellka is the most beautiful woman I've ever seen, with skin like copper and black hair that swishes around her hips. Her eyes are a haunting shade of green, almost jade. She smiles as I approach, then waves her guards away, leaving the two of us alone.

As soon as the door closes, she descends the steps and stops in front of me. "Jack."

Removing my hat, I dip into a bow. "Rani Ellka."

She grins wickedly, descends the last step, and kisses me.

Ellka took the throne after her father's early death two years back. She's my age, in her early twenties, but since her father never had a chance to marry her off, she rules alone. I pull back and cup her smooth cheek. "Would it kill you to call me husband?"

She taps a finger to her chin. "I don't know. But I don't plan on dying today." Ellka winks, and I chuckle, pulling her in for a hug. She speaks softly against my ear, "How long can you stay?"

"Only a week."

I feel her body deflate in my arms, but it isn't my call, and the more I'm around her, the more people will start to get suspicious.

The Rani isn't supposed to marry anyone outside of her people. I never meant to fall in love with her, but I was even more surprised when she fell for me. I asked her to marry me only three months back, and so we married in secret. No one knows of our marriage, especially not my captain. It isn't the perfect life I imagined, but I also can't picture a life without her.

We walk along the gardens behind the palace, talking as if ears are listening—because there's always someone listening.

"There will be a feast tonight," she says, keeping a good few feet of space between us. I desperately want to reach out and push her up against the wall and kiss her until we're both gasping for air. Instead, I tuck my hands behind my back and nod.

"That sounds lovely, I'll tell my captain."

She blushes and lowers her head to hide her smile, like she knows *exactly* what I was thinking. I love that smile, the way her nose crinkles and her eyes sparkle with life. "Very well." She pauses next to a rose bush. "I'll send a few guards to Captain Blacktip's ship to help unload the goods."

I do a quick sweep to make sure no one is around before I pluck a rose and hand it to her. Leaning in closer, I lower my voice to a whisper, "I look forward to tonight, my love."

She swats me away like a fly and turns to leave, then pauses. "Oh, and I have something important I wish to discuss with you, Jack."

I bow, then watch her walk away.

Later that night, I walk with the crew to Ellka's palace. Captain Blacktip tugs on my arm before I can go inside. He waves off a few of the others, telling them to go ahead and enjoy the feast. When they're gone, I pull my arm back.

"What?" I hiss.

Blacktip lets go and steps back, running a hand through his blond locks. "Don't get an attitude with me, little Jack."

I snarl. Blacktip isn't that much older than me, but he always treats me like a child.

"I just wanted to tell you to have fun," he says over his shoulder as he continues toward the feast. "Loosen up and dance with some pretty girls, for god's sake."

The walls are tan stone, adorned with golden mirrors, paintings, and floor-to-ceiling tapestries. I walk along the golden carpet, down the hall, and to the ballroom. The floor is marble, with flecks of gold scattered through it that shimmer in the candlelight. Chandeliers hang above, dripping purple wax onto the many gems that dangle below the candles. I spot some of my crew already drinking golden goblets of honey wine. One slips the goblet into his jacket, then catches me watching. He presses a finger to his lips, and I roll my eyes, too anxious to see my wife.

Stopping in front of a mirror, I adjust my navy-blue jacket and pull at the high collar. It was a gift from Ellka last time I came to visit. It was a little eye-catching for my style, but I'll wear a fluffy pink dress if it will make Ellka happy. The high collar is stitched with golden leaves and vines that swirl around the back and spill out over my right shoulder. Black buttons line the center, though I leave the jacket unbuttoned and wear a plain white shirt underneath. I slick back my midnight hair and tie it off at the base of my neck. A flash of green catches my eye, and when I turn away from the mirror, I see her.

Ellka stands in the center of the room in a sea-green dress that dips down her back, stopping just above her hips. Her black hair is braided and swirls atop her head, looking like a braided snake that runs down her spine. When she turns, her black earrings brush against her bare shoulders, and she looks in my direction. Ellka bows her head in greeting, then slides her eyes to a large glass door that leads out into the gardens. I bow in return, then move away to fetch us some drinks. One of the guards watches me as I step up to the bar and order two glasses of champagne. I think I know what Ellka wants to tell me, and so I think a celebratory drink is in order.

After the bartender takes his time getting my drinks, I make my way back through the crowd of dancers and slip out into the night. The air is cool and refreshing, perfumed with the hundreds of flowers that grow here. The full moon lights my way down a small dirt path that stops in a private part of the garden, where high bushes create walls around a stone bench. Setting our drinks down, I move over to a bush and pick a few tiger lilies—Ellka's favorite.

I start thinking about the future and what will become of Ellka and me. She has a city to run and can't just leave her people, but what if she can? Surely the council will be able to handle things until a new Rani or Rana is chosen to take Ellka's place.

I once heard of a ship that can control the sea around it and only requires a skeleton crew to operate her. What if it isn't just a story? What if the legends are true, and I can find this ship for Ellka and me? Then we'll be free to leave this place. I can leave Blacktip's crew and take her away, and no one will be able to stop us. It sounds a little ridiculous in my head, but I make a mental note to do more research about the ship once we leave the Constellations.

After a while, the champagne starts to grow warm, and I wonder where Ellka is. She's always getting caught up at these feasts, cornered by her council members or someone else. It makes it hard for her to slip away, but I know she'd never miss a secret meeting with me.

Finally, I hear footsteps coming down the dirt path. I stand up, tucking the flowers behind my back, and wait, but it isn't my wife that rounds the corner. It's the guard who watched me as I ordered our drinks.

"Jack," he greets me.

I drum my fingers behind my back and eye him coolly. "Guard," I address him. "Can I help you?"

He shrugs, stepping further into the clearing. "Why aren't you at the feast? The Rani put forth quite the effort on your captain's behalf." His tone is dangerous.

"I needed some air," I lie. "I'm not one for big celebrations."

"Ahh, yes. And tonight was meant to be a celebration, wasn't it?"

My heart begins to thump harder as I try to pick apart his meaning. I stay silent instead of walking into his trap. He scratches his black beard and picks up Ellka's champagne, downing the whole glass. His golden armor shines in the moonlight, and my eyes fall on his curved sword. "It's too bad you won't be celebrating now."

I smile. "I don't know what you mean."

He eyes the other glass of champagne. "Waiting for someone?"

Again, I don't answer.

The guard begins circling me, and I hear him chuckle when he spots the flowers in my hand. He pauses behind me, his hot breath filling my ear as he hisses, "Perhaps, your *wife?*"

I crush the flowers in my hand and let them fall to the grass.

Everything in me goes still and cold. I spin around and stand face-to-face with the guard. His brown eyes are wide, like a cat when it locks onto its prey. "Too bad she can't make it," he continues. He steps even closer until all I see is the hate in his eyes. "How long do you think it will take Rani Ellka to bleed out now that she has a baby in her belly?" And then he holds up her wedding ring, a small gold band with a ruby in the center.

Horror and panic mix in my stomach, and before I can move, he grabs me by the neck and lifts me clean off the ground. I kick but only strike armor. The guard slams me to the ground, knocking the wind from me and creating sparks of white that float across my field of vision. I thrash against him, bucking my hips, but with his armor on, he weighs a ton. "Wait until I tell everyone," he hisses, spittle flying from his lips. "You thought you were so sneaky, didn't you?"

Tears form in my eyes. I drive my fist into the crook of his elbow, then head-butt him. The guard snaps back, clutching his hands to his nose, which now oozes blood. I scramble to my feet, breathing heavily. "Where's Ellka?"

He smiles crookedly, then slides his curved sword from the scabbard. "We have no Rani now, Jack."

No. This can't be. This *isn't* happening. I refuse to believe it.

Snarling, I lunge forward, just missing the blade that slices for my throat. I drive my elbow into his ribs, where the armor exposes his side. He grunts, then swings again, just missing the top of my head. Dropping and rolling out of the way, I grab my whalebone dagger from my boot. The guard spots it and smiles. "There are no weapons allowed in here."

"Where is Ellka?" I demand, though my voice is shaky with panic. *"Where?"* I scream. "Or I'll call for the guards and tell them what you've done."

"Ha! Go ahead." He throws his arms out. "Tell me, what do you think they'll do to you once everyone finds out that our Rani married an outsider." He steps closer, lips snarling around the words. "An outsider who fucked her and put a baby in her belly.

You expect people to accept that? And let some half-breed rule after her reign is over? No, young Jack."

My hands tremble as I hold the dagger. He's right. The people will never accept Ellka's child if they know. And what did she plan to tell them once she started to show? The people here are strict in their traditions, and even if this guard did kill Ellka, he'll likely be praised for it, not punished. To them, Ellka would have been seen as a traitor, and it's all my fault. Tears streak down my cheeks as I hold the dagger between us.

He chuckles at my sorrow, then lifts his sword. "When I bring them your head, I'll be a hero. It's too bad, though." He licks his lips, and a wave of rage burns a hole in my core. "The Rani was a beauty, perhaps I'll go back while her body is still warm—"

A scream tears past my lips as I throw myself at him. The guard raises his sword to block me, but I'm all rage and adrenaline. I don't even feel it as his curved blade slices my arm or nicks my cheek. I deflect his sword with my dagger, then slash my blade across his throat. It isn't deep enough to kill, but now panic fills his eyes, and he falters for a moment.

I twist around him and kick out the back of his knee. The guard crashes to the ground, throwing his arm back to try to slice me, but I cut the hand that holds the sword. It drops to the bloody grass, and the second he's unarmed, I drive my blade through the back of his neck. A gargled cry escapes his lips as blood spews into the cool night air. I yank the dagger back out, then grab him by the forehead from behind and tilt his head back.

"Where is she?" I growl.

The guard gurgles some more, then the light in his eyes goes out. I let go, and he drops face-first into the grass, dead.

I take off in a sprint back through the gardens, wiping the blood from my face as I go. Stopping at a nearby fountain, I wash my hands and rip a piece of cloth from my white shirt, then button up my jacket to my throat. I dip the cloth in the water and press it to my cheek, then run toward the palace, but I'm too late.

The ballroom is in full-blown chaos. People run and shout in every direction, trying to escape through the many doors. Panic fills my eyes as I search the room for that sea-green dress, but I can't spot it. I snatch someone by the collar as they run past and scream over the commotion, "What's going on?"

The man trembles in my grip. "The Rani... she was found dead in her chambers."

My fingers release the man and he takes off running again as guards shuffle everyone out. I sway, catching myself on a pillar before I can fall on my face. Tears burn in my eyes, and I have to stifle a sob.

Dead.

Ellka is dead, and it's my fault.

A wave of guilt crashes down on me so hard that I stumble, smacking into someone as they run past. My vision blurs, and I don't think I'm breathing or moving, but then I'm outside. I spot members of the crew heading back to the docks and hear Captain Blacktip calling orders.

I pull Ellka's wedding ring from my pocket and run a finger over the ruby. I spent hours picking out the perfect ring for her, and now she'll never wear it again. How can this be happening? We're supposed to start a family, and though I didn't tell her, I planned to take her away from here one day. Nothing in this world makes me as happy as she does, and now Ellka is gone forever. Never again will I see the smile that makes my heart skip or hear her laugh. I'll never feel her hands on me or get chills when she whispers my name. Nothing.

I slip her ring on my right pointer finger, then force my legs to move toward *The Flying Tide*, where she sits docked in the harbor. Captain Blacktip is calling orders from where he stands at the helm, but I avoid looking at him. I need to change and wash the blood from my face before anyone notices it.

Some time passes, and word spreads of the Rani's death. The

only living family member left is an uncle named Maryn, who will now rule the Capital. They found the guard's body in the gardens but deemed him a hero who must have tried to stop Rani Ellka's killer. My stomach churns when I hear that, and it takes everything in me not to scream, but I can't. If anyone even finds out who Ellka was to me and that she'd been pregnant with my child, I'll be dead. Captain Blacktip might even turn me over himself to claim a reward from the people of the Constellations. It will ruin me before I even make a name for myself. I can't even imagine the horrible ways they'd torture me before finally letting me die.

I wake from one of my usual nightmares in a pool of sweat. Pushing off the bed, I look down at my wooden hand and picture Ellka's ring on my finger. I try not to think of my wife often, even though that might sound cruel, but I just can't take it. That ship, the one Blacktip stole from under me, was meant to be our escape. I wanted to find it, take Ellka away, and sail the world for the rest of our lives, living free. But then she was taken from me, and the only thing I could do was find the ship for myself.

I thought it would be some salvation for me. Like I might finally be able to sleep at night and not see her face frowning at me. Or perhaps I'm still doing this for her, even if she isn't here.

Pushing open the back doors, I step out onto the balcony. We've been sailing for a few days now, licking our wounds after what happened on the island. Tsu's death is still a hole in my heart, and I doubt it will ever be filled again. She's always been important to me, the only one who I shared my secrets with. Though now Hraefn knows of my wife.

Later that night, after some drinks, I told him more about her. I spilled everything, and Hraefn was so shocked that he didn't say a word. My crew will never say anything to an outsider, but honestly, I told Hraefn just to ease the screaming in my head. I planned to name our new ship after her, so when that, too, was taken from me, I felt her death all over again.

"Captain?"

I glance over my shoulder to see Caspian approaching. He sidles up beside me, standing awkwardly. "What is it?"

"Well," he starts, "I've been talking to Hraefn—"

I give him a sideways smirk.

"Not about that!" he quickly says, then, "I mean *yes*, about that. But I mean… we were… He told me…"

"Spit it out."

Caspian's cheeks flare, and he clears his throat. "He told me about… your wife."

Anger spikes inside me, and I whirl on him, but before I can yell, he throws up his hands.

"Wait! I'm sorry, I was prying and it just… slipped?"

"Try again."

"Fine, I *was* prying because I saw you two talking the other night, but he told me. I haven't said a word to anyone, I promise."

Grunting, I turn back to the sea we left behind. "So what? You want to leave the crew now?"

Caspian looks at me like I'm crazy. "Leave? No. Never."

His answer is so confident and final that I can't find any doubt in his voice. "Then why are you here?"

"I know how much you loved her—" My eyes close slowly as her face flashes before me, but Caspian goes on. "And I know you lost something after her. Ellka's wedding ring. I know where it is."

My eyes fly open, and I grab him by the shoulders. "Where? How?"

He smiles. "My father's shop back in the Sunken City." He turns his eyes down, shyly. "It's still on your… your pointer finger."

I'm too shocked to even ask how the hell his father has my

hand, but that doesn't matter right now. I let go of Caspian and shake my head. "That can't be."

"It's true. I used to look at it all the time." He touches my arm gently. "We can get it back, Jack."

I can't help but smile as I clap my hand on his back hard, knocking him into the railing. "I knew you'd be useful."

Caspian grins, then turns to leave. "I'll tell Sundance to keep tracking Blacktip, then once we have the ship—"

"No," I interrupt, turning to face him. "Tell Sundance to head north. We're going to pay your father a visit."

ABOUT THE AUTHOR

Brittany Czarnecki is a self-published author of YA and NA Fantasy novels. She's currently working on the third novel in her Blackbourne Series, while finishing her BA in English at MCLA, and working at her local Barnes and Noble. When she's not doing any of those things, Brittany enjoys watching anime, cooking with her husband, and reading. Sometimes she even has a moment to write a little something about herself.

brittanyczar.wixsite.com/brittany-czarnecki-b

facebook.com/brittanyczarnecki
instagram.com/brittany_czarbooks
tiktok.com/@brittanyczar_books

ACKNOWLEDGMENTS

Welcome aboard my acknowledgment page!
It's time once again to thank all those amazing people who have helped me along the way.

Let's get started, shall we?

ARC Readers:

You. Guys. You're all just so amazing! Thank you to every single reader who took time out of your schedule to give this book a try, and for all the love and excitement you've shown for this story. I can't tell you how much I appreciate your support and what it means to me.

Thank you all.

Family:

First of all, thank you April for being my first reader. I always enjoy discussing my characters with you and hearing your thoughts—even if they're sometimes angry because I kill off good characters! To my mom and dad, thank you both for being some of my biggest fans and being open to reading fantasy. It's awesome, isn't it? Thank you, Gramma for always checking in about my book process and for your genuine love and interest in what I do. There are too many names to list, so thank you to everyone in my family who supports my books!

Crystal (AKA #1 Fan): You're such an amazing friend. Every single time I have any sort of news on my books, you're the first person I tell. Your love and excitement for my books help me to keep going and push through the difficult parts of being an author. (Did I "Pierce Brown" your favorite character?) Thank you so much for everything.

Liz:

I've been able to ask you countless questions throughout my publishing process, and you've always been there to help me. Your guidance and support mean the world to me, and I'm so grateful that you had a part in bringing this book to life!

Thank you so much.

Vaughan:

Okay, so a few years back I was reading Adalyn Grace's "All The Stars and Teeth" and I told you about the ship in the book that was named the Keelhaul, and you said, "Keelhaul Jack would make a great pirate name." And so this book was created from that one comment. This series has been really fun to discuss with you, and you helped me a lot with Ace, Tetra (your favorite), and some other characters. Thank you for always listening and helping me when I'm stuck on an idea.

Creators:

To my editor, Crystal, who did an amazing, thorough job of polishing my manuscript. My amazing book designer, Franzi— thank you for creating such a beautiful book and bringing my (not-so-helpful) ideas and input to life! You're work continues to amaze me. To my map maker, Dewi, who took my original map and brought it to life. I look forward to working with you in the future. To Liz, thank you again for formatting my book! Christina—who read the first version of this book and loved it, thank you for the excellent work in doing one final read-through of my manuscript.

Readers:

I have the best readers. You all are so supportive and your excitement for all of my books just warms my cold little heart. Thank you all for loving my characters and yelling at me when I kill them.